INTO THE WOODS
AND OUT AGAIN

ALSO BY DR DINA GLOUBERMAN

Life Choices, Life Changes: Develop Your Personal Vision with Imagework (1989)

The Joy of Burnout: How the End of the World can be a New Beginning (2002)

You Are What You Imagine: Three Steps to a New Beginning Using Imagework (2014)

To contact Dina Glouberman, order books and CDs, download MP3s of Imagework exercises, find out about courses and events, or set up workshops and speaking engagements, please visit www.dinaglouberman.com

To find out about Skyros Holistic Holidays, please visit www.skyros.com

INTO THE WOODS AND OUT AGAIN

A Memoir of Love, Madness, and Transformation

Dina Glouberman

SPHINX

First published in 2018 by Sphinx, an imprint of
Aeon Books Ltd
12 New College Parade
Finchley Road
London NW3 5EP

British Library Cataloguing in Publication Data

A C.I.P. for this book is available from the British Library

ISBN-13: 978-1-91257-306-6

Typeset by Medlar Publishing Solutions Pvt Ltd, India

Printed in Great Britain by TJ International Ltd, Padstow, Cornwall

www.aeonbooks.co.uk

www.sphinxbooks.co.uk

To
Yannis, Ari, Chloe,
and Shira

CONTENTS

PART IV
THE CREATIVE YEARS: GAINS, LOSSES,
AND THE RADICAL IMAGINATION

PART V
FROM BURNOUT TO NEBBISH WISDOM

ABOUT THE AUTHOR

Dr Dina Glouberman is the visionary co-founder of Skyros Holistic Holidays, in Greece and worldwide, author of the classic books *Life Choices, Life Changes, The Joy of Burnout,* and *You Are What You Imagine,* and an international trainer, coach, and psychotherapist. Formerly a Senior Lecturer at Kingston University, she has been a pioneer for over thirty years in creating, teaching and practising the use of Imagework to tap into the imagination that guides our lives, and  make creative life choices and profound life changes (www. dinaglouberman.com, www.skyros.com). She is also a member of the Board of the Association of Humanistic Psychology in Britain (www.ahpweb.org).

ACKNOWLEDGEMENTS

Gratitude is so good, but where to begin? And where to end? You are all part of my story; indeed you have made this story possible. I thank:

Yannis Andricopoulos, who was my husband and partner through most of this story, and without whom most of this would never have happened, my children Ari and Chloe who were such a big part of it all, and my sister Shira who shared my childhood world. And to all four of you for being willing to have me publish what is not just my story but ours.

The late writer Sue Townsend, who read an earlier version of this book, and loved it and encouraged me to make it happen.

Writer Nell Dunn, who sat with me lovingly for hours and hours helping me to shape this book, through two incarnations of the manuscript.

Wanda Whiteley, my absolutely brilliant manuscript doctor, or perhaps manuscript surgeon, without whom this book would never have seen the light of day, and who has accompanied me every step of the way.

Rod Tweedy, the editor who welcomed this book, Cecily Blench, my new editor who has worked closely with me throughout, and everyone at Sphinx.

Judy Piatkus, who has given me invaluable advice, recommendations and support since the beginning of the project.

Jane Barber, who has helped edit and format the book, so that I could do the fun part of writing, and Suzie King and Clare Manifold who each spent hours doing a line-by-line edit.

Ari Andricopoulos, Yannis Andricopoulos, Pam Chaplin, Kate Daniels, Naomi Jaffe, Robin Shohet, and Manya McClew, who read the manuscript, and helped me enormously.

Debby Greenwald Harder, for her support throughout my breakdown and beyond, and for sending me a wonderful photo of our post-hospital high tea at Fortnum and Mason with James, Giorgos, and his Great Dane.

The people of Skyros, who gave a home for a magical community, and helped change the lives of all who came there. I am very sad about the difficult times Greece is going through.

The teaching staff, permanent staff and participants of Skyros Holidays who have worked together over the years to create that amazing world, and especially those who were pioneers with me in the early days.

All my family, past, present, and future, my partner, Lorcan, my friends, my colleagues, my students, my clients, my teachers, my favourite authors, and all those who have offered me a word, a touch, an insight, an encouragement, a hug or a life commitment. You've kept me going and growing.

All that holds me in the light, both in this dimension and in the dimensions of Spirit and Imagination.

And if you are still reading this, I thank you, dear reader.

FOREWORD

Sue Townsend

One of the great privileges of my life has been my friendship with the late Sue Townsend, who, aside from being an amazing writer, was the most loving, wise and generous human being. Her incredible grace of presence and profound humanitarianism touched the lives of everyone she met. Not surprisingly, she also had a wicked sense of humour. She taught in Skyros year after year until her health made it impossible and wrote in the Guardian, "I fell in love with the place, as everyone does. I kept thinking I am an actor in A Midsummer Night's Dream; *this is Arcadia, I want to live like this forever." Sue actually advised me to call this book* Confessions of a Psychotherapist, *but in the end, it has become* Into the Woods and Out Again. *She wrote this piece about an earlier version of the book, and asked me to save it and use it whenever I wanted. So here it is, published in loving memory and gratitude to Sue Townsend, a true aristocrat of the spirit.*

—Dina

*

This wonderful book is the story of a woman's inner life, written with at times heartbreaking candour. We are all to some extent innocent victims of our life experiences. Dina respects this, but she also reminds us that we can discard some of the lousy cards we have been dealt and still enjoy (and sometimes win) the game.

Dina is that rare person, somebody who is genuinely and selflessly interested in others. She will take infinite pains to help people to accept who they are, whilst also urging them to make their reach outstretch their grasp. She has enabled many people, including me, to validate their lives. She has helped me to illuminate areas of my life that had previously been in shadow, to accept negative past experiences and to look forward to the future.

She also has another truly precious gift: She is able to be in two places at the same time. She can be the person in need of psychotherapy and she can also be the therapist. In this book we can watch Dina doing for herself what she has done for so many others. The whispered implication is always: Try it, you can do it too. Thus, although this is not a self-help book, it could be read as such.

As somebody who is interested in storytelling and narrative, I find the visualisation exercises in this book particularly fascinating. And because Dina has the gifts of empathy, wisdom, high intelligence and humour, this book is never less than seriously entertaining (or entertainingly serious).

I hope you enjoy this brilliant and funny book and find something in these pages that reminds you that it *is* still wonderful to be human.

PROLOGUE

This memoir takes place over about eighteen extraordinary years of my life, beginning with when I was twenty-five. It is written with the understanding that the more honest I can be in telling my personal story, no matter how embarrassing it may be, and the deeper I can go into the heart of it, the more I can strike a universal chord of truth.

Where I keep silence or gloss over events it is because the story concerns others and doesn't feel mine to tell. This is also why I have changed the names of some of the people in my story.

Through it all I have understood that it is not possible for me to confine myself to the safe zone of standard conventional "rational thought". I, and many others like me, have needed to go where angels fear to tread, off the everyday maps of reality. We have catapulted ourselves, or been catapulted, into dimensions of madness, spirit, and imagination that are a radical re-imagining of these conventional maps.

We have gone, willingly or not so willingly, into the woods, "where nothing's clear, where witches, ghosts and wolves appear; into the woods and through the fear, you have to take the journey".[1] And, if at all possible, we have returned to bring back wisdom.

I call the wisdom I have brought back from those dimensions "nebbish wisdom". What this is will become clearer by the end, but for now, I offer the thought that if you consider yourself a *nebbish*, a nothing, a self-deprecating Yiddish version of The Fool in the Tarot deck, you have so little to lose that you can afford to take that very risky path of following where truth leads.

On this path, everything in life is, as they say, "grist to the mill". Even birthdays can have an important role to play.

When I think of birthdays when I was a kid, it is my friend Joanie's birthday, not my own, that I remember, because she had a surprise birthday party. I have a vivid picture of the moment she walked into her basement, stopped and smiled delightedly, as we all popped up, waving balloons and shouting: "Surprise! Happy birthday!"

Birthdays, I believed, were the day that gave people a chance to show you how much they loved you by showering you with just what you wanted—without your having to ask or do something about it. Real love was love that came from the outside, unsolicited. Real love was a surprise birthday party.

Why birthdays? It may have something to do with the day of my birth itself, which wasn't much of a celebration. There is a history to this, to do with the sudden death of my sister Ora a few days after I was conceived. More about this later, but suffice it to say that if I was hoping for a grand welcome, loads of loving attention, and a demonstration of how special I was, birth must have been quite a disappointment. Birthdays had a lot to make up for.

Every year into young and middle adulthood I hoped that something special would happen on my birthday, and every year nothing quite special enough did happen, and every year I felt a deep disappointment in my heart.

One day, I decided not to have another unhappy birthday. I just took my birthday into my own hands. I would do what I wanted on my birthday and not expect anything from anyone to come unbidden from the skies.

I had my first happy birthday.

My birthdays were totally turned around. Every birthday in the years that followed was not only a happy birthday, but also a deeply significant day, often the day when I suddenly saw a new pattern for my year or for my life. Instead of being a day that will be good if I am unexpectedly showered with love, it was by definition a good day, because it was *my* day.

And so, it became everyone's day.

I had wonderful parties, where people were invited to come and go whenever they wanted, and which started early in the morning and finished late at night. The pink champagne started to flow early, and the food was something along the lines of bagels and lox, New York style, bought around the corner with no fuss and fanfare. Whatever happened was just perfectly right.

It is as if I was able to say on the day of my birth, "This baby is welcome and is being made a fuss over by life itself."

What about the other 364 days of the year? Learning to have a good birthday became one of the portals into the discovery of how I could live at the centre of my own life. There have been many such portals.

Going mad for a few amazing months was one. Having to find my way through the dreary wasteland of "normality" and everyday life was another. Creating magical communities on the Greek island of Skyros, the home of our holistic holiday venture, was another. Marriage, births, deaths, and spiritual awakenings were others. Mothering children, yet another. Learning to illuminate my everyday life with the mysterious world of the imagination is in there. Burning out because I couldn't burn through is also on the list. Dismantling what I had created so carefully, still another.

In the deepest sense, my own life, or to be more precise, my consciousness, has always been my most important work. Some people are fascinated by the stars, others by music, and still others by history. Understanding and becoming my truest self—and helping others to do the same—happens to be the love of *my* life.

In particular, I love the wondrous shifts and expansions of consciousness that have moved me inexorably from one cycle of my soul to another. I am in awe of the profound beauty of the way consciousness rearranges itself into a breath-taking new pattern when some insight, some sudden change within or without, takes me to a new place and opens up a new set of choices. At that moment, my mind, and the whole world, are born anew.

It is my belief that, to invert a common phrase, I learn what I need to teach. Everything I figure out that makes a difference then becomes the teaching material of my next course, my next lecture, my next therapy session, my next book, my next encounter.

And, since social justice has always been a core principle of my life and work, being part of the transformation of consciousness and culture is also my way of contributing to the spiritual and social fabric of the world.

As I look back at the experience of these years of being me, it is suffused with an underlying, almost secret joy. This is the incredible joy of transformation, and of the knowledge that no matter how bad it all gets, something will emerge to light the way, and then there is more light for the next bit.

On my seventieth birthday, I too got a surprise birthday party. When it was over, my friend Naomi told me sternly that I am never allowed to complain again. So, with no complaints, and lots of joy, I offer you the inside story of becoming myself.

PART I

OVER THE EDGE AND
BACK AGAIN

CHAPTER ONE

Preface to madness

It is August 1971 and I am having a hellish time. Then I go crazy, mad, psychotic, insane—or whatever you want to call that state of being out of touch with normal reality such that you see, hear, and understand things in a confused, hallucinatory, and delusional way. The official diagnosis is psychotic depression. Once that starts happening, I am really in hell, or perpetually worried about how to avoid landing in hell.

I was twenty-five, living in Child's Hill, North-West London, with Yannis, my boyfriend and future husband, in a small flat at the top of Mrs Cohen's house off the Finchley Road. A New York Jewish psychologist, I was lecturing in psychology and training in existential therapy, as well as doing my PhD, writing a book, and seeing therapy patients, not to mention paying visits to my analyst.

Yannis was a Greek journalist, in exile from the dictatorship in Greece. Just before the coup, he'd been sent to England as the London correspondent of *Avghi*, his left-wing newspaper. It was pretty good timing, because as soon as the coup took place, the police came knocking on his family door in Athens, and had he been there, the colonels would have put him in prison. His paper was closed down, and he was now working wherever and whenever he could and doing a doctorate in History.

Our flat cost £6 a week, a surprisingly low rent even then. We had to walk through Mrs Cohen's house to get to the flat, and if we had too many visitors, she would complain we were wearing out her carpets. It was heated by a paraffin heater, so you either froze when the room door was open, or suffocated from the fumes when it was shut. After New York City, with its centrally heated, indeed overheated, apartments, this was quite a shock.

At that time, you could get a rather good flat in Hampstead for £14 a week, as did my friends Sylvia and Norman. We could probably have afforded it, but it wasn't my way. I prided myself on the bargain, and didn't notice how much it cost us.

I could have spent a bit more on clothes, too. I was still mainly wearing the same jeans, old sweaters, and wool coat that I brought over from America and that dated from my college days. When a friend commented on this, I couldn't understand what she thought was odd about it.

I was my father's daughter. He was always happy to spend money on education and books, but not on restaurants, taxis, clothes, or good bananas.

Indeed, the only expensive thing about my life was my therapy with top psychoanalytic training analyst, Dr S, at seven guineas an hour three times a week. Twenty-one guineas a week would have got us a penthouse in those days.

It was not the done thing in the UK at that time to be seeing an expensive analyst, or indeed any therapist at all. But in my neck of East Coast psychology-mad America, it certainly was. At Brandeis University, where I did my undergraduate degree in psychology, we lived in a hotbed of Jewish, radical, existential, humanistic, psychological intensity. If you didn't go through the counselling department and get a spot of therapy, you were an exception.

Besides, understanding the psyche, and transforming consciousness was lifeblood to me. There was nothing more important than that.

4

It is against this backdrop that I lost and then gained my sanity.

My journey into madness seems to call for a preface. It is, after all, a subject that is neither easily talked about nor readily understood. Certainly, it was many years before I spoke of these experiences. I was afraid that I would lose my right to be taken seriously as a psychologist and a psychotherapist or even as a human being.

I was studying at that time with the existential antipsychiatrist RD Laing and the Philadelphia Association. Ronny Laing's brilliance lay in making madness understandable. But I'd heard people whisper about him disparagingly that he himself had been mad. I was sure that if I told people about my psychosis, they would similarly dismiss me. "She's a loony of course," I pictured them saying, and then shrugging their shoulders.

And yet, so many of us have been mad, or are connected to people who have gone mad. I have also met many people who, even with no direct personal experience of mental illness, are so haunted by the fear of going mad that they put their lives and their attitudes in a preventive straightjacket.

We keep madness, rather like death, poverty and abuse, as far away from us as possible, yet we sense its potent and dangerous presence.

But times are a changing and so am I. I now talk openly and publicly about having been crazy, and I have been received with fascination, respect, and often a profound relief at the exorcism of the humiliation and terrors surrounding insanity.

It seems important to state publicly that I have been insane, or psychotic, and that what I retrieved from that place has stood me in good stead ever since. Without that experience, I wouldn't be able to do the work I love, which involves accompanying people into their terrifying and often unconscious inner worlds.

Having lived for months in the constant presence of an over-whelmed and overwhelming unconscious and having come through, I'm not afraid of my own madness or that of others. I feel completely at home in dimensions that are considered irrational or even unmentionable.

Why do I prefer to call it "madness" rather than by a more psychiatrically acceptable label?

It is because this is the word that is most vivid to our psyche. We do not fear "going psychotic" unless we've been around the block a few times in the world of mental illness. We fear going mad. And it is how I can best sum up the way I felt.

I did not feel like someone with a diagnosis and a prognosis. I was simply a young woman facing a frightening reality with-out much guidance as to what it meant and what I could do about it and believing without doubt that it was a life sentence. Meanwhile, the people around me were living light years away in what is conventionally called the real world.

My madness has distinguished antecedents. I was not the first in my family to be mad, and the ones that I know of all died with it or of it. Their pain was, in general, kept secret, including by me. We were all ashamed and frightened.

The only reason I know anything at all is that my sister Shira met my cousin Jane at university, and because Jane's family were much more open, Jane could tell her a bit about the family. Yet, when I later met my aunt Esther, Jane's mother, and Jane herself, they wanted to talk to me about the family history, and I either changed the subject or promptly forgot what they told me. Indeed, when I heard about someone named Glouberman living in London who was possibly from my family, I was ter-rified of meeting him, shook when I thought of it, and put it off until he left the country.

The family ghosts, imbued with death and madness, were too powerful for me to confront.

I want to take this opportunity to honour the family mem-bers I knew or know of, and those I do not know of, who went

6

through madness, and were not fortunate enough to come through it as I did.

I honour my uncle Roland, my father's brother, who went mad at a time that lobotomies were all the rage. His brain was massively cut into so that he was what they called a vegetable the rest of his life. I have heard that my grandfather Solomon, a Russian communist Jewish dentist, had wanted his youngest son to become a dentist, and the pressure was too much for Roland.

Roland apparently stayed incredibly young looking until the day he died. My grandfather used to visit him in hospital and bring him cigarettes; one day, I saw him carrying a carton and as my grandfather didn't smoke, he was forced to tell me that he had a son in the mental hospital.

This is all I know about Roland. He was never talked about in my family. Indeed, I remember the moment that I asked my father how many children there were in his family, and he hesitated and said two—he and his sister. It was considered that shameful.

I honour my grandmother Sophie, my father's mother, about whom I know absolutely nothing, only that she went mad and died in the mental hospital. I've never even seen a photo of her.

I honour all the members of my family who went through madness, whether I know of them or not. Above all, I honour my brother Emmet, older than me by two years, who was labelled schizophrenic, and was in and out of psychotic states—and mental hospital wards—from the time he was a teenager. Nine years after my own period of madness, he was to jump to his death from his balcony. He was only thirty-six years old.

The weekend he died, I was running a personal development group, and I neither cancelled the workshop, nor even told the group about my loss. How could I, a psychotherapist, admit that I had a mad brother who had committed suicide—or perhaps thought he could fly?

I loved Emmet so very much, and felt I failed him. This story too comes later, but let me just say that like so many women with multiple demands coming from family and from work, I was juggling too many balls and he was the ball that I dropped.

Yet, if only he had lived a little longer, or had been born a little later, the improved psychotropic drugs and therapies might have gained him enough sanity to keep him alive.

Emmet, I will love you always, and I dedicate these chapters to you.

I also want to honour my father, Isaac, who lived in the midst of the madness and death of his mother, brother, and son, and yet remained sane, however anxious and troubled he might have been, and who continued to do his best to be of service to others. I don't think he ever knew what a wise and courageous man he was. And I honour my mother too, whose family of origin was more "normal", and yet she was able to accept all of this with an open heart.

This period of my own madness was one of the most magnificent, intense, illuminating experiences I have ever had. The events of those four or five months are more alive in me now than those of any other event of my life. I was in hell, but I was also blessed.

Not only did I not die of it, but I moved through from neurosis into psychosis, that state of mind otherwise called insanity or madness, and back into a kind of health that I had not known before.

Health was not a concept that I was too familiar with.

At Brandeis University, neurotic was normal. Psychotherapy was normal. Woody Allen would have been normal at Brandeis.

When I later joined the psychology PhD programme at the University of Michigan, I discovered that not everyone thought like this. My new friend Debby who was on the same programme told me that she didn't consider herself neurotic.

At first, I thought she was joking. Then I thought she must be boring.

She wasn't. She was brilliant. But I hadn't met anyone in years who would have described themselves as healthy or normal or non-neurotic. I couldn't imagine what it might mean.

Yet once I had the experience of going into and through insanity, I knew that henceforward there were only two main categories for me: sane and insane. I was now, and I intended to stay, uncontrovertibly sane. Whenever I would fall into old patterns of stress or self-attack, I would stop myself by saying, "That way madness lies."

It wasn't just that I had a new category system. Living on the edge of normality, as I had been before I went mad, was a thin, taut existence. It didn't take much to push me over the edge. Now, having faced some of my monsters and come to some understanding with my unconscious, it is as if there was more of me to be healthy with.

Besides, when you have faced death every night, as I did when I was mad, just being alive is a burstingly healthy state.

I imagine that madness comes most easily to those of us who live on the edge of conventional realities at the best of times. When our experience of life and of ourselves becomes too barren, starving, pressurising, terrifying, and/or unbearably painful, we go to another dimension to find a way out. Or more precisely, another dimension comes and finds us.

How people then fare depends on many factors, many of which we do not understand, and which range from the genetic to the chemical to the spiritual, from their own self-healing resources to the medical, psychiatric, and psychotherapy resources available. I am very grateful to be one of the lucky ones who survived and flourished.

Madness is not just madness. As I see it, when the filters between the conscious and the unconscious mind are lifted, we can gain access both to our personal unconscious, which is often where our demons lurk, but also to a dimension of spiritual truth that is variously referred to as the spiritual unconscious, the super conscious, the collective unconscious, the higher self, or the transpersonal.

We go mad when the personal unconscious floods the conscious mind, and daily life is like being in a dream, or, more usually, a nightmare. But deep insights from the spiritual unconscious can come mixed up with the mad fantasies so that it is hard to tell which is which. My brother Emmet's madness was flavoured with enough positive heightened awareness and wisdom for him to seek out altered states with drugs.

I remember him talking to me about how truth was like a prism and his aim was somehow to get to the essential truth at the centre. But because he was so vulnerable, he would have done better to keep himself as safe and as sane as possible.

It is not always easy to tell enlightenment from madness. In my experience, enlightened or wisdom states have an inclusive quality that makes you feel part of the world, and the world, part of you. Mad states have a more paranoid quality where you believe some people are okay and some are not, or that you personally have a special heroic role to save the benighted world. Alternatively, if you are depressed, you may feel deeply and terribly at fault.

Whichever way it goes, whether hero or sinner, if you are at the centre of the story rather than a part of it, it is probably illusion.

In general, we need to be strong and balanced enough to safely hold these out-of-the-ordinary energies and stay sane. Also, we need wise and experienced guidance of a kind that is not taught in most medical schools nor, for that matter, almost anywhere else, as well as the ability and willingness to trust someone at such a vulnerable moment. I have found that you can sometimes help people head off psychotic states and come back to reality with as little as a wise word, the suggestion of a sleeping pill, or an imagery exercise, as long as there is some connection and trust.

Going to other dimensions in order to shed light on the world of everyday reality, has played a pivotal role in my life. Madness is one way I've expressed my inability or unwillingness to confine myself to the dimension that is called "the real world", and once was definitely enough.

I've also had several mystical experiences in which I felt happy and peaceful and as if I'd come home. These experiences turned my life around, and introduced the element of soul or spirit into my understanding of life. Some people achieved these mystical wisdom states through drugs. Mine came through to me in the context of important life experiences. Drugs always seemed to me too dangerous for my delicately balanced psyche.

Many of my perceptions in these mystical states were similar to when I was mad, but they were in a form that made wonderful sense. It was as if the truths could come through in their original undistorted form. For example, being mad I was confused and couldn't tell what century I was in, while being in a mystical state, I knew I'd lived before and was participating in more than one lifetime at once. But even in wisdom states, I needed to be open to feedback from loving and wise others, so as not to stray from inclusive truth into ego bolstering paranoid states where I thought I was special and there to save the world.

Another way in which I regularly move into another dimension is through my work with imagery, which I have called Imagework. Imagework is a kind of technology of the imagination that I have developed in order to help myself, and later others, to gain access to and work with the deep level creative images that can help us understand ourselves and guide our lives.

When I am opening myself up to this imagery, I am willingly and consciously choosing to enter into another dimension, rather than being pushed or catapulted. And I love showing people who are frightened of being overwhelmed by

11

their inner world how to don a diving suit, dive safely into the sea of the unconscious, and come back with treasures.

Even setting up a magical holiday experience on a Greek island, as we did some years later in Skyros, was an attempt to illuminate everyday life by creating an extraordinary world with different rules and indeed a different approach to what is conventionally called reality. And it did sometimes feel like another dimension, full of powerful dreams, amazing coincidences, and extraordinary events.

So, the story does have a happy ending.

But in the summer of 1971, I felt doomed forever.

CHAPTER TWO

An adult life

I originally came to England in 1968 for a six-month stay and never left. There is an age when you tend to get stuck into life, and it becomes hard to uproot yourself again. This was mine.

But it felt more like stuck than like living. I was unhappy, but I was tightly held by the life I had begun. Partner, job, therapy training, postgraduate work, my own therapy, and the therapy I was offering all came within the first year or two of coming to England.

Besides, there was not an easy niche for me to go back to.

My mother died just before I left America, and my father was heavily involved with my brother Emmet who was having psychotic episodes. I wanted to stay as far away as I could from the family problems, which I feared would overwhelm me.

Then, in 1969, I went back to the States, and for a variety of good reasons, I quit my clinical psychology doctorate programme in Ann Arbor, Michigan, and split up with my boyfriend there. If I'd wanted to return to the States, it is not clear what I would have done and where I would have gone.

I met my future husband the minute I returned from that trip.

I had had some awful experiences trying to meet men, like a trip to see the tulips in Holland with what felt like a busload of

Jewish dentists with no detectable sense of humour, Jewish or otherwise. I'd decided during my flight home from the States that I was not going to go anywhere to meet men. I'd just do my thing and hope the right man would show up wherever I was.

It's not clear whether the gods thought that was funny and decided to play a trick on me, or whether they thought it was laudable and clubbed together to give me a present.

I arrived home from the airport, walked into my flat, and there was Yannis.

My flatmate Tonia was a left-wing film-maker who happened to be one of Yannis' Greek friends who were based in London, in exile from the dictatorship. She had invited him to meet me, and he had taken some convincing because he figured if I was an American psychologist I must by definition be either right-wing or nutty.

Yannis was a bright, attractive, intense and fiery Greek journalist, mainly unemployed since the Greek dictatorship, though he did have some support from short-term grants. He was living in a flat in Clapham with broken windows, subsisting on packets of biscuits and going daily to the Public Record Office, then in Chancery Lane, to work on his PhD.

His very limited English seemed to be based on the documents he read there. He knew the word "blaze" but not the word "fire".

He asked me out and suggested we go to a pub with live music. He had a London guidebook with the address of such a pub in Tottenham Court Road. We walked up the whole length of Tottenham Court Road, from Oxford Street to Warren Street, and then down again, looking for the number. We finally discovered the pub right across the street from where we had started. We hadn't noticed it because it had closed down long ago. It was a very old guidebook.

I was undeterred. I went back to his place and then he came to mine, and eventually we found our flat together at the top of Mrs Cohen's house in North-West London. We just fell in with each other, as you can at that age, and we never really parted for twenty-something years.

Did we fall in love? It wasn't exactly like that. It was more as if a force of nature drew us together and kept us together. We certainly loved and admired each other, shared our present and future unreservedly as if we were one and not two, and wanted to protect each other when the going got rough. It wasn't so much that the bells were ringing, but that a powerful discordant symphony played in the background and made it all dramatic and worthwhile.

We went together to Spain, hitchhiking and sleeping out with only our sleeping bags. He was anxious about our safety sleeping out at night so unprotected. I wasn't. I was worried about all sorts of things that had to do with my inner world of feelings. He wasn't. As he put it, he worried about the real things and I worried about the imaginary things.

He wanted to have coffee at the most expensive cafes overlooking the sea, and then if we ran out of money we'd go home. I wanted to eat at the cheapest places and stretch our money. Greek pride met New York Jewish bargain-loving abhorrence of waste.

Just at the moment we thought the Costa Brava was all there was and wanted to go home, we discovered and fell in love with the then almost unspoilt Ibiza. We drank too much wine, which was cheaper than coca cola, and we talked of the future.

When we returned to London, I'd visit him at the Public Record Office and we'd go to the ABC bakery and eat rum babas. Our idea of a Sunday morning was to go out and buy a bag full of sweets from the local sweet shop, including those large pink and white striped coconut bars, and eat them together.

Yannis was astounded at how messy I was—particularly at first when we shared a small room in my flat and the floor was so covered with clothes and papers that there was no space to put your feet. He had few possessions and kept them very neat. For some reason, he tolerated my mess, and we rubbed along together.

Both of us being outside our own culture, with no family around, we had to be all things to each other. Of course, we didn't always succeed.

We were both rather passionate and eccentric idealists, ill-suited to the British world around us and following our own stars. We had that in common. And we both had a touch of the Mediterranean in us, in my case through my Israeli mother.

But being from such different worlds, we hadn't got a clue about what made the other tick, and didn't have a clue that we didn't have a clue. His focus was on the outer world of politics, and mine was on the inner world of psychology. But more important, I was from a New York Jewish non-sexist family, and I'd hooked up with a macho Greek male.

I had no idea what being macho was all about. After all, he was nothing like my father or brother or any of the men I knew from college or graduate school in America. In the radical existential atmosphere of Brandeis University, where I'd done my undergraduate degree in psychology, we really did believe that men and women were the same.

And here I was with a Greek archetypal warrior.

I didn't know what his version of maleness meant to him, or what expectations he might have of a Greek wife, any more than he knew what I expected of a partner. And I had no one to talk about these things to.

I had very few friends of my own. I found it difficult to find people with whom I could have the kind of intimate relationships I had heretofore taken for granted. I didn't really understand the British and they didn't understand me.

He and his friends spoke Greek among themselves even when I was there, although they knew I couldn't understand a word. I stayed away from these social events when I could. I did help quite a lot with the English language anti-dictatorship news bulletins he was sending out.

Add to this, my PhD supervisor, Dr M, lived in my neighbourhood, and because I visited his house for my supervision, I never became part of university life. Nor did I meet my fellow supervisees until years later.

Not being in my own country, nor even living with someone from my country, I did not feel a resonance with the world around me beyond the little universe of my flat and my job. I was a stranger, isolated, and lonely, becoming a stranger to myself. There were no cubbyholes to disappear into, only the painful one I lived in.

And I was working much too hard, juggling my lecturing, PhD, therapy training, clients, and group work against a pretty sterile background.

Too much work, not enough love, has always been my recipe for disaster.

Or is it too many inner expectations, not enough self-love?

Ironically, my original PhD topic, later dropped, concerned families with a schizophrenic child. I was so disconnected that it wasn't until years later that it even occurred to me that, given that my brother Emmet had already been labelled schizophrenic, I myself came from a family with a schizophrenic child.

It is interesting, too, in the light of the mental health breakdown I was about to experience, that I was attracted to the radical existential Philadelphia Association therapy training, founded and headed up by RD Laing, who spoke about madness so beautifully. Indeed, madness was fashionable in those circles.

One of the most painful discoveries in that period was that I couldn't feel part of the world surrounding RD Laing. An existentialist by nature, I loved their approach to psychology and psychotherapy, and thought they must be like me. Why wasn't I getting on better with them? I didn't realise that, despite all its virtues, this was a trendy world with a charismatic male leader, and I was never going to make it.

I have never been a good groupie. I neither knew how to flirt with these charismatic men, nor to stroke their egos, and I've tended to veer between fighting and pleasing them, not a good combination.

Of course, once I went mad, I was a bit more glamorous.

Before I ever came to England, I had turned down two other trendy worlds with charismatic male leaders. Fritz Perls, charismatic pioneer of Gestalt Therapy at Esalen in California, invited me to join his first training programme in San Francisco. Maxwell Jones, who had founded a pioneering therapeutic community in an NHS hospital called Henderson Hospital in Surrey, offered me a job as clinical psychologist at Dingleton Hospital in Scotland where he was now the Head Psychiatrist. Two wonderful opportunities.

Instead I chose work in the rather menial role Maxwell Jones had called "social therapist", at his original therapeutic community in Henderson Hospital. Maxwell Jones had thought you couldn't create a sense of community in a hospital unless you subvert the medical hierarchies, and he brought some young beautiful women from Scandinavia with no nurses' training to be "social therapists". By the time I got there, each of the male psychiatrists, including Maxwell Jones, was married to one of them, and you no longer had to be a beautiful blonde Scandinavian to be a social therapist.

Why did I make such an odd choice? After all, in the official hospital hierarchy, I would be the equivalent of an assistant nurse.

The truth is that I didn't even remotely think about the advantages of status, or the disadvantages of being too highly qualified for a relatively menial post, but only about where I thought I would learn the most. I reasoned to myself that since my perspective on the world depends so much on my language and culture, which was the subject of many of my college essays, I'd get closer to the "truth" if I came to England rather than staying in America, because I'd find out about a different culture. Furthermore, if I worked in a low status job rather than being a psychologist, I'd gain something by being closer to the patients.

I didn't realise that I would face the tyranny of conformity to the minute rules, roles, and attitudes of an assistant nurse job, which I wasn't good at and couldn't take seriously. Punctuality was next to godliness, while being good with the patients was a nice extra. Being seen to be completely unselfish was particularly valued. When I took a long-awaited weekend off to go to Paris, I was told in no uncertain terms how selfish I was. That weekend, I found myself in the midst of the extraordinary first day of the 1968 Paris Revolution. I took loads of wonderful photos, but, to my eternal regret, I hurried back to work as soon as I could find a ticket for fear of getting in more trouble with my colleagues.

No one believes me when I tell them I came to England seeking truth.

Maybe I was also scared. "You know," said one of my friends in Ann Arbour Michigan where I was doing my MA at the time, "if you go and work with Fritz Perls you'll have to sleep with him". Maxwell Jones was the same. When I did go and visit him, he chased me around the table, despite the presence not far away of his beautiful young Scandinavian wife walking romantically with a lamb in the garden.

This was before the days when such behaviour would be considered unprofessional, indeed a matter for legal action. It was just the done thing.

Yet, having avoided the glamour of two charismatic men, I was now surrounded by more charismatic and/or power-ful men with whom I had ambivalent relationships. These included RD Laing as well as my PhD supervisor and my ana-lyst. I ran around, trying to cover all the bases and be a good professional, secretly believing that this meant wearing a skirt and never smiling. Nowhere did I have a sense of being seen and recognised, of being at home.

Finally, I found my natural place. I got involved in a new wave of personal development work inspired by people like

Abraham Maslow, founder of humanistic psychology, who had taught at my college in Brandeis University; Jacob Moreno, creator of psychodrama; Fritz Perls, creator of Gestalt Therapy, whose training offer I had turned down; Carl Rogers, creator of person centred therapy; and Erich Fromm, psychologist, psychoanalyst, and humanistic philosopher.

This was a very different psychological world. It was very much less professionalised, verbal, or boundaried than academic psychology, psychoanalysis, even existential therapy. The humanistic world invited us to burst our boundaries so that we could expand into our best selves, and to do this through drama, imagery, catharsis, dance, direct confrontation, and the like. Here, I didn't have to pretend to be a conventional professional. Just being myself was what was wanted.

On one of my visits to New York, I'd gone to a mini-workshop called Psychodrama of Death run by a wonderful psychodramatist named Hannah Weiner. It was part of a groupwork conference in New York that my father took me to. My father, who was an adult educator but also a seeker, was into this new personal development world before I was.

When I told Hannah that my mother's presence was hanging around in a negative way, she played the role of my mother. "I want you to be alive somewhere even if I don't see you," I told her. She answered, "I can't do that for you." I said, "Then I want you to be dead!" With tremendous force, I pushed my "dead mother" out of the room, slammed the door a few times, and was cheered by the group. It was extraordinary, taboo breaking, and powerfully healing.

I went back to see my analyst, and told him I had finally dealt with my mother's death in this way. He said to me, "You must have been very disappointed in our work here."

In one of the courses I took at that time with the personal development guru Will Schutz, we all had to get undressed. I suppose it was part of being in touch with our true nature and letting go of our masks. Later, when I was admitted to hospital, one of the psychiatrists believed that that undressing must have been either a symptom or a cause of my madness.

Of course, it was neither. But it is true that the many worlds I was part of were colliding with each other, and I was running between them trying to make believe I belonged to each one, yet sensing that I couldn't fully belong anywhere.

I had begun what one might call a successful adult life. Unfortunately, there wasn't enough adult in me to carry it off.

My professor now asked me to co-author a book with him. I was flattered and I agreed, but didn't realise that as usual in the academic world, it meant that I would do the writing and he would supervise, possibly edit, and list his name as first author.

I began to be tormented by the spectre of all I had to do. I told myself, or rather wailed to myself in the middle of the night, that I'd have to be a perfect machine to get it all done, and that I was a very imperfect machine.

Perhaps the final straw was that my analyst, Dr S, was not only away for his August break but had suggested before he left that we finish the analysis in December. He felt he had helped me as much as he could.

In my mind, seeing Dr S had been my last-ditch attempt to get the best that money could buy and find out once and for all whether I could reach perfect emotional health. I believed, like so many Americans of my generation and subculture, that therapy should be a cure-all for whatever life throws at you and lead you to Nirvana or at least permanent happiness.

It was perfectly obvious I wasn't going to get to Nirvana by December. The fantasy collapsed and with it my hope drained away.

CHAPTER THREE

Slipping

I started waking up early in the morning, desperately looking back at my life in order to figure out at what point I had gone wrong. Every day I had a new theory.

I was obsessively making plans for the past.

Then it began to get worse. I started thinking the American FBI were after me and were bugging the house. We had little door closing gadgets on our door frames, and, having forgotten their purpose, I looked at them closely and decided they must be bugging devices.

There was actually some reality background to the FBI fantasy. On my last trip to America, two FBI men in those classic suits had visited me at my sister Shira's house to enquire about the whereabouts of my friend Naomi, who was at that time a member of the Weathermen, an "underground" radical left-wing political group.

I told them I had no idea where she was and hadn't seen her in years. They reminded me politely that she'd visited me in England on her way back from Vietnam. "Sorry, I forgot," I said, realising fearfully that they knew a great deal about me.

All this time, Naomi was sitting crouched in the bedroom wardrobe.

They finally left, but returned a few minutes later to tell me that they thought I looked like her, and they wanted to take my fingerprints to make sure that I was who I said I was. People did say we looked like sisters, so they may have been telling the truth, but the fingerprinting terrified me.

At the time, I thought my role in this event was relatively straightforward and simple, and Naomi was the one who was in danger. In a way, of course, that was true. But I didn't realise till later that because I hadn't chosen her way of life, as she had, I was totally unprepared for a visit from the FBI. I was so focused on protecting her that I didn't realise how psychically unprotected I myself was.

So, it is perhaps not surprising that in my vulnerable state that summer, the FBI were figuring pretty heavily in my fantasies.

I was surrounded by psychologists and psychotherapists as friends, colleagues, and therapy supervisors, but it seemed as if no one really got what was happening to me nor had any idea how to deal with it. Yannis was the best, in a way, because he took a simple common-sense approach, endlessly trying to cheer me up and point out the simple pleasures in life. It was not that this did any good, but I could see that he was trying to take care of me.

Because Naomi was "underground", we were not in touch, but I wrote regularly to my American friend Debby, telling her what was going on in my mind. She would write long letters back, responding carefully to what I was telling her, trying to introduce some reality into my crazy theories.

But these were the days of what we now call snail mail, before email and before cheap international phone calls. By the time her letter would get to me, I had already discarded the theory she was refuting and was on to the next one. I'd read her letters and feel a bit sorry for her because she just wasn't getting the "real" truth I was into now.

However, I knew very well that I was slipping into mental illness. My biggest fear was of ending up in an American state mental hospital where all they did was sit around and watch television, and (this was almost an internal scream) I don't like television! I begged everyone not to put me in hospital.

Years later, when I saw the film *Midnight Express*, I nearly went into shock during the scene in which prisoners shuffled around and around hopelessly in a bare room. I was pregnant at the time I saw the film, and my blood pressure zoomed up dangerously. It was probably the closest thing I'd seen to my image of a pointless life in an American state mental hospital.

The fear and horror of this mental hospital back ward vision of my future was probably one of the worst aspects of the whole experience.

I believed that I would never be able to work again, and I thought that whatever money I had would have to last me the rest of my life. I'd go into a shop to buy an envelope and find that you had to buy five. I'd pace back and forth trying to decide what to do, and finally walk out empty handed. I couldn't afford to waste money on the four extra envelopes.

Like many other aspects of my behaviour during this time, this was an exaggeration of what was already a tendency of mine. I'd always been careful about money, wanting to make it last as long as possible, and now it was extreme.

Somehow in the middle of all this, I got myself on a plane to Amsterdam to attend a psychodrama conference that I had booked some months before. Finding myself in Amsterdam on my own, I realised I couldn't cope. I started walking backwards because I thought if I walked forward I was walking towards my execution.

I knew this was mad, and I managed to get myself on a plane to come home again. It was characteristic of this whole period that I somehow got myself places and did things that seem impossible given my confused state of mind.

When I arrived in the airport in London, I walked out of the airport building through a side door without ever passing immigration and customs. I found myself in a back alley, got very scared, and then figured out where the buses and taxis were.

These were the days before modern security would make the whole event unthinkable. But even so, I would have thought this was pure fantasy, were it not for the fact that some months later, when I was well, and travelling back from France, the immigration official was studying my passport in a puzzled manner, and told me that he couldn't figure out why there was no sign of my having returned from my previous trip.

When you are in any kind of abnormal or altered state, strange and serendipitous things seem to happen, not just in your fantasy, but in reality. It is as if certain doors open, or perhaps you are open enough to see them.

When you walk through the cracks of reality, reality shows you another face.

CHAPTER FOUR

Falling over the edge

By September, my mind as I knew it seemed to be gone for good. I couldn't even do the simplest arithmetic. Without a working mind, I felt completely worthless.

Yannis uncovered some unused free train tickets, and took me to Cornwall. I'm not sure where we went but it was pretty bleak. It was past the tourist season, and it seemed to me to be full of old people wandering around looking as forlorn as I felt.

My analyst finally came back from his holiday and I went to see him. God only knows how I got myself there in the state I was in. Dr S took one look at me and saw I was pretty gone. I told him a bit about what was happening to me. I also said that I couldn't pay him anymore because I would never be able to work again and my money had to last the rest of my life.

The first thing he said was that he couldn't have foreseen this when he left. It sounded to me as if he was reassuring himself that he was blameless. Then he told me that I was not in a suitable state for analysis and that I should see a psychiatrist friend of his at the Middlesex Hospital who would prescribe drugs for me. I could return to him when I was better.

I don't know what I was expecting, but it was not this. After seeing him three times a week for three years, at the moment

I most needed his unconditional love, he handed me over to someone else to fix me until I was once again normal enough to see him.

At the time, I thought it was because I said I couldn't pay him. I now think that he simply had no idea how to extend his boundaries to care for someone who could not be dealt with according to normal analytic methods.

He was a specialist. I needed a human being.

Funnily enough, he was known for his writings about the importance of a sense of trust in forging the therapeutic alliance. Yet for me, that moment was a real betrayal of my trust in him, and a failure of both imagination and love.

Later he was to visit me in hospital, and leave me devastated once again.

I did go to the psychiatrist he had recommended, hoping that I'd got it wrong and I would get help. The psychiatrist was stiff and unwelcoming, and prescribed some drugs I didn't take. That was the end of my relationship to the psychotherapeutic and medical establishment until I was actually admitted to hospital.

All this time, I was seeing therapy patients. None commented on the fact that I was a bit strange, or not as helpful as I used to be. I probably sat there silently and listened as well as I could, and they concluded I'd become very wise. Or perhaps more like a psychoanalyst?

Then again, maybe they did notice, but were too polite to say anything. Those days it wasn't done to make personal comments to your therapist unless you thought that your reactions had something to do with your unconscious fantasies and were "grist to the mill" to be worked on in the therapy. If the criticisms seemed real to you, you shut up.

One of my clients, Jesse, was an exception. Jesse had come down from Motherwell, Scotland, to bring her son Colin, who had been diagnosed as catatonic schizophrenic, to receive therapy from Laing and his colleagues in the Philadelphia Association. He stayed for some time in one of the therapeutic houses created by the Philadelphia Association.

Unfortunately, their focus was on fascinating interactions with brilliant mad people. If you were called catatonic, it generally meant that you were pretty frozen and said next to nothing. So, Colin was not exactly the most exciting person to interact with, at least on the surface.

As Jesse told it, he was ignored to the point of practically starving. I can't vouch for the truth of her account, but this sort of neglect of someone who seems relatively "boring" might well have been an unfortunate by-product of madness being trendy in those circles at that time. Jesse eventually took him back home to Motherwell.

Jesse was her own person and a marvellously wise, loving, and intuitive woman. She was working in a hairdresser salon, giving lovely massages with her healing touch. Eventually she couldn't stand it because, as she put it, the women all walked in as individuals and walked out looking alike.

Jesse really loved me and, knowing nothing of therapeutic protocol, used to call me her "wee girl". She now looked in my eyes and saw I was in bad shape.

"What is it?" she asked. "Is it that man? He's not worth it."

We spent the rest of the therapy session talking about me. When she got up to leave and began to pay me, I naturally told her she wasn't to pay me. She insisted. She said she had learned so much from seeing my vulnerability as well as my strength.

Later on, when I was in hospital, she sent me a card with a chain I could wear around my neck and the inscription, "Thank you for being you."

It was a touching vote of confidence in me when I was in such a sorry state.

Things went from bad to worse. I was crossing the street at busy junctions without looking; Yannis was terrified of leaving me to walk in the street on my own. Then I started to suspect Yannis himself of trying to kill me.

My friends Sylvia and Norman came around. Sylvia, who was also a psychologist and a psychotherapist, had been my flatmate before we had met our partners, and Sylvia and Norman had been my closest friends. By now, however, they had two children, and we'd been out of touch. Yannis must have phoned them for help.

They appeared with a plastic container of minced meat, presumably to cook us some hamburgers. I couldn't understand why they had come, and I thought the meat was poisoned.

I went to the next room to phone 999 and told them to come quickly before I was killed. They said they would come but no one appeared.

Then I left the house and went on a long walk up the nearby Finchley Road. It was raining heavily and I was wearing only my all-in-one brown polka dot jump suit. I didn't know what century I was in, and didn't know how I could find out. I looked at what the women were wearing, and some were dressed in mini-skirts and others in long Victorian dresses. I was very confused by this.

I stopped in a bakery to get a bun and took out some change to pay. I feared I didn't have the right money for this century, but they accepted the money and gave me the bun, so I thought I'd somehow got away with it.

I sat on a bench for a while, and then the rain got too much and I headed back. This walk is retained in my memory as a kind of dreamlike sequence. Yet I know it happened, because some time later my friend, psychotherapist John Rowan, said he had seen me sitting on a park bench looking strange, but he had been in a hurry and had just waved hello.

I came home drenched and took my clothes off. The jump suit had shrunk tremendously and now looked like a large babygrow. This was not a hallucination, and I've since discovered that there is a form of natural viscose that shrinks when wet and needs to be ironed to regain its size. At the time, these child-size clothes just fit seamlessly into my fantastical world. Reality and the dream were interpenetrating.

Everyone was very relieved when I returned home safely, but decided that things had gone too far. Later, Yannis described that moment, "You were as wet as if you had emerged from the sea, and totally lost. The world around you seemed not to exist. I have never, before or since, been so shocked."

Despite my fear of mental hospitals, Yannis phoned my GP surgery. He told me later that when he told the doctor I'd gone nuts, the doctor said, seemingly humorously, "Maybe you drove her crazy. Have you asked yourself that?"

My GP organised for me to go to Middlesex Hospital, a general hospital in Central London with a psychiatric ward. When they admitted me, I kicked and bit the doctors. I thought that they were representatives of the FBI and that their plan was to take me back to America to stand trial, because they thought, or pretended to think, that I was Naomi. I was terrified, and fighting for my life.

The doctors seemed surprised and hurt by my attacks on them, or that is how I remember it. Maybe, because they knew I was a psychologist and psychotherapist, they thought I should know better. But they proceeded to get me under control and bring me to the ward, where I had my own room.

I berated myself for being in this situation when I hadn't even done anything. What I meant was not the obvious, "I'm innocent and it's not fair." I meant that I wished I had done something, put myself on the line, been courageous, since in the end I was going to be standing trial.

My friend Debby commented to me years later that both paranoid and depressed people might think someone is after them, but if you're paranoid you think you're the good guy and they're the bad guys, whereas if you are depressed you think you're the bad guy.

So being depressed, even though I was innocent of the crime I was accused of, I felt I was bad because I hadn't been a political activist. But even in that state, I don't think I thought the FBI were the good guys.

The patients on the psychiatric ward got wind of the story of my violence. They got up in arms, saying I was too ill to be on their ward. Couldn't I be sent to a proper psychiatric hospital?

Luckily someone with more power decided differently. A proper psychiatric hospital was, of course, the thing I was most terrified of. In an odd sort of way, Middlesex Hospital became the womb of my journey through, and recovery from, madness.

CHAPTER FIVE

Seeking asylum

When you arrive in a good mental hospital or psychiatric ward, there is a sense in which you can feel that you are home and dry, having reached the end of an inchoate, uncharted, indescribable, and incredibly painful period. Now it is clear. You are ill and you are in hospital.

This is one of the reasons that people in great mental distress often want to go to hospital. That will clinch it, finish it, define it, let you rest.

Of course, it isn't quite like that. The journey doesn't end until the internal process, like a great sea monster, carries you to the other shore and regurgitates you onto the sand, battered but safe. Or until you get stopped short and brought back to normality by means of drugs, shock treatment, and the like.

The effect of such a treatment, and of the way you are treated, can be to close you down and alienate you from your experience. And you do get a diagnosis on your medical records for all to see. This is why so many radical thinkers at that time, including Laing and the anti-psychiatrists, were so against drugs and mental hospitals.

Nowadays, when there are so few hospital beds, and "care in the community" is usually devoid of either care or community, the views have changed. Indeed, finding a hospital bed for someone who really needs it is often impossible, and they are left to sink or swim, and, in some cases, sink their whole family.

Despite all my fears, a good hospital can sometimes be just what the doctor ordered—a safe haven where you can carry through an inner journey that has become too threatening in the outside world. I was lucky, or maybe statistically speaking, I was young, middle class, white, living in London, with an acute rather than chronic mental illness, and with a good GP. For me, the hospital was an asylum in the best sense of the word.

I was lucky to be on a mental ward in a general hospital in the middle of London. The patients tended to be less ill, and in acute rather than chronic states. Hence the uproar among the patients when I came in kicking and biting; in their view, I didn't belong here if I was so much trouble, so obviously insane.

I think also that the staff were less dismissive and condescending than they might have been in an isolated mental hospital. And we were able to feel less stigmatised, less institutionalised, and more part of the urban world around us. Indeed, life in London in the early seventies was unconventional enough that, mad or troubled though we may have been, we were not completely off the map.

Best of all, when we felt well enough, we could go to the café a few doors down, and look, act and even feel just like the other people in the café.

I am eternally grateful that the hospital team, though they didn't understand me, did in general pay me enough respect to give me a choice about what was right for me, and even left it to me to decide if I would take any medication. They never depersonalised me or ordered me around or forced me to do anything.

The respect of the staff was an interesting phenomenon. Was this their general policy? Or did they see I was extra sensitive to coercion because of my fear of the FBI, police and interrogation, and not want to tangle with me? Or, perhaps because I was a psychologist and a psychotherapist, I was, so to speak, in the business?

The healing power of the hospital was not, I hasten to say, due to any therapeutic skills on anyone's part, least of all the psychiatrists. None of them had a clue how to understand me, create safety, or guide me through the process I was in. I never heard the other patients say anything good about them either.

In general, the level of understanding, kindness, and humanity of the staff was in inverse proportion to their status in the hospital. The psychiatrists were hopeless, the nurses were better, and the women who served our food were friendly and delightful and treated us like human beings. Best of all were the patients, who were my real healers. Naturally and easily, they formed a community within which I came back to myself.

In my intake interview, the psychiatrist veered between treating me like a colleague and treating me like a madwoman. His therapeutic skills, even the most basic, were conspicuous by their absence. The whole interview would have been situation comedy material if I hadn't been so very vulnerable and frightened.

"As a psychologist," he asked, "what do you think were the causes of your breakdown?"

"Well," I answered, "that depends on your theory. If you believe in transference related psychosis, it's because my therapist was away, and he was about to finish the therapy. If you believe in real-life effects, I was working too hard. If you believe in genetics, it was my family history." And I went on to elaborate a number of other theoretical possibilities.

On one level, this ability of mine to juggle theoretical perspectives was quite complex thinking—probably too much so for that psychiatrist, who looked at me aghast. But it was also characteristic of my madness that I had one theory after another about what was happening to me and around me, and not all of these were strictly rational.

I myself was oscillating between psychologist and madwoman.

He proceeded to take a case history of what had been happening to me, in a way that felt to me like a police interrogation. He knew that I believed the hospital were colluding with the FBI, and also, that in reality, and not just in my fantasy, Naomi was "underground". But he wanted names and dates. "What is her surname?" he asked when I mentioned Naomi, writing everything down furiously.

As it wasn't clear to me whether he was a psychiatrist or an FBI agent or both, I did my best not to reveal anything that could be used against anyone.

Then he became fascinated by the fact that I had been in that encounter group with Will Schutz where we had taken our clothes off. Did this have anything to do with my breakdown, he asked me.

Even in my confused state, I thought his fascination with our undressing in the workshop was not purely professional. But it did set me wondering whether there was some meaning to nudity that had to do with the disintegration of the social self. It was another one of my psychologist/madwoman theoretical enquiries.

Back on the ward, I had a small drab light green room with two single beds and a desk. It was a typical hospital ward room, but it was mine, and I knew I could retreat there, so I loved it. It was my haven.

The next day, I was asked if I wanted to take anti-depressant pills. Because I was heavily into the anti-psychiatry movement, I thought pills were the pits and ECT was abusive. But I talked to the patient next door to me, whose day job was as a BBC director, and who was depressed but not psychotic. He told me that he'd found them useful and why not give them a chance? So, I did. No one ever suggested ECT. Indeed, they were so careful not to constrain me that they didn't always protect me from the potentially dangerous consequences of my delusional thinking.

There was the little matter of how I almost threw myself off the hospital roof.

The day after I was admitted into the hospital, I wandered off the ward, which was after all just a floor of the teaching hospital, and walked through deserted laboratories and teaching rooms, picking up notes that people had dropped on the floor. In my mind, I was following the clues left by these notes.

Somehow, I managed to find my way to the top of the hospital and onto the roof. I believed that the clues had told me that I should jump off. It wasn't that I wanted to kill myself, but it was what I thought I was being told to do.

Then this thought flashed into my mind, *I can't bear the idea of my beautiful body lying splattered on the pavement below.* I turned and ran, my heart beating loudly, till I managed to get back to the ward. One of the nurses greeted me, asked me what was wrong, and realised I was in trouble. They did keep an eye on me a bit more after that.

It is interesting to reflect that doing what I thought I should do almost killed me, and it was only my self-love—or my narcissism—that saved my life. Doing what I should do was, in fact, one of the factors that had pushed me into madness to begin with.

The fact that I might have jumped off that roof even though I didn't actually want to commit suicide, also makes me unsure what my brother Emmet really had in mind when some years later he did jump off his balcony and die. He was certainly more ill than I was, and might have had less of an ability to counteract the dangerous thoughts.

For the most part, I lapsed into a private world and basically stopped speaking, except for minimal polite responses. I didn't know whom I could say what to. My reality was just a bit too different from the reality of the people around to know how and what to communicate. Besides, I still thought I was in danger.

Being almost completely mute did not stop me from thinking I should go back to lecture, now that the academic term was about to start. No one told me what a bad idea that might be. I phoned my head of department to tell her I was coming in to teach. She sounded a bit doubtful, but didn't actually say not to come in, though she knew I had had a breakdown and was phoning from hospital. Perhaps politeness ruled.

On the day I was supposed to go in, I started to get dressed for my college teaching. One of the nurses walked in and looked at me sympathetically and said, "Maybe not?" My reaction was instantaneous. I stripped off my clothes, put on my dressing gown, and went to phone my head of department.

She was probably delirious with relief. I can't think what would have happened if I had gone to college. But for days afterwards, I regretted the fact that I had not done the teaching and was angry at the nurse who had so easily dissuaded me.

It is quite amazing to see the tenacity with which I held on to my social and professional world, determined to do what I was supposed to do. Work has such a powerful pull on us that having a breakdown could almost be defined as, "when you stop being able to go to work". I was most definitely having a breakdown and even so, I was thinking I could go to work.

Meanwhile, I was still alternating between being a bright psychotherapist and being a rather mad patient. As psychotherapist, I was a character in search of a theory that would make sense of what was happening to me, and I did know my psychological theory. I just couldn't seem to find a theory to account for the mess I was in.

And in my saner moments, I could definitely see the humour in my situation. I had been seeing clients almost until the day I went into hospital and, since it must have been obvious that I wasn't well, I marvelled at how little comment I had from any of them except for Jesse about the state I was in. I laughed to myself as I imagined myself strapped to an ECT machine (I'd never actually seen one so this was how I pictured it) and my clients coming in one after another and telling me about their problems without seeing, or at least without referring to, my unusual situation.

Apparently one of my clients actually came to my flat the day I went to hospital, and upon not finding me there, talked to Yannis for exactly fifty minutes and then left. He later said that in the extremely unlikely event that he would ever have considered becoming a therapist, that fifty minutes would have been enough to convince him to give up the idea.

On the other hand, I was also delusional, and needed—but didn't get—an enormous amount of reassurance. Mainly I needed to be told that I wasn't going to be killed. It could have been something like, "I know you are frightened of the FBI. We have nothing to do with the FBI. No one is going to put you on trial or kill you. You are safe here. We will protect you from anyone who might want to hurt you."

I also needed some realistic practical information that would have sorted out some of my fears and confusions. The most important bit of information was: "You are suffering from depression. Depression is always cyclical. This means that you will get better. Everyone who is depressed comes out of the depression and gets better." Certainly, someone should also have told Yannis this, given that he thought I might never get better, and had started searching desperately for full time work, thinking he'd have to stop his studies and support both of us.

More generally, I needed someone who could help me distinguish between my madness and my wisdom. I'm not saying I would necessarily have believed them. There were times when I would have totally discounted what I was being told, but there were others when my mind was lucid and open to new information and their words would have sunk in and helped me.

A good all-purpose question to me would have been, "Tell me what is worrying you." And a good all-purpose response to my anxiety would have been to explain how and why I would be okay.

After all, if the psychiatrists thought I was sane enough to give them a theory about why I was ill, I must have been sane enough to get some reassurance, information, and guidance from them.

It is difficult to convey how important all this was at this vulnerable moment.

Months later, when I was about to leave the hospital, I thought I could help future patients by telling the psychiatrist what would have helped me. He quickly came back with, "You wouldn't have believed me."

I gave up trying to educate him. He was certainly never going to believe *me*.

CHAPTER SIX

The hospital as community

I magine a world in which you simply cannot take anything for granted, not in the material world of reality, not in the social world of convention and conversation, and not in your inner life. There are no guidelines to go by. Nothing is impossible. You have completely lost that mysterious knowledge that is called common sense.

This is what it was like for me those days when my hold on reality was so poor.

Much of what might sound like a hallucination had to do with this loss of common sense, this inability to decide what can be ruled out, and what cannot be ruled out. For example, I announced to a visitor that the wall was talking. Amazingly, she believed me enough to go to the wall and check what was happening. She discovered that there was a radio program being piped into the room, and the headset was hanging off the hook. I was not hallucinating. There was a voice coming from the wall. I just didn't know that since walls don't in fact talk to you, there must be some other explanation.

If you can't judge what is possible or impossible, it is also difficult to recognise a joke or a metaphoric turn of phrase. One of the main ways we know something is a joke or a metaphor is if it isn't possible for the person to be saying it literally or seriously. "I'm going to kill you" is clearly a joke if your good friend says this after you've hurled an insult, and probably not a joke when said by a stranger you meet in a dark alley at night. Whether they smile or not is irrelevant.

But when nothing is impossible, this test fails.

One of the nurses saw I was frightened and smiled reassuringly, "Don't worry. I won't eat you." What did this mean? I wasn't sure. Did she usually eat people? Did she consider eating me because this was the standard treatment but decide not to? Why not? Would it be polite for me to offer to be eaten? It was, after all, not impossible that she would be seriously considering eating me.

I found a paper bag from a chemist which had the same name as my friend Naomi's surname. I threw it away fearfully. I thought someone was leaving a clue that they were onto me.

I thought the Cornish pasties had the consistency of dried skin and believed they were the burnt flesh of Jewish concentration camp victims. I choked on them when I was told to taste them.

A friend accompanied me to the synagogue on the Jewish New Year and I was sure the Rabbi was giving me a piercing accusing stare because he knew I was the sinner in their midst. I ran out of the room and didn't go back. But when I watched a television programme and thought it was about my life, it was rather exciting.

Above all, the generosity of some of the patients on my ward was phenomenal. In a world with no boundaries, having a caring community is a great gift, even when they can't help you sort out the confusion. Where they could, they offered. Where they couldn't, their kindness made the world feel safer.

James was probably the patient who became most important to me. James was a big good looking sophisticated man from an upper-class family, who claimed that the Turkish authorities were after him because of some kind of drug smuggling suspicion, and that he had to stay incognito. He said he had press cuttings to prove it. His handsome young Greek boyfriend

Giorgos used to come and visit him accompanied by an enormous Great Dane.

I was entranced.

James sympathised with my confusion, which he put down partly to the fact that I was a foreigner. I think he may well have been right. He talked of how hard it was to understand that in England a public school was what would in America be called a private school, while an American public school was a state school. "Public is private and private is public," he joked. Given my difficulty with jokes, I had no idea what he meant. But I appreciated his kind manner.

Much of my take on reality came from the books I was reading at the time, which included novels by Agatha Christie, Doris Lessing, Graham Greene, and John Fowles, and quite a lot of science fiction. I tended to think that they were, or at least could be, true stories.

This was very like my childhood relationship to my fairy stories. When my cousin Isaac gave me a wooden doll whose arms and legs could bend and which had two noses, one longer for when he told a lie, I became confused and wondered if this doll was the real Pinocchio that came alive in the fairy tale, since it was after all made of wood. Similarly, I knew for certain that one day I would become a princess and marry a prince and live happily ever after. Every night I'd go to bed lying on my back with my hands folded which I called "sleeping like a princess".

Now in my hospital room, I compared myself to characters in my books, or learned about reality from science fiction novels and crime or spy thrillers.

As I read Doris Lessing's book *The Four-Gated City*,[2] I was terribly envious of Mark Coleridge's mentally ill wife, Lynda, because he had given her a self-contained flat in his big house to live in permanently. How would I pay for a home when I would never be able to work again?

When I noticed that my watch was ticking, I thought it was a time bomb about to go off. I ran out into the lounge to get help, and found Phil, a very depressed patient whose day job was physicist. He used to sit on the couch with his head on his shoulder barely stirring. Phil saw my distress and roused himself to tell me that he was a scientist with a lot of wartime experience with bombs and there were no bombs small enough to fit into a watch. I was perfectly safe and was not to worry.

He didn't know that I had just been reading a science fiction novel in which there *were* bombs that small. I thought sorrowfully that he probably wasn't up with the latest scientific discoveries. But again, I knew he was being kind. I waited for the bomb to go off, but it never did.

My main concern was with death. Every night I went to bed and prepared myself to die.

I needed to know more about death and the afterlife, and about how to die. I asked to see the hospital Rabbi, hoping that he could teach me. But when he came I thought he looked like the psychiatrist that my analyst had sent me to, but with a longer beard. This might be just another role he was playing.

I was used to this kind of thing from John Fowles' novel *The Magus*,[3] in which every time the hero thought he knew what was happening, that turned out to be simply a story, and there was another story behind that, and another behind that.

I asked my visitor, "How do I know you are the Rabbi?" He started to give me his qualifications and credentials. He realised that I didn't believe a word he was saying, and he went away.

Unable to get a definitive version of death, I had to work things out myself. I had a lot of questions—and a lot of theories—that would not normally occur to anyone with a taken for granted sane reality. And yet there is nothing in the theories that is strictly impossible. Since even at my sanest I have always refused to assume that the publicly accepted version of reality is correct, this theory creation was another exaggerated form of what came naturally to me.

One theory was that death was an alternative world in which dead people believe they are alive and that we are dead. Maybe my mother believed she was alive and I was dead, while I believed I was alive and she was dead. This was a theory I actually raised years later with Elizabeth Kübler-Ross, expert on death and dying.

Then there was the question of purgatory: What was it? How do you get there? The Jews don't do purgatory and I didn't want to end up there just because I didn't know the rules and had broken them inadvertently.

More worryingly, why do we assume that dead people don't feel anything? We only know that they can't tell us. Perhaps being cremated is experienced by the dead person as if he or she were being burnt alive. It might be over in an instant, but, after all, there was a line in one of Graham Greene's novels about an instant being an eternity. Was being cremated what is meant by burning in hell for all eternity? I got everyone to promise that they wouldn't cremate me.

In my effort to protect myself from hell and purgatory, I remembered how some weeks before I went into hospital, my friend Robin quoted a story from Dostoevsky's *Crime and Punishment*[4] about a wicked woman whose one good deed was to pull up an onion from the ground and give it to a beggar. Upon the intercession of an angel, she was pulled up towards heaven holding onto the onion.

What was my onion? I figured I had better do a good deed before it was too late. I would wander out into the hallway saying to people, "Can I help you?"

Here too, James tried to come to my rescue. He pulled out a puzzle he was working on, and asked me to help him solve it. I can't do puzzles at the best of times, and in that state of mind, I was unable even to begin to look at it. I fled back into my room feeling hopeless. Yet again, I knew he was being kind.

I date the turning point in my healing as a moment when I sat with James at a café near the hospital, and he talked about

45

his problems. He told me he was confiding in me because he respected and valued me.

I was amazed. How could anyone could value a nothing like me?

To be crazy meant above all the devastation of my self-esteem. So much of my sense of being of value was tied up with my ability to think, and I couldn't get my mind to work properly. I had even lost my ability to do simple arithmetic. I was nothing and no one.

Of course, I was reading novel after novel, and spinning theory after complex theory, but that didn't seem to count.

Then James added, "You know more about groups than these psychiatrists."

What he said was self-evidently true. The psychiatrist's idea of encouraging group interaction was to say something like, "Mrs Jones, how is Mr Smith today?" It was obvious to me that I knew more than he did about running groups, but that wasn't saying much. I laughed, and dismissed what James said. I had so little respect for these psychiatrists that I didn't know why he thought it was a compliment.

And yet, at that moment, something took hold in me that one might call a sense of self. I was once again a person of value.

James, wherever you are, thank you. You had no idea how important you were.

CHAPTER SEVEN

Signs of spring

As I start to get better, I become part of the camaraderie on the ward. We have our little group that hangs out together, talking, listening to music, enjoying each other's company. Sometimes, if you're lucky enough, psychiatric wards can be fun.

The divisions on the ward were probably mainly along social class and age lines, though that wouldn't have occurred to me then. We were youngish, white, middle or upper class, and mostly professionals. We were also pretty unconventional types. When an older woman whose day job was Nursing Sister came on the ward, she was too conventional for us, and we were probably too weird for her. She kept herself to herself and never mixed with us. I have a feeling that there were a number of patients that we never got to know at all.

Besides James, there was the BBC director Jerry, my "next door neighbour" who advised me to go on anti-depressants. He had an absolutely beautiful girlfriend whom I used to stare at star struck.

Then there was Sally, a lovely young woman with long blonde hair who used to cut herself. Indeed, she cut herself after every interview with the psychiatrist, convinced that he was laughing at her. Knowing what he was like from my intake interview, I told her he probably was. But maybe it was his version of flirting with her.

Sally had the new Carole King *Tapestry* record, and we all sat around and listened to "You've got a friend" and all those wonderful songs.

Where possible I tried to be helpful myself. I was particularly concerned about James, because I knew how lax confidentiality was, and when I saw the groups of psychiatrists and psychiatry students coming to interview him, I feared that he would tell all, they would write it all down thinking it was a fantasy, and then someone would realise it wasn't and report him to the authorities.

I warned him to say nothing. I don't think he listened to me. Then again, maybe it *was* all his fantasy. That didn't occur to me then.

Another woman who was not in our little group is vivid in my imagination because she never got out of bed. At some point in her life at home, she had decided to retire to her bed and her family had given her a bell to ring when she needed something.

I had a secret admiration for her. How did she get her family so well trained?

Decades later, author Sue Townsend, with whom I had become friends at our centre on the Greek island of Skyros, was writing her book *The Woman Who Went to Bed for a Year*.[5] I told her about this patient on my ward who seemed to have done it successfully and urged her to give her heroine a bell. Sue rather reluctantly put it in her book, probably because she never liked saying no. Her heroine got rid of the bell almost immediately.

I remember a moment when I was standing in the hospital lobby and watched a woman who had come to visit one of the patients. She looked well dressed and confident, and she hailed a taxi to go back to work. I found this extraordinary, as if she had stepped out of a world I didn't know. Taxis are still my special luxury, and I always think back to that woman who gave me the idea.

I also had visitors. Yannis came almost every day faithfully, though neither of us quite knew what to say, particularly as I was so silent most of the time. He did tell me that his mother, who had been depressed herself, had told him to take good care of me, and he was determined to do so.

One day he brought me a present, a favourite poetry book of his by the Greek poet Constantinos Cavafis.[6] He hoped it would keep me company and inspire me. Instead, I opened the book straight to the poem: "There is no ship for you, there is no road. As you have destroyed your life here in this little corner, you have ruined it in the entire world."[7]

A number of my friends also came, and so did one of the trendier therapy trainees from the RD Laing Philadelphia Association. He had heard I was psychotic and in hospital, and though he'd never shown any interest in me before, he now had more respect. Or this is my ungenerous interpretation?

My sister Shira came over from Brooklyn. Shira is six years older than me, and was working as a probation worker in New York after years of living in Jerusalem. She is no more conventional than I am, but she is not someone who dwells on feelings, and has always stayed relatively sane and down to earth in her own rather eccentric way.

Growing up, Shira and I had had surprisingly little contact with each other, though of course our early experiences are profoundly linked. She became alienated from the whole family when my sister Ora died.

Let me explain. Shira was six and Ora was almost four when she died. Shira was close to Ora, so she was devastated at her loss. But my parents never talked to Shira about how she felt about the death of her little sister, and Shira, as is not unusual for young children in families where there is a tragedy, felt sure they wished she were dead, and not Ora.

49

In Shira's view, Ora had been the golden child, while she had been the difficult and rebellious one. She blurted out something like, "I'm glad she's dead," and when my usually gentle father became furious at her, Shira decided this family was not for her.

My parents were of a generation that didn't know how to talk to children, particularly around such difficult subjects. And they were feeling not only desperately sad but also guilty that they hadn't got to the hospital in time.

My given first name, Zohar, was in memory of Ora. In Hebrew, Zohar means shining light or radiance while Ora means light. Yet, no one told me about her until, when I was about twelve, I asked my mother about the age difference between Shira and Emmet. "You had a sister," she said. I was shocked. When I asked why she hadn't told me about Ora, she said, "I thought you don't talk about painful things."

All in all, Ora's short life and death marked our family more than any one of us knew at the time. My mother became old almost overnight, Shira turned away from the family, my brother Emmet was overprotected, and my father lived with guilt and high anxiety, rushing home whenever he'd been out for a walk, fearing something had happened. In the midst of it all, I was neglected; it is striking that there are no baby photos of me at all, while there are of the other kids.

I have very few family photos of any kind, but I do have one beautiful one with my parents and two daughters, neither of which is me. They are of course Shira and Ora. It is heart stopping to see it. My mother looks so well and happy, my father seems a bit uncomfortable as if children are not his forte, Ora looks peacefully happy and loved, and Shira looks excited and full of fun. It is the last photo in which the family has a glow about it. In photos taken after Ora's death, my mother looks prematurely old and a bit sad, and Shira is the one who is looking away.

Shira was actually responsible for my middle name, Diane. Shira didn't like her own name, which in Hebrew means *song*.

She was about six when I was born, and realising that I was about to be given an embarrassing Hebrew name, said, "Give her an American name." I was always called Diane, for which I was very grateful to Shira, because I used to imagine sinking through the floor if I had to say my name was Zohar.

Then in high school, my friend Joanie, the one who had the surprise birthday party, started calling me Dina, the Hebrew form of Diane, and it stuck. So, I ended up with a Hebrew name after all, just not one quite so outlandish as Zohar. Now I love the name Zohar and have gone back to it, at least to the extent that is possible given that my professional name is Dina and that this is what my friends have always called me.

Having absented herself from family life, Shira was only vaguely aware of me when we were growing up, and whatever little I knew about her was by secretly reading one of her diaries. Yet later, when I looked at the strange parallels in our recent life stories, it was clear that the bond was unconscious and deep.

We met our husbands around the same year; she an African American and me a Greek. We later separated from them around the same year. Despite Shira being six years older, the due date for the birth of her first child, Erika, was exactly the same as that for my son, Ari, though their birthdays turned out to be different. Then, in the next generation, the actual birthday of Erika's first child and of Ari's first child is the same day though a different year.

Shira and I see each other very seldom, and yet, when we do, we take up in this close sisterly way. At this moment, Shira must have realised I needed her, and she flew over and was absolutely loving and warm from start to finish. I cried when she left. She was the closest thing to mother that I had experienced in a very long time.

Where was my father in all this time? I really don't know. Maybe he had his hands full dealing with my brother's illness. Perhaps my sister came *in loco parentis*.

The worst moment for me in the hospital was when my analyst Dr S came to visit me. The last time I had seen him was when he had sent me off to see his friend the psychiatrist and get pills. He was the analyst attached to this hospital as a consultant, so it was quite normal for him to come to see patients. When I was told he was coming to see me, I was thrilled. Now things would be different.

But when it came to it, he walked into my room, sat down on the opposite bed, asked me rather politely how I was, stayed a couple of minutes to hear my polite answer, and then said goodbye and walked out.

I was shocked that this was all he could say to me, this man to whom I had told my deepest secrets for three years. Didn't he care enough to want to go beyond politeness to listen to me now? After he left, I sobbed and sobbed at this renewed betrayal.

Again, the failure of imagination was astounding. He was doing his usual thing, and I was outside his remit because in a world where the analyst is a blank screen, you never have interactions outside the office. Once, when he realised that we would be travelling on the same flight from America, he was visibly uncomfortable and made clear in advance that he would not be chatting with me on the plane. Then, it turned out that we were on the same train to London and I made a move to sit near him and his family. He got up, again uncomfortable, and went with me to sit far away so he would not have to introduce me to his family.

This was probably normal psychoanalytic practice, at least at that time, and perhaps had a point in his world, though not in mine. But in these abnormal circumstances in hospital, this kind of emotional distance felt almost unforgiveable.

After I got out of hospital, I went to see him to talk about my perception of what had happened and to hear his. I so hoped he would understand and say he was sorry. He simply defended himself. What he did later in his mind and heart I cannot know.

While still in hospital, I also went to see my PhD supervisor, Professor M, the one who had asked me to write a book with him. I talked to him about how difficult it had been before I had the breakdown, doing all this plus a book with no real emotional support from him. At first, he went silent, particularly when I collapsed in floods of tears in his home.

But amazingly, he did tell me that he had been depressed himself during the period before my breakdown, hence he hadn't been able to be a support to me. This willingness on his part to be transparent was an immense relief. I remember standing on the escalator in the tube on the way back from seeing him and having this wonderful awareness that I had sensed something true. It was another step towards regaining confidence in myself.

It took a long time before I was able to do anything slightly difficult without collapsing in tears, and, as was my wont, I kept doing challenging things a bit too early.

Slowly but surely, I began to recover my mind. I even went to a seminar at the Philadelphia Association about the nature of psychosis. The lecturer talked of how the psychotic keeps asking "Why?" and behind that there is another "Why?" He was exactly describing my Magus-like experience.

I became able to do a bit of arithmetic, a magical achievement at that time. I could even go and study in the library.

Coming back to myself was like the thawing of the winter ice at the beginning of spring.

In the real world, it was winter, and by Christmas, I was out of hospital, home and dry, so to speak, amazed and joyful to be alive, but still a bit stunned and wounded. After I got out, Debby, my friend who had written me endless letters trying to help me clarify my thinking, came to see me. She had suddenly thought that she didn't need to just write letters—she could come. It was a lovely visit.

And the best bit was when we met James, also out of hospital now, and his boyfriend Giorgos, and that big beautiful Great

Dane, to have tea at Fortnum and Mason. James and Giorgos probably did that sort of thing all the time. But for Debby and me, it was the height of glamour.

It was a great way to celebrate my safe return home after a terrifying yet wonderful trip.

NOW AND THEN

I'm sitting here writing on my up-to-the minute big screen computer in my North London flat, looking back at twenty-six-year-old Dina ensconced in her drab little light green hospital room, not believing she would ever be able to afford a home of her own because she would never work again.

I love her. I feel akin to her. I recognise that basement world where she lives in the immediate presence of death, the FBI, torture, the end of hope, the mistakes that can never be rectified or forgiven. I don't live there anymore, and where possible, I don't even visit. But it still has a place in the landscape of my inner world, particularly in the middle of the night, when my defences are low, and the inner world holds sway.

That young girl is sitting on her bed, long straight hair in a mess, wearing jeans and an old sweater, looking a little cold. Her eyes are stupid with terror. I can almost see her mind teaming with plans for the past—what she should have done if she hadn't been so bad and dumb and how it is now too late. I can see her trying to turn reality around to the world she might have had if she hadn't got it so wrong.

I feel immense gratitude to her for having faced the monsters and survived and grown and learned, and made it possible for me to have a better life. I also have great compassion. She looks so alone and frightened and confused.

I want to have a conversation with her, to help her with all my experience and knowledge. I reach out my hand. I say,

"Dina, do you know who I am? I am the grown-up Dina whom you will be. I call myself Zohar now. I know what you're going through and it is hell. But look at me. I'm happy now. You are not going to die tonight. You will get better, better even than before you were ill. We will never live in the back wards of an American state mental hospital. We do have a home that we can feel safe in, and will not be kicked out of because we can't pay the rent. I have children and grandchildren and a partner and a good life, and have had some amazing times.

I promise you, I am okay, and thanks to you, I have never again had to go through what you have just gone through. This is your future, not the one you are picturing. I love you. So much."

Then I imagine I am younger Dina, meeting this strange woman who says she's from the future. As young Dina, I am thinking:

I'm in my little room. I'm feeling safe, or at least, away from pressures. I can read. The food comes to me. The dinner ladies are nice. But I've got to prepare to die. Can this lady help? Can she tell me how to die? But she is saying I don't have to die. And she does look alive and even happy and she's smiling at me in this rather lovely way.

I think it's a lovely smile. But maybe she is making fun of me.

After all, she has nice clothes, and a stylish haircut and earrings. She looks like one of those proper ladies, the kind that goes to hairdressers and takes taxis. Where did she learn all that?

I worry. Why is she visiting me? I know how pathetic I am. Does she really understand? Of course she couldn't. She's okay. I'm not okay.

I say ...

Nothing.

It's all such a tangle I can't find the beginning of the thread. What can I say? What can't I say?

56

But I smile a little. She's a nice lady. Hope? Maybe?

I go back to reading some more of Doris Lessing's books about going mad. There is a key in there somewhere. Maybe Doris Lessing can help. She seems to have gone ahead of me into these worlds I am living in.

I come back to being today's me, and I give young Dina a big hug. I kiss her on the forehead and tell her softly, "I am sorry if I have confused you. I'm going now, but I'll be back soon. What would you like me to bring you? Is there anything you would like to ask me?"

She still says nothing. She looks terribly sad. I hate to go. But I know she needs to read her books. I also know I've got through to her just a little.

I'm a bit scared myself. It's such a powerful world. I don't want to be pulled in. It's like going into a labyrinth that you may never escape from. But I'll come back soon.

And now that she knows about me, maybe she'll dream a lovely dream about the future, and see herself in a sunlit meadow with me, James, Giorgos, Debby, and that enormous Great Dane.

PART II

THE CHRYSALIS YEARS

CHAPTER EIGHT

Preface to sanity

Madness is easy, almost, compared to having to tolerate sanity. Anyway, it is easier to remember, describe fondly, even enjoy in retrospect.

I'm reminded of a seminar with Ronny Laing where he was asked why he had only written about families with a schizophrenic child. Didn't he realise he needed some kind of control group? He confided that he had fully intended to write a follow-up book to *Sanity, Madness and the Family: Families of Schizophrenics*[8] which would be about "normal" or "sane" families who didn't have a schizophrenic child. However, he found the experience of being with "normal" families so excruciating, he just couldn't do it.

It was like that.

The five years of a kind of barren sanity were bookended by my recovery from madness in December 1971, and the birth of our children and of our centres on the Greek island of Skyros, in the years beginning January 1977.

Perhaps this sounds odd to say, but I considered both the period of madness and the period of birthing babies and centres to be intensely creative times. I was really alive, no matter how painful it was. The years in between were to my mind vast spaces of going nowhere. There was nothing romantic about it all. I simply felt diminished.

And yet, it certainly wouldn't have looked to anyone else as if I was just marking time. I got married, bought a house, got a full-time lecturing job, worked on my PhD, started but didn't finish at least three books, one with a signed contract that had had two publishers interested, ran regular weekend workshops called "The Open Circle" groups, and even got pregnant.

But inside was an anorexic-like diet of a daily desperate struggle to be responsible, get it all right, and move my life forward, without much nourishment coming from anywhere. I needed family, community, nourishing love, a creative project that mattered to me, everyday magic. I needed connection and meaning. All this seemed beyond my grasp.

At first, when I got out of hospital, I did have months and months of feeling quite high, when I felt that I had been saved from death, that spring would go on forever, I was happy, and both I and life were a very good thing. But then life set in with the tyranny of the everyday. I've never been good with the everyday. This time there was no community to bring me back to myself. It was as if I was in some vast institution, so big that I could not see the walls, where I had to either toe the line, or get out.

Except that since it wasn't clear where the walls were, I couldn't be sure where was out, and indeed if there was such a thing as out—besides being out of your mind, or out of your body, neither of which option I could afford to take. And there were no grades to let me know how I was doing, so I felt I must be failing. Not only that, I sensed that I had chosen to be there, so I couldn't complain.

This vast institution was after all what they call adult life, and I was in a nuclear couple. It was how it *should* be. I found myself wondering whether the "nuclear" in "nuclear families" got its name from the fact that you could be so devastated and destroyed.

It was not unlike the years before my breakdown, except that going crazy was not an option.

The death of my mother before I came to England still left a hole in my life. My family was in New York and Yannis' family was in Athens. Nothing much was coming to me from my family; my sister Shira and I never wrote or rang each other, my brother Emmet was in and out of mental hospitals, and my father was distraught. Nor was Yannis' family able to do much to help us.

In my professional world, it was much the same. My PhD supervisor, Professor M, was not particularly interested in me personally and I never met any other students. My lecturing job was so filled with power play and manipulation that I was constantly trying to heal my wounds. The organisations inspired by the notion of community that I had tried to join, including the Henderson Hospital where I had worked as a social therapist, and the Philadelphia Association, where I was still training as a therapist, felt more like cliques than communities. It was difficult to find friends in England with whom I could feel really intimate. I could leave England and no one, except for Yannis, would care.

But maybe even more than all this, I was missing a sense of what it was all about, where I was going, what I was doing. What was the point?

To put it another way, I was in the chrysalis years, and no one told me that I was about to become a butterfly.

I can't charm myself or you with storytelling about those years. After those colourful three months of madness, which my memory preserved in vivid detail, there are these five years of which I remember almost nothing. I have a few memory pictures of getting married, and others of my life at K Polytechnic, and a bit about my imagery and group work. Not much else.

The lack of stories is itself a statement. These were not dramatic times of high colour and clear focus. Just a lot of murky greys and browns and blacks, and some piercing lines of blackish red self-hate.

On an outer level, I plodded on as resourcefully as I could. Inside, there was a kind of double exposure: me feeling desperately uncomfortable about almost everything, and me looking at me trying to figure it all out, make it okay, turn the right switch, get it right.

You could call it depression, or perhaps, a dark night of the soul.

I started a diary inspired by a lecture by Anais Nin, which I had attended on one of my visits to New York. She had talked of her diaries and likened them to a Japanese spirit house in the garden. She also pointed out that it was a way of turning negative experiences into something creative. I began it on April 24th 1972; seven years later, April 24th became the birth-date of my daughter Chloe.

I didn't use my diary to record the events of my life; my marriage day isn't in there for example. It was my therapy. I wrote about how awful I felt, conducted conversations between the adult in me and the child in me, made decisions from choosing a plumber to planning my groups, and made up fairy tales and images.

There was a whole series of stories that began: "Once upon a time there was a little girl who lived by the sea." I remembered those stories when we set up our second Skyros Island centre, Atsitsa, right by the sea. Even today, I sometimes write little stories about that little girl who lived by the sea.

One of the most striking things I notice in the diary is that at twenty-seven, I felt old and past it. *I can't help thinking how empty my life is, how routine, how old I am getting [...]. I live with a foot in the past and a foot in the future and none in the present. No excitement. No joy. No adventure. No becoming.*

I couldn't bear the fact that time was passing in this barren way. I'd find I'd written a cheque or a letter and dated it with a date months or even years earlier. I'd give my phone number, and it was a long outdated one. I took to walking around with a stooped back. I was trying to stop time, go back. I was too old, and it was too late.

Aside from the general feeling of being past it at twenty-seven, there were a few pretty constant themes of torment in the diaries. There was the daily torture of trying to get myself to sit down at my desk for an agreed upon (with myself) time of five hours a day, to work at my PhD, lectures, books. There was the humiliation, anxiety, tension, and upset I felt around various people, including Professor M, many of whom made me feel literally as if the ground was being pulled out from under my feet.

There was also my relationship with Yannis who himself was getting more depressed as he had trouble finding work. Then there were all the major and minor decisions of life, which I simply didn't know how to deal with. I ended up obsessively attacking myself night after night for getting the smallest things wrong. Regretting not having bought the second-hand gold velvet easy chair I later thought would have been perfect could occupy hours of my time.

I was still making plans for the past.

Years later, as I lay awake in bed regretting something I had done, I began to wonder why I have always felt so unforgiving of myself about making mistakes. I tried to go to the heart of that feeling: "I've made a mistake." I moved from fear to rage, and then a picture came to me of my parents trying to get through to the doctor to save my sister Ora. Their terrible "mistake" had become mine.

It was only when I burrowed down through their guilt, and their rage, that I found their underlying feelings of sadness and loss. And I too was able to find my sadness and loss, and whisper to Ora, "Oh Ora, I wish you'd lived. Our family would have been so different." Only then could I let go of the self-attack and come to rest.

I was born into a traumatised family, but since nothing was talked about, I just thought if only I were a really good girl, then they'd pay me more attention and love me. Was this the beginning of my "too much work, not enough love" pattern that marked my descent into madness, and has consistently pushed me beyond my limits?

When I was in graduate school, I watched a family therapy video and my immediate comment was, "People can live in the same house for so many years and yet be total strangers to each other." The professors were impressed by the comment. But that must have been how I felt in my family.

Probably, my life now was evoking all those old feelings. I desperately needed a therapist, but my last therapy had ended so traumatically that I couldn't imagine trusting anyone. So, it was up to me, and I was determined to fix myself, make it all better, pull myself through.

One of my main methods was conversations between the adult me and the child me. In the early years, these were not so much conversations as spine chilling battles. Long paragraphs of tirades in capital letters grace the pages: *LISTEN HERE, YOU BITCH. I'M SICK AND TIRED OF YOU, SICK AND TIRED OF YOU, SICK AND TIRED OF YOU. WHY DO YOU THINK YOU CAN HANG AROUND BEING A DRAG ON THE ECONOMY? GET TO WORK AND MAKE YOUR LIFE WORTHWHILE. OTHERWISE YOU DESERVE TO BE LIQUIDATED. LIQUIDATED. LIQUIDATED.*

Then there is the "Dialogue of the Refuse and the Worker" in which the part of me that wants to get my work done is calling the refusing part of me "refuse".

Thankfully, the conversations get kinder over the years, and eventually become more like that of a teacher telling a young pupil why she shouldn't feel bad rather than a killer parent and child. I like the line about a year later that calls work, "a stop-gap against eternity".

But it is not pleasant. It is not a joy to read.

Living in a vacuum, just Yannis and I, not held by a loving family or community, I had only myself to attack and blame and persecute. There was no defence against the monsters of loneliness, worthlessness, pointlessness, helplessness. There was only the whip.

There seems to be this golden rule: When I am out of contact, I turn around and attack myself. Feeling abandoned, I abandon myself. I am reminded of how my young friend in hospital used to cut herself to stop the pain.

And what made it much worse was that I believed that I should be happy, successful, confident, flourishing. Other people were out there working hard, playing hard, being wonderfully happy. I was the failure.

The patterns that had driven me mad were still there, but I was too strong to break down. Was this what they call normality? If so, it wasn't remotely good enough.

And yet, let's not be totally convinced by the negative cover story. These diaries were my therapy, so they only contained the blackest bits of my life. The happy, positive stuff didn't need working on, so it didn't appear.

And the best thing is that I didn't go crazy. I persisted until I found a way through. And in so doing, I built a foundation for what was to come.

Not trusting a therapist, I developed the self-help technique I call Imagework to be my own therapist. Not being part of a community, I jumped at the chance of creating a short term "symbolic community" on Skyros Island. Disliking the power play in the institution where I worked, I found a way to create a world that was healthy for me and for others.

Out of the desert come very special blooms: cactuses. The "Sabra", the native-born Israel, is named after the cactus: tough on the outside, sweet on the inside. My mother, born in Jerusalem, was a Sabra. And so, it seemed, was I.

In a sense, my work eventually became to create therapies and communities for cactuses: for people who like me feel deserted by the social structures' refusal to welcome their true self, or feel oppressed because of who and what they are, and who respond by creating inner resources to sustain them.

Like the early pioneers in Israel, I had to make deserts bloom.

CHAPTER NINE

Educating Dina

However painful the struggle on an inner level, nothing could stop me from going for all the things I believed were right or necessary—a marriage, a home, a PhD, a job, a professional life, a book. I didn't always function in a balanced, well-put-together way, but I did function.

I got married almost by accident, and neither of us bothered much with the normal wedding rituals. As with other institutions, until I was in it, I didn't realise how powerful it was.

It was August 1974 and I had to go to the American Embassy to get my passport renewed. There I saw some signs on the walls that referred to marriage to "aliens".

This apparently meant terrestrial beings who were not American.

I came home and said casually, "Should we get married?" Yannis shrugged his shoulders in his utterly Greek fashion and said, "Yes." He added that since the Greek dictatorship had just ended and he was about to go back to Greece for the first time, being married to someone with an American passport might be useful in case of political trouble.

It wasn't quite as bad as it sounded. Or maybe I was just used to his macho style. I hopefully translated it as: "I'd love to marry you, darling."

We got married at a Registry Office a few days later, on August 15th. Yannis suggested that date because it is the biggest Greek holiday in the year, the Assumption of Mary, and that way he would remember our anniversary. Unfortunately, as I was to learn later, it was also the name day of every Greek named Maria, and name day parties often took precedence over our anniversary.

I knew you needed a ring for the ceremony, but I didn't know you normally have to have one each. I walked up and down Oxford Street looking for the cheapest silver ring I could find. I had still not discovered the art of spending money. I found one which cost less than £2. Mission accomplished. Yannis later told me he would have liked a ring too.

I wore a long flowery blue dress with ruffles and Yannis wore a light blue brushed denim jeans suit. To be honest, if it weren't for my friend Robin, I would have grabbed some old thing from my wardrobe. She put her foot down and took me shopping.

We have photos of the wedding, looking like two incredibly young and innocent hippies. The only reason we have any photos is that a photographer at the registry office offered to take them and told us we didn't have to pay for the photos if we didn't want them. In the end, of course, we bought all of them.

We invited a few friends, and held the reception in the sitting room of the new house that we had just bought which was still more or less a building site. There was a big second-hand wooden table for the food, and people were asked to bring food to share, as you would in a personal development workshop. I think Robin brought the wedding cake.

We didn't think of inviting our family. Surely it wasn't important enough for them to come from Athens and New York?

We weren't actually hippies, as neither of us had ever really dropped out, and we weren't making a statement. This was just how we lived. It never occurred to us to do it differently.

It was a time when it was possible to be non-materialistic and not be thought a failure.

Immediately after the wedding, Yannis went to Greece to see what was happening after the dictatorship. I stayed home alone. It did occur to me that this was rather an odd way to have a honeymoon. But in a way, it worked quite well, because right after the wedding, all my ambivalence about being married started to hit me, and I was glad to be alone. I also decided to keep my name, reasoning to myself that I wasn't Greek, and a double-barrelled Glouberman-Andricopoulos wasn't going to work.

Despite this incredibly casual approach however, the fact of being married had a profound effect on me. Somewhere inside, I decided to become a proper "wife", or rather, to fit into my notion of the role of wife in a conventional world. This was not a good idea. I didn't know how to do it without losing myself.

Buying a house had been possible because I had found a full-time job lecturing at a polytechnic some months before and so could get a mortgage. I had sat down and phoned every college in London that had a psychology department to ask if they needed a part-time psychology lecturer. When I got to the Head of Psychology at what was then K Polytechnic, now K University, he had asked in amazement, "How did you know?"

I was to stay there for seventeen years.

At the time, psychology was part of the sociology department. When I joined, the sociologists were all male White Anglo Saxon Protestants, or WASPs, with the exception of my friend Bridget, a left-wing female sociologist of Irish descent. The psychologists, though headed by a blond WASP, had all the oddballs—women, foreigners, and/or Jews. I was all three.

One sociologist, Paul, made a list of the members of the department and divided them into two teams, The Fascists and The Foreigners. It was like that.

Luckily, we Foreigners became allies, and Bridget and I in particular felt we owed our sanity to being able to compare notes with each other and confirm our perceptions of the mad things going on. It was so painful sometimes that my life lesson in my diaries was, "If they stick a knife in, don't stick it in again yourself." The attack was so bad that I had to ban self-attack.

But K Polytechnic offered me an education, best referred to as *Playground Politics for Dummies*.

Take staff meetings for example: at first, when issues were raised, I'd contribute my honest take on them. A deathly silence always followed. I didn't know that the deals were done outside the room, and saying what you thought was beside the point.

It is hard to describe the rowdy atmosphere in which business was conducted. The Head of Department memorably said in the middle of a particularly unpleasant staff meeting, "I don't care. I'll be the last to go." He wasn't. As soon as he started to be aggressive to those above him in the hierarchy rather than just to us below him, he was thought to be having a breakdown, and was kicked upstairs.

The politics of envy ruled unashamedly. Paul and I seemed to be speaking honestly and openly to each other, and then he immediately went around to his friends to report what I'd said and make fun of me. I was sincerely puzzled.

"Why?" I asked his friend Ray.

"He'll feel better about himself if he pushes you down."

I laughed. Why would anyone want to do that? Ray looked insulted. "But it's true."

Later when we started Skyros Holidays, and there were articles about us in all the major newspapers, I heard that people talked about it—and me—in the common room, but not a single person would give me the satisfaction of referring to it. No one even said, when we came back from our summer holidays, "You look tanned."

Ray kindly explained to me: "It worries us when you seem to be doing something that might get you ahead, if we aren't."

Meanwhile, the students were also trying to educate me. They weren't happy with my lectures because, as they said, "We don't know what is important. What do we need to underline?"

I thought "important" meant it would help you make sense of the world in a new way. They thought it meant that it would help you pass your exams, which, most believed, was the whole point of these lectures.

"What about learning?" I asked.

"Oh, we can do that later."

Eventually I restructured all my lectures so they knew what to underline for exams, and the whispering died down.

My seminars were another matter. Here I was determined to offer the option of an experiential workshop, influenced by my humanistic group work. I started by running what we used to call "t-groups" or "leaderless groups" which meant that I did very little besides making the occasional wise interpretation, and told them to observe the group interaction and keep a journal. The idea was to learn about group process by direct observation rather than theory.

My first experience of this kind of group had been when I was an undergraduate at Brandeis University, in Massachusetts. There it was avant-garde. Here it was unheard of.

The students got up in arms. This wasn't proper teaching. They weren't learning anything. They'd meet in the cafeteria and plan revolution. I didn't mind. I thought it was all part of the process and was certainly good for group cohesion.

However, when they handed in their journals, I discovered they were right. They weren't learning anything. I had underestimated the minimal level of psychological sophistication you need in order to be able to observe the process.

But I didn't give up. I was more successful with all the visualisation sessions where we went into the future to set goals, found wise consultants, explored how to make a life change, talked to inner children and the like. We even threw dice in a role-play that was inspired by the then cult novel *The Dice Man*.[9] It was all new and exciting. Years later, I was to meet students who still practised the exercises.

I'll never forget my Eritrean student. His English was poor, and study skills even worse, but he was determined to pass his exams and return to his country to make his contribution. He came to me for help, and we had a series of sessions in which we visualised his success in studies and exams and looked back to see how he did it, and we generally practiced successful attitudes rather than content. Foreign though it all was to him, he sensed it would help him and was willing to do what he had to do.

From being the student other lecturers talked of failing, he not only passed, but was given an award for being the student who had showed most improvement.

I've often thought of him and wondered what happened to him when he went home, given the subsequent history and politics there.

For some students, the seminars were indeed life-changing, and for their sake, I am glad I took the risk of defying the culture there. Just yesterday, an old student, Stephanie, contacted me through my website, writing: "I watched a programme last night of an interview with Carl Jung and remarked to my son that listening to him reminded me of a lecturer I had for social psychology at K Polytechnic in 1984, and suddenly I told him your name without knowing I remembered it! He looked you up and here I am writing to you now."

When I responded, telling her it was one of the best compliments I had ever received, she went on to tell me how important I had been to her, concluding with: "You started me off on my journey of discovery and now you have popped back to check to see how things are going."

In a later email, she added: "You were not aware that my younger sister came to visit me for a week. She was deciding what A levels to do. She sat in on one of your lectures and from that moment she decided she wanted to be a psychologist. She went on to do a doctorate and is presently a clinical psychologist working with adults with a learning disability."

It's as if *she* popped back to remind *me* that it was all worth it.

It is interesting that in those days we had the kind of freedom where we could run the courses and seminars we wanted, no matter how counter-cultural they were, and indeed we could write our own exams with some minor oversight by external examiners. In that sense, it was a golden age.

This freedom did have a down side, though. The truth was that no one really cared what lecturers were actually doing in their classes. Education as I understood it was not the point anyway. As in any institution, running a department with students who passed and didn't complain and keeping the staff in good jobs was the main objective. This was probably obvious to everyone but me.

Perhaps what was a little unusual was how baldly and openly all the power and status machinations were admitted to. I used to thank my lucky stars I wasn't in some prestigious institutions where the same power play would be glorified in the name of "academic excellence".

I might have believed them.

CHAPTER TEN

Fool or trickster?

I need to own up to the fact that while the teaching staff at the Polytechnic wouldn't give me the satisfaction of honouring what I was doing in and out of college, I also didn't give them the satisfaction of paying lip service to the institution, its politics, and its values. I thought this didn't matter as long as I did my job.

I was a bit like someone who has walked right into the middle of a life size Monopoly game. Everyone around is getting excited about houses and hotels on Park Avenue. I've never heard of Monopoly and I think games are silly.

"A house?" I say. "Could I have one with big windows please?"

Then they trample all over me trying to get to the next deal.

K Polytechnic wasn't the first institution in which I was stepping into a vast monopoly game, refusing to play, and saying games were silly. I'd had the same attitude in almost every institution I had studied or worked in. I was always the Stranger, alienated by the rules and the roles, and since I didn't even observe what was going on and use it to my advantage, I was also the Fool. It emerged later that I was the Trickster as well.

Brandeis University, where I took my undergraduate degree, was the only academic institution that didn't have this effect on me; it was such an existentialist, left-wing, and unconventional world that I fitted right in. And before that, my summer camps, which were run as communities, gave me a taste for worlds in which I could belong, and became part of the inspiration for the Skyros holidays I was to become the founder of. This split between institutions and communities has been one of the leitmotifs of my life.

When I look back at my childhood, I can see that it all started in the playground of the Yeshiva of Flatbush. My mother, who was born in Jerusalem, wanted us to have a Jewish education and so sent us to this Yeshiva, which was an Orthodox Jewish school considered modern because it was co-educational. My father went along with it.

It was not a wise move. The school was indeed modern compared to ultra-orthodox male-only Yeshivas, but it wasn't exactly free-thinking. I was being thrown into a highly conventional world by my highly unconventional parents.

Going from home to school was a trip into an alien world. There were a million ways in which I was an outsider, and never learned to play the game.

My Israeli mother was worlds apart from your typical middle-class American Jewish stay-at-home mother. She had two jobs teaching Hebrew, and only Israeli friends. She spoke Hebrew to us at home, while we answered in English. Although she came from an Orthodox Syrian Jewish family, she had rebelled against their traditional values. As a young girl, she used to throw her books out of her window to get to school because girls were not supposed to get an education. She had also challenged the Scouts and demanded she be allowed on an all-male hike. She gave up her religion one day when she travelled on the train on a Saturday, which was against Orthodox Jewish law, and, as she put it, "The sky didn't fall in." All this was before she ever came to America.

My father was American, but he knew nothing about being Jewish, having had an anti-religious Russian Communist father, and he knew even less about being an Orthodox Jew. He was also an eccentric adult educator, part time poet, and spiritual seeker, with no social skills.

She was not in her own country, and he, having been incredibly neglected as a child, was hardly in his own universe.

My parents didn't keep a Kosher kitchen until I insisted that they do so because I wanted to be Orthodox like my friends, and to be seen to come from an Orthodox family. Even then, they were only medium Kosher; I learned not to ask too many questions about their practices as I wouldn't necessarily get an honest answer.

I had to keep friends away from my house on a Saturday in case they saw my parents breaking the Sabbath rules. I had to keep them away anyway because my house was so messy, unlike their perfect middle-class homes. If a friend did come, I'd spend hours trying to clear the house.

At the High Holidays, the most important dates in the synagogue calendar, when you have to buy a seat to attend, I had to throw myself on the kindness of a friend to sit next to her family in a little half seat in the synagogue. My parents weren't going, and I never thought of asking them to buy me a seat.

All my clothes were hand-me-downs. The only other girl who dressed like me, or worse, in this expensive private school, was the caretaker's daughter who attended for free. My parents were willing to spend quite a lot of money on education but not on ephemerals, and didn't realise what sort of world a private school was and why you needed to spend a bit on clothes if you want the education to be relatively pain free.

I did get given a gift of a lovely gold hand embroidered Israeli dress, so I wore that to school every day until my friend Anne said to me one day, "No insult intended, but are you poor? You're always wearing the same dress." She meant no harm, and was just curious. My mother found me crying and when she heard the story, took me shopping.

Unfortunately, no one in my family explained to me what the differences between home and school were, and why my family's attitudes and values were a positive thing, which of course I now think they were. As a result, I thought of myself as an orphan, looking at the "real" families of my friends. I thought they were normal, while my family was nothing like them, and had loads of secrets, ranging from not being observant Jews to all the death and madness.

This feeling of being an orphan with my nose pressed against the window of a normal family persisted in the background of my mind way into adulthood.

On top of all this, I had been skipped one year and was younger than the other kids and so was behind in all the changes happening to the girls as they flirted with boys and manipulated situations to get what they wanted. I was completely out of my depth and was successfully elbowed out of situations I would have liked to be part of.

When my classroom seat was next to Gerald, who seemed to like me, Debbie noticed and got jealous. I watched her walk up to the teacher, whisper to her, and get her to change our seats so that Debbie sat next to Gerald instead. After that, I wasn't invited to Gerald's Bar Mitzvah, or indeed any of the Bar Mitzvahs; the same six girls got invited to them all.

That was the first of many such incidents. The most vivid was the one which involved my friend Hannah, who wanted to throw a party with me and exclude the popular girls as a kind of revenge for all the parties we weren't invited to. Then she got schmoozed by said popular girls who couldn't bear to be left out. I happened to overhear Nora trying to convince Hannah how much they liked her, but I thought she sounded so phoney that Hannah couldn't possibly take her seriously. I was wrong. As it turned out, Hannah held the party, invited them, and left me out instead. I said nothing, dismissed her in my mind, and never spoke to her again.

Then there was all the flirting on street corners, which I was too young to have a clue about. What was that vibe in the air? I didn't get it. My friend Joanie and I would walk together until we reached her home, she surrounded by admiring boys, and then I'd go on to my own home alone. Nora had two boys bringing her flowers and fighting over her in the middle of the classroom. What?

Apparently, Nora later became a well-known feminist.

Things changed when, as a young teenager, I went to the community oriented summer camps of Habonim, a socialist Zionist non-religious youth movement. This was a time when you could be both socialist and Zionist, when we still believed that an ideal society could be created in Israel, before the politics there made it impossible. I loved it and felt inspired by it.

The camp was set up with a community atmosphere, we sang Hebrew and other folk songs, did Israeli dances, and worked in the cornfields. I felt completely at home.

My camp experience was not miles away from what was to happen in London after I tried unsuccessfully to fit into the normal psychological and psychotherapeutic worlds, and then discovered humanistic psychology and the human potential movement.

I began to think of myself as having two personalities. In school, I was quiet and a good girl; in camp, I was vivacious and very popular. I didn't know why. But this was the start of the split between institutions and communities.

Then I went to Brandeis University, where I again felt in my element, and had a sense that I could find resonance in the world around me. I began to emerge, become known, have good friends and boyfriends, and have an impact.

As an undergraduate in college I wrote a paper entitled, *The Fool and The Trickster*. It started out being about the archetype of the Fool; I was actually dealing with my feelings about being an incompetent, a fool, someone who never knows the social rules. When I discovered that the other side of the Fool archetype is the Trickster, I was puzzled. Surely, I was never a Trickster?

I didn't recognise the Trickster in me that turned social situations upside down.

My anarchic innocence was strangely powerful, indeed threatening to the status quo. I created chaos around me with all the best intentions in the world.

This became a serious problem when I started the clinical psychology PhD programme at the University of Michigan. My final term in Brandeis had intensified my anarchic tendencies. I had already been accepted for my next degree and as I only had to pass my exams, I reasoned that I might as well just do only what I enjoyed doing. Surely, I'd manage to pass. With this rather cavalier attitude, to my surprise, I got exactly the same grades as I had before.

By the time I found myself in a very conventional professional training programme, and had to conform to their structure and values, I had forgotten why and how.

To say that I found myself there is a bit misleading. I chose it, for all the wrong reasons. I was actually wooed by the University of Chicago clinical psychology department, who thought I was great, and would have been much more suitable for me. But given my perpetually low Groucho Marx type self-esteem, I reasoned that if they wanted me so much, there must be something wrong with them. I literally said something like that to the gentleman who came to see me from the University of Chicago. I can still picture the insulted look on his face in response. I chose the University of Michigan, who accepted me, but didn't care much about me either way.

At Michigan, I got along well with the social and community psychology professors and with my fellow students. They had a broader perspective and sensed what I was on about. But the clinical psychology professors definitely expected me to toe the line.

When we started our first seminar about the history of clinical psychology, I felt bored and puzzled and said that I could understand why we might want to study the history of how people think, but not the history of a particular profession. The two professors teaching the course looked at each other in astonishment.

Then I had a statistics exam on the day I was going to New York to see my boyfriend and I actually forgot about it, didn't study and came in at the end of the class, apologising to the professor. He told me not to worry—he could give me the exam in his office. I sat there on my own in the office, looked at the paper, and wondered why the professor was asking questions he knew the answer to.

I hadn't only forgotten the exam. I'd forgotten the whole *raison d'etre* of exams.

I left the paper blank, and walked out. As I climbed into the taxi to the airport, I had the feeling that I was possibly going a bit mad. I knew exams were normal and my behaviour was not.

My statistics professor cleverly hooked me back into the system. He gave me a zero on that exam, and told me I had the rest of the year to get my average up. I began to work harder and bring up those grades.

The other professors were less successful with me and we seriously antagonised each other. I got called in by my clinical supervisor and told that I needed to be more committed. He pointed out that I was going back and forth to New York much too often. I responded, "You can't really tell me how I should be; only that if I do that I'll fail." I really didn't understand why he thought he had a right to tell me how to live. He couldn't understand why I didn't respect his authority as my supervisor.

Most damaging of all to my reputation was the time our psychopathology professor asked us to tell him honestly what we thought of his exam. Having experienced the thought-provoking examination style of Brandeis, I had been astounded that the exam simply required us to parrot what was in the book or on the course. I took him at his word and stood up and said,

"I thought it was like a sixth-grade spelling test."

The professor grimaced. "It's a good thing I am well analysed."

Not quite as well analysed as he claimed, he hated me after that, and he was incredibly powerful in the department.

My wonderful social psychology professor, Dick Mann, called me in and told me: "I've been hearing the name Dina around in a way that's a bit disturbing. All your teachers are in roles, which are like boxes, and you refuse to recognise this. You've got them rattling around in your brain without any walls between them. They don't like it. You'll get in trouble."

It was a brilliant analysis, and totally true, but, as usual, I just didn't believe what didn't make sense to me. I thought that since they were psychotherapists they would want to understand me. And why would anyone like being in a box?

I became known as difficult, rebellious, a troublemaker, just as I later did at K Polytechnic. I got assigned the strictest and most critical supervisor in the department, who treated her students like children. They thought she might keep me in line. It was exactly the opposite of what I needed. A more open and compassionate supervisor could easily have kept me aligned with the course and brought out the best in me.

At the end of my first year, despite being one of the top students academically, I was the only one who didn't get a clinical placement for my second year. I later heard that my psychopathology professor had a lot to do with that, as did my supervisor.

My community psychology professor told me that summer, "You were rocking the boat." Who me? I didn't think I was powerful enough. I saw myself as Fool, not Trickster.

I was so upset by what felt like a failure experience, my first failure in an academic context, that I developed a bleeding ulcer within days. Fainting in a bookshop, I literally saw stars.

This combination of being critical and yet wanting and needing approval always ended up with my getting very hurt, and not quite knowing why. If the rules didn't make sense, I tended either to dismiss them and manoeuvre around them, or try so hard to fit in that I lost myself. It never occurred to me to do what I believe most effective change makers do—accept the reality, pay at least a minimal respect, and then find a way to make my own statement within that.

I could have told the Emperor that he wasn't wearing any clothes and then felt awful when I didn't get an invitation to the palace.

My inability to adapt effectively to conventional institutions cost me a great deal over the years. Yet this failure of normal socialisation is what later made me so successful at creating unusual contexts that welcomed people like me. I instinctively knew how to create a world with the kind of rules that would make deep sense, one where people could feel at home with themselves and others and be truly encouraged to flourish.

Now, despite my difficulties fitting in at K Polytechnic, I was able to create alternative worlds which ran alongside my day job, and would later enable me to leave the institutional world for good. I started to run a personal development group called "Open Circle", a one-weekend-a-month group where I used humanistic psychology methods and developed my imagery techniques. It was our little community, and it was honest and loving.

I felt valued by my group members in a way that was new and wonderful. I found myself thinking one day: *I can't be nothing, became I am something for my group members*. But when I'd return to work on Monday morning after a weekend workshop, just walking down the corridors could feel physically painful.

The sad thing was that I loved teaching and I was good at it. I loved my students, or at least the ones who had retained their curiosity and love of learning. I particularly enjoyed working with the mature students who were studying to be social workers and probation workers. They had no academic confidence when they started, indeed they were terrified, and in fact they were fabulous students, eager to learn, eager to become as good at their future work as they could be.

I was by now learning first hand so much about institutional rules and roles that I didn't really want any part in them. When I later researched burnout, I discovered that in most cases, when people burnt out at work it was not the work itself that was the problem but rather the internal politics of the institution they worked in. I pictured institutions as bounded by rigid walls, and as indifferent to our coming and going; you couldn't have much impact, but you could vote with your feet and go. Communities had walls made of people, so each person could step in and step out and make a difference to the shape. Of course, this was an idealised picture of community, but it inspired me.

Later, the basic shape of our Skyros holidays in Greece was to be rooted in the determination to create a "symbolic community", one in which participants could have a life-changing experience of being in community. I knew that a community atmosphere had made me happy in my Habonim summer camps, at Brandeis, and in the humanistic psychology world. Even in the Middlesex Hospital, it was the community of patients that had been most responsible for my healing.

I assumed that others would feel the same way, and they did. Our first advertising slogan, and perhaps our most successful, was to be: "Sun, Sea, and a Sense of Community."

NOW AND THEN

When I look back at young Dina, I admire her, and I want to say:

"You're a bit mad but I like you, or rather, you're a bit mad *and* I like you. I admire the way you walk into institutions and create chaos without quite knowing why. You're real and you're honest and you're a breath of fresh air in these closed down places. And you do have the right idea about what makes human beings happy and what doesn't.

I only wish you weren't quite so naïve about it all, so uncomprehending when people don't like being challenged, so wide open to getting hurt."

But the admiration kind of dribbles away when I see Dina sitting and writing these terrible notes to herself. I just feel this devastating dumb pain in my heart. She is like a young girl who is old enough to pass for a proper adult, and yet is more like a motherless neglected child having to step into her mother's shoes. She is persistent, and determined to make her life work, but it never quite works for her.

I overcome my desire to close down and turn away from the pain and helplessness and shame she feels so that I can reach out to her with an open heart. Then it occurs to me that I have been so horrified by her life as it is revealed in the diary pages that I have not paid her the respect of tuning in and hearing her side of the conversation.

I step into the younger Dina to get her response. As young Dina I find myself saying: *Oh, it isn't that bad. The diaries tell every moment of pain and inner argument. They don't tell you about the bits that are good. I'm enjoying having a job as a lecturer for the first time, creating a home, having a husband and a stable life. There is a lot that you have forgotten that is really okay. Don't waste your sympathy on me. Save it for yourself!*

I am surprised at how gutsy she is. I have been awarding her A for effort. Why not A for her whole range of solid achievements? There's a saying in Hebrew that my mother used to use: *Kol hakavod*. It means: all respect to you.

"*Kol hakavod*, young Dina. You cleared the ground, tilled the soil, and planted the seeds for all that was to come. Thank you for doing the backbreaking work so that I could reap the harvest."

That harvest was not long in coming.

PART III

THE CREATIVE YEARS:
BIRTHS AND REBIRTHS

CHAPTER ELEVEN

Preface to the creative years

After the parched desert times came the deluge.
Births, deaths, and spiritual experiences came, like buses, almost at once. There was a cycle of about twelve years when it all happened—between January 1977 and Autumn 1989.

The cactus burst into flower.

If the previous years were full of events and achievements that didn't nourish my soul, these years were so full of experiences that touched and expressed my soul, crowding each other so close, that at one point I became convinced that the only way to solve my time and energy problem was to have two of me. And for a few mad hours, I thought this was a real solution, and began to ask around about cloning.

In these years, I finished my PhD, gave birth to two children, moved into a new house, started two centres on a Greek island, lost my brother and my father, had a series of spiritual experiences that turned my life around, created my Imagework approach to therapy and transformation, left my full-time lecturing job, wrote and published my first book, helped Yannis launch a new magazine, and then burned out. Meanwhile, I continued seeing clients and running groups. I was also having an insight a day to help me cope with a life that was so utterly beyond my limits, and yet seemingly wasn't, because I was doing it.

And in all that time, I thought I wasn't working hard enough, wasn't efficient enough, didn't have enough energy, and why wasn't I also hosting dinner parties?

No wonder you burned out, you are probably thinking. No, the truth is that I burned out because I didn't know how to stop. Or rather, just when I was about to stop and rest, something came along dripping with everything I was addicted to and I said, "Just this last time."

This became the subject of my second book, *The Joy of Burnout*,[10] which I wrote many years later, in 2001. It was only then that I heard the word burnout and suddenly knew that this was what had happened to me.

Here is the approximate chronology of the events, but remember that each event or project had a preparation period and a follow up, so that events that look separate were actually overlapping each other:

January 1977: We signed the contract on the house in Skyros, I was awarded my PhD, and I gave birth to my son, Ari.

Summer 1977: We spent a month at the house in Skyros.

Summer 1978: I was catapulted into an altered spiritual state.

April 1979: I gave birth to my daughter, Chloe.

Summer 1979: We had our first Skyros Centre session.

May 1980: My brother, Emmet, died.

Summer 1984: We had our first Atsitsa session.

November 1988: My father, Isaac, died.

Spring 1989: I took a Sabbatical year from K Polytechnic never to return.

Autumn 1989: I published my book about Imagework, *Life Choices, Life Changes*,[11] helped Yannis launch *i-to-i* magazine, and then burned out.

How to talk about all this? It requires some semblance of an order that real life doesn't always offer, that is to say, one thing separate from another, rather than everything all at once.

Though brief, the creative years fall into two sections for me:

Part III: The Creative Years: Births and Rebirths is the action-packed two years from 1977 to 1979 which included the PhD, the birth of two babies, my spiritual breakthrough experiences, and the birth of the Skyros holidays with the establishment of the Skyros Centre on Skyros Island in Greece.

Part IV: The Creative Years: Gains, Losses and the Radical Imagination covers the years from 1980 to 1988, which begin with the death of my brother and end with the death of my father, and include the founding of our second centre, Atsitsa, the development of Imagework, my marriage conundrum, and an insight a day to survive and thrive.

After the creative years, comes a new cycle described in *Part V: From Burnout to Nebbish Wisdom*, which looks at the years from 1989 when I stepped into burnout and beyond.

But before I talk about it all, I want to honour the miraculous creativity inherent in the cycles of life, such that at every point when it all seems so hard that you want to give up, you turn a corner and have a new vista, even a whole new life. And this new life has the capacity in turn to change and transform other lives, including those of people who at that moment are finding it so hard that they want to give up.

My life of extremes would not, I admit, suit everyone, or perhaps, almost anyone. Indeed, for many people the years of building a stable life would have been wonderful, and the months of madness and years of creative excess, nightmarish.

But the fact remains that the moment that we are most tempted to give up hope, is also potentially a vehicle to a new beginning. And, likewise, unfortunately, the moment we are tempted to stop and sit on our laurels, might also be the moment before the crash.

Anyway, so it has been for me.

New beginnings later became the subject of my third book, *You Are What You Imagine: Three Steps to a New Beginning.*[12]

Let's begin with a birth.

CHAPTER TWELVE

A baby is born

It is a Saturday night in mid-January 1977, a month before my son Ari is due. I am running my Open Circle weekend group.

Just days before, I have been awarded a PhD. My thesis[13] is enormous. Overdoing things as usual, I have done research on a psychological theory called Psychological Differentiation, as well as on family systems, on class differences, and on differences between entrepreneurs and bureaucrats. To top it all off, my main interest is a metatheoretical argument about the class bias in psychological theories.

At the oral exam, my main External Examiner confided in me that the professor had told her, "It's brilliant, but it's like three PhDs in one. Don't bother to read the whole thing." Only three people, or maybe two and a half, read this thesis that had taken me seven years or so to write. No one encouraged me to publish, though many interesting papers could easily have emerged from it.

Sad to say, but as a woman, the greatest advantage of having a PhD turned out to be that when you were asked whether you were Mrs (someone's property), Miss (either very young or on the shelf) or Ms (a raging feminist), you could say "Dr" and they would say "Sorry" as if they had suddenly realised you were worthy of respect.

We had also just signed the contract to buy a derelict house on the Greek island of Skyros. This significant moment somehow got lost in the midst of getting my PhD and giving birth to our first child.

The early months of the pregnancy had been very hard, because I found myself full of depression and fears. A fear of losing the baby was a big one, and stopped me from preparing pleasurably for the birth. I preferred to say to people "I'm pregnant" rather than "I'm expecting a baby". I couldn't bear the fear of disappointment.

Strange frightening pictures came to me. The one I remember most, because it was so peculiar, was a terror of being shut up with a baby in a little flat in a high-rise tower block. I was living in a house, and indeed, have never lived in a high-rise flat.

Where did these pictures come from? Were these my mother's fears that I had somehow picked up in the womb? Or was it a symbolic image of an ancient unconscious fear of being trapped with a baby without community or social value?

When I phoned my sister Shira to tell her I was pregnant, I discovered that she too was pregnant, and, though six years older than me, her due date was exactly the same as mine. I was touched by this strange unconscious bond between us.

I attended classes of the National Childbirth Trust. I don't know about how these classes functioned generally, but in mine we were taught week after week about how to give birth naturally. What about before? What were these strange feelings I was having? Was this normal? What about after? What do you do once you have a baby? The teacher didn't seem at all interested in these questions. The birth process was all.

Luckily, by the sixth month, my mood and energy greatly lifted. Now, coming to the end of the eighth month of the pregnancy, I was on maternity leave from work, the PhD was done and dusted, the fears and depression were mostly gone, and I was happily running this last weekend group before the birth.

One of the members was doing a psychodrama role-play in which he was carving up his mother. I suddenly started having terrible continuous pains. The baby must have hated that psychodrama; in fact, my son Ari still wants as little as possible to do with personal development groups.

I thought the baby was sitting on my bladder. It got more and more painful. I phoned the hospital and I was told that I should take an aspirin and go to bed. I didn't believe them. When I started vomiting, having diarrhoea, and just naturally getting everything out of my system, I figured it was getting serious.

I phoned my doctor who, to my eternal gratitude, rushed right over, saying, "How could the hospital possibly know?" He immediately called an ambulance to come, saying, "Quicker than quick, if you know what I mean." He reassured me that if I gave birth in the ambulance they could handle it. It was that immediate.

The labour was so quick, unexpected, and scary, only three hours in all, that I forgot everything I had learned all those months at my childbirth classes, and I just screamed. No one seemed to mind.

In those frantic moments in the ambulance, Yannis somehow got the idea that we had to come up with a name quickly, and he suggested Ari if a boy, and Chloe if a girl. He didn't know that Ari is not only a Greek name, but also a Hebrew word, meaning lion. He came up with a name that brought our two cultures together. I later learned that it is also an Icelandic word meaning eagle.

There was no one around to say, as my sister Shira did, "Give him an English name."

We got to the hospital in time. The nurse came in to ask if I wanted my husband in at the birth. I knew Yannis was nervous about it, and it was not a thing that Greek men normally did at that time, so I said, "If he wants to." He appeared, partly because I had said he didn't have to.

As was my wont, I now worried about him rather than myself. "Are you okay?" I asked him in the middle of my painful birth process. He flushed with embarrassment.

My fears were also surfacing during the birth and I kept asking if the baby was alive, but didn't believe their answer, "You wouldn't tell me if he wasn't" I said.

But the tiny infant was alive and well, though premature. Life shone on us.

As I came out of labour and was being wheeled down the corridor, I was handed a telegram from one of the group members which said, "What a way to end a group."

Because Ari was premature, he got jaundice, and needed to be in Special Care. It turned out to be a welcome opportunity for me to have a kind of special training from the nurses, as I hadn't a clue about what you do with a baby and had no family around to cushion my ignorance.

I had an incredible feeling as I stepped out of the hospital with Ari in my arms that I had walked in as one person and walked out as two. I moved into a wonderful altered space in which I felt totally peaceful and wonderfully clear.

It was a rather blessed time. People seemed to come streaming towards the house. Some were friends I hadn't seen for ages who had just decided to drop in, not knowing that I'd had a baby. And I got great pleasure from the fact that everyone wanted a turn at holding this amazing being.

After all my worries, my experience of having a young baby felt like a pure delight.

Funnily enough, though, the four months of maternity leave were enough to raise the "only a housewife" spectre that women who don't work outside the home have to contend with. I found myself wanting to tell the shopkeepers that I had a PhD.

Mostly, during this period, I was absolutely thrilled. I was particularly fascinated with the development of Ari's language and thinking. All my college papers had been on the subject of language, symbol, and thought, so here it was, unfolding before my very eyes. I read everything I could and was in awe of the process.

Totally unprepared for the wonder of having a baby, as I sat at breakfast with Ari gurgling happily in his arm chair, I felt, perhaps for the first time, that I was a very lucky girl.

CHAPTER THIRTEEN

Seeds of Skyros

Summer 1977. Yannis, I, with six-month-old Ari, spend the summer camped in the garden of a house on the Greek island of Skyros. Two summers later, this house is to become the home of the Skyros Centre, our first holiday community on Skyros Island.

Creating Skyros Holidays was and is one of the miracles of my life. How often do you get the chance to create a mini-world with values you believe in, and on a Greek island?

Like so many creative endeavours, it was born in a moment of despair.

We need to backtrack a bit to the previous winter, when Yannis and I spent a weekend at my friend Bridget's home. She got a telephone call from our colleague Ray who at that time was responsible for the rooming of seminars in our department. He told Bridget that he wouldn't give her a good room for her seminars because she had supported me at the staff meeting. They had been trying to sabotage my timetable to make it more difficult for me, and she had done some fancy manoeuvring so that I could get the class times I wanted.

Getting a bad room for her classes was her punishment.

The whole thing sounds almost funny now. And even then, I told myself that it was nothing new, just one more spiteful incident. But, for some reason, it seemed more awful than usual. Things had gone too far.

It was the way of the world. But it wasn't my way. My soul was crying out for a better world.

That night I dreamt two dreams, from which I awoke crying.

The first: *I'm on the front line in a war. I've just been shot and I'm dying. I am telling myself that it doesn't hurt to die. But it does.*

The second: *I am sitting at a table in the college cafeteria with our head of psychology. I tell him about something terrible that is happening to me at college. He keeps saying rather distantly, "I don't understand." I can't get through to him, and I feel desperate.*

The pain I felt in both dreams was the same: deep, dull, hopeless.

That weekend the idea of creating a centre in Greece emerged. I had just come back from a wonderful experience being on the first year of a therapist training course at the Pellin Centre in Southern Italy, set up by Peter Fleming. "You seemed so happy when you came back," Bridget said. Why not do something in Greece? Yannis could organise the Greek side, I could run groups, and Bridget could run sociology seminars on related topics.

It was a wonderful idea, but Bridget dropped out soon after, and I doubt that, left to my own devices, I would have actually carried out the plan. It was Yannis that made sure it became a reality.

Yannis was suffering from the seventies. The academic world, so lush in the sixties, had dried up. Lecturing jobs were like gold dust. As I read somewhere, a PhD in History was not so much a stepping-stone as a millstone.

He was working again as the London Correspondent for a Greek paper, *Eleftherotypia*, but the pay was derisory. He did some sums and figured out that running a centre might be a viable way to earn a living. No sooner seen than done. Within days he was out in Greece looking for a place.

I remember reading that the Findhorn Foundation community in Scotland would not have been founded if co-founder Peter Caddy had not been unemployed at the time. If Yannis had gotten one of the lecturing jobs he applied for, or if I had liked the one I had, there would have been no Skyros Centre.

As I was falling asleep the night after he left for Greece, I had a kind of waking dream. I was walking on a beach and a wise man came walking toward me. He took my hand and let me know without words that there was hope, and dreams could come true.

Yannis went straight to the Sporades Islands, a constellation of islands north-east of Athens, popular with the Greeks but little known abroad at that time. It includes Skiathos—the most touristic of this island group even then, and more recently the location for the film *Mama Mia*—as well as Alonissos, Skopelos, and Skyros.

He came to Skyros last and there he found a large derelict house that had been a school. The minute he saw it, he said to himself, "This is it." He phoned me and we agreed to buy it. It cost about £5000, and we had to take out a Greek mortgage to pay for it.

The Skyros adventure was about to begin for real.

This project could only have come out of that unlikely partnership between an American Jewish Psychologist with a background in Socialist Zionist communal summer camps and personal development workshops, and a left-wing Greek whose career trajectory in journalism and politics had been messed up by the Greek dictatorship just when he was beginning to make a name for himself.

I had the ability to create the kind of social, psychological, and spiritual world that is a hothouse for transformation, plus a personal yearning for community, connectedness, meaning, and consciousness change. Yannis was able to create the

103

bricks and mortar physical world to house this symbolic venture, and also had a tremendous drive to begin and to expand at moments when I might well have given up.

What we shared was our quirky individualistic creativity, and an underlying set of values to do with social justice, plus a basic ability to do the sums. Less favourably, we shared a serious lack of experience with business management, a weakness that became more significant as participants stopped being tolerant of our foibles and began to have more conventional expectations.

Years later, I read an article in which a business angel talked of what she needed to see in a business to make her feel it was a good bet for investing. She looked for the presence of one visionary, and one accountant type to run the show.

We were two visionaries and no accountant type.

But it worked, beyond our wildest dreams. My original picture as I described it to myself was of bringing "twelve people to a Greek island", and I expected it to go on for three or four years. Now, almost forty years later, more than 30,000 people have passed through our doors. Increasingly they have included conventionally successful mainstream professionals rather than the eccentric alternative types we tended to attract in the early pioneering years, and a large majority of them have made profound life changes as a result of their stay in Skyros.

Indeed, there is something I cannot fully account for by simply describing what we did. People laughed, danced and played, as well as sinking into a deeper part of themselves than they thought possible. Miracles were commonplace. Relationships were formed in a kind of crucible so that people felt they had known one another forever, and often became friends for life. So many felt it was their best holiday ever or a turning point in their lives, or both. As one participant told me, if you met anyone anywhere in the world and they said they had been in Skyros, you immediately knew you could have a deep connection with them.

I believe that this something emerges when we intend to create something from the soul, and are willing not only to foster love and truth, but to work towards our own transformation. My friend and colleague Max Furlaud used to say, "In Skyros, every Thursday night at the end of a two week session, the angels gather round." This is a kind of grace, the gift of the soul.

My view now is that our souls brought us to Skyros and sensed what was to come, while we, in the sense of our everyday personalities, had very little idea what we were about to set into motion.

At that time, the world of New Age therapies, complementary medicine, and the notion of mind, body, and spirit had not yet become big business. Nor did special interest holidays of any kind have a significant presence in the tourism world, with the exception of Club Med, founded in 1950. What we were doing turned out to be not just an idealistic professional venture but a new kind of tourism.

We were pioneers at the forefront of a sea change in holidays.

Journalists from all over the world came to see for themselves what the fuss was about. Full-page spreads appeared in all the major papers and magazines. The journalists often came to mock, and then stayed to praise us. Almost consistently, the articles were paeans to this life-changing, laughter filled, joyous experience.[14]

The usual story, especially if the reporter was British, would be that they were at first incredibly cynical but eventually they themselves had a wonderful life-changing experience and had made friends for life. The British were so allergic to anything to do with the inner life or alternative living at that time that even sympathetic journalists felt they wouldn't be believed unless it was clear they were not hippy dippy themselves.

As we became known and successful, and as it became clear more generally that people were bored with beach holidays, new special interest and all-inclusive activity holidays burgeoned. A number of smaller centres featuring one or another of the alternative approaches began to appear. These were quite often started by people who had worked or had been participants in Skyros, and who shared many of our ideas. I don't think any had the wonderful range of holistic activities combined with an intentional community atmosphere that made Skyros so unique.

The Guardian called us, "The first and still the best."[15]

Looking back, I am struck by the way that I, a young woman from Brooklyn already living in a country that was not my own, could go to a relatively remote village in Greece to make it the home of a spiritual venture. Yet I never had any doubts.

Perhaps it is because it represented on some level the coming together of the worlds I had inherited from my mother and father. My mother was a Mediterranean woman imbued with the pioneering spirit of the early days of Palestine and Israel. My father was a spiritual and psychological seeker, as well as a natural educator, and was particularly taken by the whole new world of humanistic psychology.

Put them together, mix in this unique partnership between myself and Yannis, and voila, Skyros.

CHAPTER FOURTEEN

Skyros summer

The following summer of 1977, we take a plane to Athens, and then a hot, crowded city bus to Skyros, carrying a six-month-old baby on our laps. We have not thought about where we will stay, although we are travelling with a baby and we know the house isn't habitable.

We were good with the big ideas and plans; the rather crucial details sometimes eluded us. Then again, those days were before the web made everything so local, so if you were going anywhere a bit remote, it was kind of normal just to show up and assume you'd find somewhere to lay your head.

The bus stopped in front of an amazing Greek square that looked like a film set, and I saw the cobbled streets, and the tiny white houses and shops. I felt as if I had entered another dimension. Women crowded around the bus, saying, "Rooms, rooms." They were, of course, the local landladies. But we didn't know that this was how you normally got yourself a room and we just said no to everyone.

Soon we were left standing on our own in the street at night with a six-month-old baby, not knowing what to do next. Someone Yannis vaguely knew from the past recognised him, took pity on us, and offered us a bed for the night.

Thereafter we slept in sleeping bags in the garden of our new house.

Sleeping under the stars in sleeping bags was not new to us. We had done this during our first holiday together in Ibiza. At least here in Skyros we were safe, and did not have Spanish policemen waking us up to say, "*arriba, arriba*" as happened then. We were in our own garden, and we were pioneering a new venture that was about to change our lives.

Being on Mediterranean soil was also not new to us. Yannis of course was Greek, and I had not only spent a year in Israel, but had an Israeli mother, and ancient Jewish history in my blood. The dry heat, parched land, olive trees, the fig, pomegranate, and lemon trees, the blue skies, and the smell of herbs all felt like home to me. More than that, it was as if some deep archetypal memory emerged and made me feel I was back in biblical times where I was meant to be.

Skyros, like many Greek villages from the same era, is built amphitheatrically on the slopes of a hill, with the white cubic houses clustering on the sides and around the base of the medieval castle, in order to protect themselves from pirate raids. Skyros has a history that dates back to the stone ages, and is dotted with stories from Greek legend, the most famous of which is the story of Achilles and the Trojan War. It is said that Achilles was hidden here dressed as a girl by his goddess mother Thetis to escape his fate, but Odysseus found him, tricked him into revealing his identity as a boy, and took him to war.

It was an amazing village, hardly touched by foreign tourism. You could still see the men wearing their traditional outfits, with sandals made from tires, riding on their donkeys, or sipping coffee in the cafes, and the women carrying jugs on their heads. I always felt it had a raw, primordial quality. I could almost smell the ancient blood sacrifices in the air.

Of course, there were also televisions everywhere as well as electrical equipment, calculators, and other evidence of the modern world.

It was as if we were living in more than one century at once.

The tiny houses normally had one or two rooms, with a "sofa", a sleeping platform like the one in our house, above the kitchen, and the toilets outside. They were decorated with plates on the wall, most of them the local pottery for which Skyros is famous, but also some willow pattern plates from England. There was talk of how the pirates had traded modern junk for the old treasures of the villagers.

Our house, unlike the tiny houses all connected to each other that dotted the cubic style village, was at the edge of the village, was large enough to begin our project, and had a garden open to the hills and the sea. Its position not only gave us a remarkable view, but also made us accessible by foot to the village as well as to the sea.

It was a traditional stone house with thick walls, wooden doors, big balconies, and ceilings with naked wooden beams. There was a small room on the left with a sleeping balcony, and a larger room and a kitchen. It had been uninhabited for years. What we called the garden was basically a small jungle with almond, pomegranate, and peach trees, as well as an enormous spreading bay tree. It had a view of the sea as well as of the barren hills dotted with olive trees, small abandoned stone buildings, and a few tiny lighthouses.

The sea was only about ten minutes down the hill, but more like fifteen or twenty if you were coming up the hill in the evening and you had had a few glasses of retsina and were carrying a baby.

When we'd go down to the beach in the hot afternoons, we thought we were doing a marvellous holiday thing, but our Greek neighbours would look at us walking with a baby in all that heat, and say, "*Oi Kaimenoi*", meaning, "Poor things". Only mad dogs, etc.

Wherever we went, people made a fuss over little Ari, smiled at him and talked to him. A Skyrian woman might walk up to us, grab him from our hands, without asking permission, and go for a little walk with him in her arms. I loved that.

109

Ari slept in a little suitcase we had brought for the purpose, as had been suggested to us by one of our health visitors. It wasn't great advice. Whenever we went out to eat in the evenings, we had to carry him and the empty suitcase instead of pushing him in a stroller, and everyone stopped to ask if we were leaving town. He slept in the suitcase during dinner, but then we had to wake him up to carry him home up what now seemed like endless steps.

Yannis' mother, Ireni, came to visit us for a few days. She was distressed and angry at the way we were raising Ari. She insisted that he be woken at six in the morning for a regular feed, and that I cook all his meals properly rather than using prepared baby food. She'd been very respectful of me until Yannis and I actually got married. As soon as I became her daughter-in-law, and even more so when she became a grandmother, she disapproved of most things I did.

She died suddenly of a heart attack not long after, and, despite all our differences, I was very sorry that she never got to meet her granddaughter Chloe and remain part of our family life.

As the days went by, we began to make friends with our neighbours, especially Nikos and Zafiroola. Nikos was a wonderfully sweet man, and like many of the Skyrian men, he did many jobs, including riding on his donkey to tend his small farm, keeping bees, making honey, and carving the small wooden chairs with Byzantine designs that villagers loved. These chairs are the size of children's chairs, yet are beautiful and very comfortable, and you could see the old people sitting on them on their balconies. We bought quite a few for the centre.

We've also got one larger version of these carved wooden chairs, the size of a normal chair, with my name carved on the back. The story behind that is that in one of my therapy groups, a participant was dealing with his anger against his mother and I invited him to imagine his mother sitting in one of the little

Skyrian chairs and then talk to her. This is a common imagery technique coming from Psychodrama and Gestalt Therapy.

He was so furious at his mother that he picked up the chair and hurled it across the room. It didn't survive. Some days later he presented me with the big Skyrian chair, the only one like it I had ever seen. He had gone to Nikos and specially commissioned it.

Nikos' wife Zafiroola, a Cretan, never felt accepted in the village, and mostly stayed home. I believe she was agoraphobic; in Greek, the agora is the marketplace, and literally agoraphobic means a fear of the marketplace. She used to say that her Nikos was the only good man in the village, and, indeed, he was the best that I knew. She was a good cook, and invited us to eat in her little kitchen. I still remember how she would call to her son Stamati from miles away. The resounding sound of STA-MA-TI echoed out any time of the day and night.

The *yia yia*, or grandmother, Nikos' mother, covered from head to toe in black mourning, would climb on the roof and tend to the plants she was growing and fruits she was drying. She was later to become my daughter Chloe's babysitter while I was holding my group sessions.

They were incredibly kind to us, and seemed to manage to understand us a little, despite the enormous cultural gap between us.

Our very next-door neighbour, Nitsa, had never married. She had big vats in her home to dye the blue cloths for the trousers worn by the shepherds. It is said that she had a secret formula for this particular blue, made from herbs she gathered in the Skyros hills. Although she was already at least in her seventies, she used to complain that she was an orphan. When we started having participants, one or two would stay in her big room with the vats, and she would feed them and worry about them and give them advice.

One or two houses down, there lived a mother and daughter who both looked ancient, though apparently the daughter wasn't because she eventually got married and had three children. They asked us to take a photo of them, and they dressed up and posed unsmilingly.

In a narrow house between Nitsa and Nikos and Zafiroola, lived Evaghelia, who whitewashed houses for a living, and had three bright children and a husband I seldom saw. Later, when we started the centre, her little daughter Maria used to steal into our courtyard when there was music and she would dance exquisitely. It always reminded me of the dancing child in the wonderful Marcel Camus film *Black Orpheus* or *Orfeo Negro*.

Most of our neighbours in this very poor part of town eventually had tragic lives. Nikos died suddenly of a heart attack, quite young. I happened to be in Japan when I heard about Nikos' death. I was devastated because I really loved him. I had a dream in which we were on his balcony and he said, "Dina was always afraid of falling off balconies." Then he picked me up, and carried me in his arms as we fell, a kind of slow free fall, from the balcony. I felt as if he had come to tell me not to be afraid of death.

Zafiroola was left desperately lonely and depressed, her now teenage son Stamati very unhappy and having to support her emotionally and financially. Eventually Stamati married and had a child, lived next door to his mother, and he and his wife took care of her as she became more ill and demented. Nitsa became ill and was sent off to a hospital in Athens, and never returned to Skyros. Apparently, she took the secret of the blue dye to her grave, a fact much lamented by villagers.

Most disturbing of all was what happened to the daughter we had photographed. She was taking a ride on her young teenage son's bike, and fell off, hit her head, and died. As far as I know, no one talked to the boy who must have felt he'd killed his mother, nor indeed to the family, of how they felt. Of course, there was no such thing as therapy in the village. I wished I could help, or at least say something, but my Greek was never good enough.

The exception to these sad stories was Evaghelia's family. Her children all got to Athens to get an education, ending up as professionals either in Athens or in the UK. I found this mysterious until years later Maria, the eldest daughter who used to dance so beautifully, came to visit us. She explained that she went to train in computer studies in Athens and then helped and supported her sisters and brothers to leave home and develop careers.

Was I nervous about the venture? Funnily enough, I wasn't. Is this to do with being a child of the sixties, when we believed anything was possible? Or perhaps it is in my nature to start new ventures with a vision and a complete blind confidence, and then the panic, worry, regret, and stress set in only when it's too late to turn back. It's rather a good protective adaptation for an adventurer who is also a worrier.

If I had any uneasiness, it was not about the future. I knew in my bones that we were doing the right thing. It was more about the fact that I felt rather lonely there, and didn't really know how to enter into village life, beyond my relationships with my immediate neighbours. Skyros is a rather insular village, where you are considered a foreigner even if you come from the mainland, and so the fact that Yannis was a Greek did not help. After all, he was a journalist from Athens, another world entirely. Many islanders had never visited the mainland.

Some years later, I was talking to a taxi driver who came from another island and had married a Skyrian woman. He said to me, "Sometimes when they are drunk, and only when they are drunk, they turn around and call me a foreigner."

The Skyrians as a whole did not have the reputation of being friendly open-hearted people. The Greek army had a base in Skyros, and they complained about the villagers. The Skyrians were typical of a certain type of isolated islander, proud, passionate, envious, stubborn, and often quicker to want something from you than to do you a favour. I kept waiting for the traditional warm Greek villager I'd read about in novels, giving us grapes with a big smile. It didn't happen much at that time when we were beginning our new project, with the exception of our closest neighbours.

It does much more now, when I have some good Skyrian women friends, and when we are established, accepted, and respected and have known each other for so many years. Maybe even then there was a lot of appreciation of us I didn't hear of. I am directing a Skyros Centre session right now, and just yesterday a neighbour baked me a batch of *koulouria*, traditional Greek biscuits, and gave them to me wrapped with ribbon and love, telling me how much she has loved our family all these years. Just moments ago, a young Skyrian woman who works with us described to me how her grandfather kept talking about us to her, telling her how we had brought tourism to the island, which became their bread and butter, and how we helped foreigners to appreciate the beauties of Skyros.

Indeed, many of our participants do speak of the warmth and generosity of the villagers. I think it is also the case that when you are visiting a country, you get a different reaction from locals than when you are pitching up to live and work there. Or maybe you yourself are more open and available.

In some ways, also, I am grateful for the pride and stubbornness of the islanders. It has meant that they have been rather unwilling to assimilate into the modern Western world and because of this, Skyros has never lost the feel of a traditional island.

Anyway, as I reasoned to myself, the Greek gods themselves were passionate gods, neither kind nor moral. And, as my friend Clare said to me years later, "The reality is always more interesting than the fantasy."

Yannis and I were both a little too shy to make new friends even among the obvious foreigners. I remember sitting at a restaurant watching an enormous table of Greeks and foreigners speaking different languages excitedly and looking rather fascinating. I was longing to go over and join them, but just didn't know how.

Some years later, when we were visiting a friend of Yannis' in Athens, the distinguished writer Stratis Tsirkas was in the company. He had read Yannis' first book, *1944, Krisimi Chronia*,[16] which referred to a Greek navy mutiny in Alexandria during the war which Tsirkas had been part of. Tsirkas had been friends with Lawrence Durrell and Constantine Cavafis and he told us wonderful stories of Alexandria. It turned out that he used to visit Skyros regularly and he had probably been at that very table we had gazed at.

He died not long after, so we never did meet in Skyros. I felt sad about my lack of courage.

On our way home from Skyros, as we were sitting in the airport, Ari caught the eye of an Englishwoman, and tried to engage her with his eyes and smile, expecting the warm interaction he was used to; the Greeks, no matter how fierce they were, always made a fuss over babies. Now, the Englishwoman ignored him and looked away. His little face looked so puzzled and hurt.

It was an early lesson in the painful realities of moving between worlds.

CHAPTER FIFTEEN

The spirits are whispering

Summer 1978. It is the summer between our first stay in Skyros and the opening of the centre, and I am in Geneva giving a talk at the European Association of Humanistic Psychology conference. I am also attending the workshops and relaxing into the warm, loving, and intimate atmosphere that conferences with experiential workshops always seem to create. I meet fascinating group leaders from all over the world, some of whom I invite to run courses in my new centre. It is the kind of world that brings out the best in me, indeed the kind of world I hope to create in Skyros.

Then I attend an extraordinary lecture by Dr Elisabeth Kübler-Ross, world expert on death and dying, who has worked extensively with dying children, and revolutionized the treatment of dying people of all ages. It is a portal into a whole new world.

I remember it as if it were yesterday.

She talked of how dying children would tell her they were being visited by family members who had passed away. If they had been in an accident which involved their whole family, they would mention only those who had already died in the accident, although they hadn't been told who had lived and who had died. She also described the imagery and pictures children drew in the days and months before they died which showed their deep knowledge and understanding. This view of imagery as a pathway into the intuition was to become an important foundation of my work.

One little girl in California was eaten by a shark when she went swimming. Her mother found drawings she had done in the days before her death, and there was a series of drawings in which the waves had washed over a little girl more and more each day. In the drawing her daughter did on the last morning before she died, the little girl in the picture was completely submerged. The mother was deeply touched by her daughter's unconscious understanding of what was about to happen to her.

Dr Kübler-Ross also movingly described a little girl sitting on her dying mother's bed, and telling her "all the good things and the bad things" in order to say good-bye. This story later became part of my imagery exercise on saying goodbye. I always use her beautifully simple words, "Tell them the good things and the bad things."

I was fascinated when, speaking of the guides and the family and friends people meet when they are dying, she said very definitely, "And I take it for granted that a Jewish child does not meet Mary." It was a kind of postmodern approach to the afterlife, and solved my perennial question about how the idea of an afterlife can work when everyone is from a different religion or culture. Mind you, I myself feel very connected to Mary, and so I hope this Jewish woman does meet Mary.

Then she described how the children in the concentration camp drew pictures of butterflies on the walls. She asked in her ringing tones, "And how did the children know that death is a butterfly?"

At that moment, an energy column seemed to rise up in my spine and explode into my head. I stood up and began to cry and cry and cry. The crying had a feeling of rightness about it, though I had no idea what it was about, except that it was something to do with those children. Someone tried to comfort me, but I knew I was really okay.

And then all tension left my body, and I moved into an altered state of heightened awareness. I was fully and happily at peace with myself and with life.

Spirit and the spirits were making one of those forceful, unstoppable appearances.

Later I learned about the phenomenon that is called "the Kundalini awakening". In Eastern philosophies, the Kundalini is described as a primal energy that lies coiled at the bottom of the spine, like a sleeping serpent or goddess waiting to be awakened. When it wakes up, it rises up the spine, like an electric current, to the crown of the head, and leads to a profound mystical experience. This is undoubtedly what happened to me.

There are many ways to arouse the Kundalini, by chance or by design, but one is a spiritual transmission by a guru or teacher. I think this is what Elisabeth Kübler-Ross became for me.

With all the talk about death and dying, I remembered my strange beliefs when I was in hospital, and in particular my belief that my mother was in another dimension where she was alive and I was dead, while in this dimension I was alive and she was dead. After the lecture, I went up to Dr Kübler-Ross and asked whether there was any truth to my theory. She answered softly, "No it's not quite like that. It's more like Beethoven is playing in the room here, but we can't hear him."

When I returned to London, the experience continued for days.

The spirits were whispering constantly. Each tree and flower I met spoke to me. I wondered whether each blade of grass was a spirit or whether it was the whole lawn that had one spirit. Each blast of wind felt like winter; a ray of sun was summer. I didn't sense a supreme God figure, but rather a world of Spirit with a community of spirits of which I was part. I also felt that I was part of a spiritual network of people all over the world with whom I was in psychic communication.

Even in the realm of Spirit, it was all about community.

I was like a creativity factory, coming up with an insight or creative idea a minute, and making predictions about the future. When I walked down the street or went to shops, people would stop and talk to me, either to comment on how happy I seemed, or to allude to an experience or network that they were part of too. One asked, "How long have you been here?" and seemed confused when I went to give a real-life answer rather than one about the spiritual state I was in.

Yannis looked at me strangely and told me I was like a visitor in the house. Yet he didn't seem to think I was crazy. It was almost as if he had a respect for what was happening.

My old belief system was turned upside down. I felt that I'd been like a rat running on an activity wheel, having no idea what the point of anything was. Now I was out of the cage and it all made sense. I had a sure knowledge that I had lived many lifetimes before this one. As I pictured it, all these lifetimes put together create a kind of curve on a graph that signifies a meaning and a process. Trying to understand this present life on its own was like looking at one bit of a curve.

No wonder life hadn't made sense. I needed the longer perspective.

As I walked around London in this altered state, I had an experience I thought of as "a city in history". It was as if all the centuries were happening simultaneously. Ordinary scenes looked mysterious and otherworldly as if I was seeing the present moment set in the larger frame of lifetimes. The women standing in the bus queue chatting could almost be speaking in tongues. Extraordinary coincidences seemed normal.

I had had a sense of living in more than one century at once in Skyros, because of the ancient yet modern quality of the place. But this had a compelling power that reminded me more of that walk up Finchley Road when I was going mad. It was as if all the mad thoughts I had then were echoes of some kind of spiritual truth, distorted because they came through the illness, and now I was well enough to get the original and correct version.

Then I was confused about time, wondering what century I was in. Now, time had expanded and it was as if I had access to past, present, and future.

Then I was lost. Now I felt I had come home.

That felt like a waking nightmare. This felt like an awakening.

Then I had no control over what was flooding in. Now I welcomed it and knew I could stop it at any moment.

Even so, some of the thoughts I was having now were more flaky than wise. While I had learned the laws of scientific evidence in school, this new world required a whole new set of objective principles with which to judge what was true and what wasn't, and I had to discover it on my own. I did not want to be mad.

I figured out that the crazy stuff was whatever fed my ego and made me feel special, or was a product of wishful thinking. Predictions made with this sort of motivation did not work out. Yannis made fun of me for years about my solemn pronouncement, "You'll get a letter offering you a job" at a time that he was unemployed. Yet other predictions, which came to me unbidden and were surprising rather than sought after, did come true.

One wisdom-thought that has stayed with me is: *The important things are meant to be and the unimportant ones are unimportant.* I could relax into the knowledge that all was well, without thinking that every stray coincidence was a magical sign.

That way flakiness lay.

Until my altered state experience, I had never heard of the New Age, I thought reincarnation was a weird Indian belief, and my experience of religion came mainly from the synagogue where the women's hats often seemed to be the real objects of worship.

My only profound spiritual connection had been to the Shabbat, the Jewish Sabbath. Long after I had stopped being a strictly observant Jew, and didn't keep to the strict rules of conduct on a Saturday, I preserved one principle of keeping the Sabbath: I only did what I wanted or was necessary for that day, and nothing for the sake of the future. This is not far off from what is now called mindfulness, or living in the Now, but it had a sacred feel to it.

When the Sabbath started at sunset on Friday night, I would light the Sabbath candles, and sing songs to welcome in the Sabbath Queen and her army of angels of peace. My anxiety simply melted away and peace descended in my heart and in my home. All Saturday, I would read art and poetry books, or do things I loved, and life felt wholly good. Indeed, I felt surrounded by those angels of peace.

But what was happening now was of a different order. That experience of Shabbat was a wonderful part of my life. This new experience declared that life was part of it.

An American friend happened to visit me, and I talked to her about what was happening. She told me there was something called the New Age, and that among other things it meant that lots of people were having similar powerful spiritual experiences. I later heard that the year 1978 was an especially big year for these spontaneous spiritual experiences.

She mentioned the New Age community at Findhorn, and said that there were books I could read. She especially recommended the books of Alice Bailey, who wrote about esoteric philosophy, psychology, astrology, and healing, and whose writings were said to have been dictated to her psychically by a Master who was referred to as The Tibetan. It was all a bit jaw dropping for me. But I needed to know more.

I bought Alice Bailey's *Esoteric Healing*[17] and did indeed find in there some of the things I was experiencing. Most importantly, I found the idea of a psychically connected network of people around the world, along with beings in the other dimension, all working toward a transformation of consciousness in the world. Each Master, including God, had their own ashram, their own little community, and all were evolving. There was no fixed point anywhere.

I loved the idea that even God was evolving.

I also read a great deal else that I had no knowledge of, but which seemed to be a kind of underlying science of these phenomena. The books began to give me a framework for my strange new experiences.

Another book that helped me tremendously was *Varieties of Religious Experience*, a wonderful book by psychologist and philosopher William James.[18] Oddly enough, when I had been visiting my father in New York, I had picked up that book from the basement of my old house where all my books were stored and brought it back to England with me. I didn't know why I had chosen it, and had never looked at it. Not long after, there was a fire in the old basement, so this turned out to be the only one of my precious books that I was able to save.

Now I pulled the book out to make some sense of what was happening to me. William James described the nature of a typical mystical experience and of the people who were likely to have these.

He talked of how there were people who had two feet in this dimension of the real world, and that when they had a spiritual experience, it tended to be experienced within a conventional religion. But those of us with one foot here and one foot somewhere else, tended to have mystical experiences. These involved sensing another dimension of spiritual reality that not everyone was in touch with, but was nevertheless real. It was like a wavelength that you might or might not have the ability to sense.

Reading it, I became reassured that the experiences I was having were pointing to something real, fit into a pattern, and had been experienced by others.

I wasn't mad. I felt accompanied on my journey.

I was having a wondrous time, but I was in such a heightened state that I couldn't carry on a normal life. I asked the spirits to please stop whispering for a while and let me get some work done.

Silence fell. And they did not return, at least not at that time. The veil had fallen back in place. I was back in what is traditionally called the real world.

It was a devastating loss.

In the years after those magical few days, I had a number of similar altered state experiences, though none quite so long and dramatic. Each time I would get very high, get access to knowledge and insights, might start to have psychic connections with people, and so on. Some of this undoubtedly had a ring of truth and illumination about it. It was also incredibly joyful.

Sometimes, however, I'd move into that crazier ego-driven kind of belief that I could tell the future, heal the sick, raise the dead. When I couldn't, I'd be terribly let down and come down to earth with a bang. Or some wise and courageous friend would let me know that I seemed a bit mad or paranoid and I would choose to come down.

Always when I came down, I'd go through a long period of depression, as I crawled my way back into daily life on my hands and feet without the magic. It was rather like when you paint part of a room, and the rest, which might have looked okay before, now looks awful.

The trails of glory left everything else looking a terrible depressing mud colour.

The lows were always much longer than the highs. Yet I hungered for the highs, not caring what price I had to pay.

I finally recognised that these highs were like those crumbs Gretel left for Hansel. You could follow them as signals, but they weren't your dinner.

As in any love affair, you start with the highs and lows, but you eventually have to stabilise into a real relationship.

I needed to bring those experiences into my everyday consciousness and under my control. My way of doing this turned out to be working with the deep imagination, or Imagework. Instead of the sea of the unconscious or of the spiritual dimension coming up towards and even over me, I had to learn to don a diving suit and choose to dive in. This became one of the teaching fundamentals in my Imagework trainings.

Did I really believe? Or was it just a kind of addictive need for reassurance and escape from the pain of everyday life? This question worried me.

Years later, when I was teaching imagery in Russia, I found that when the Russians created images—from flowers to icons to panthers—the problems would be solved by the image flying in the air like a Chagall lover. We joked about this way of solving problems and I'd say: "No spiritual shortcuts."

I didn't want to allow myself a spiritual shortcut. I would test the power of my belief by asking myself: *Facing death, would I feel secure, knowing that I was going to another dimension, or scared, that I was coming to an end?*

Of course, it's hard to answer this question definitively until you are there, facing death. And yet maybe that was not really the point. Two of the most spiritual people I have known, my father and my cousin Jane, did not believe in an afterlife at all.

Jane's husband said after she died, "She's going to be mighty surprised."

What I can have no doubt about is that which has been a lived experience for me, the feeling that I am surrounded by loving spirits or Spirit, am part of something that is greater than myself, and am participating with others in the transformation of consciousness in the world. Beyond this, also, is a sense that there is a spiritual fabric to the world that is something to do with light. It is always in the process of evolution, and I am committed to contribute to it.

The world of Spirit made me feel I was not alone and I was of value. It challenged the power of the monsters of loneliness, worthlessness, helplessness, and pointlessness. And as time went on, it became simply part of who I am, a kind of extended consciousness that went beyond my personal everyday consciousness and was always evolving and transforming.

It was as if I now had a beautiful lining under my inner self. The journey might still be hard, but I was travelling in more comfort.

This image comes to mind as I think about all this: *I am learning to swim. I am terrified at first so I dip in and out. Then I get a little rubber armband that holds me up. After a while, I try to do without it but I start to sink. I put the armband on again. One day, I realise that the armband lost its air long ago yet I am still swimming.*

If I announced a moratorium on belief, swore I would never talk to a Spirit again, decided to be a rationalist, my life would now go on more or less the same way. Whatever I believe in my mind, the buoyancy is still there.

I am still swimming.

CHAPTER SIXTEEN

Mother of two

Spring and summer 1979 marked the birth of our daughter, Chloe, and the birth of the Skyros Centre within months of each other. I was thirty-three years old.

With this pregnancy, the irrational fears did not reappear, and I was taking a wonderful meditation biofeedback course with meditation master Maxwell Cade, during which I was reaching deep states of calm. At one moment, I got an image of my future baby and saw that she was a girl.

But this time a realistic fear appeared. Ari had come down with German measles when I had just pregnant and didn't yet realise it. The doctors were talking of abortion. Then a very wonderful hospital consultant gave me a test, which I think was quite new at the time, that could distinguish between old and new antibodies. He was able to see that my antibodies were old and gave me the okay to go ahead with the pregnancy.

March 1979, and I was eight months pregnant, staying home to take care of Ari who had whooping cough. Despite his illness, it was a really lovely period because it was one of the few times that I could devote myself to being pregnant and a mother, as well as having hormones to match. I felt like a contented cow, and my brain was a lovely mush.

Meanwhile, Yannis was in Greece getting the house fixed up. Suddenly I got a phone call from him. "We're doing it this summer." I didn't know what he was talking about. Then I realised he meant we were starting the Skyros Centre.

"Oh," I said. I didn't think to argue.

Obediently, I set to work writing copy for advertisements in *Time Out* and *The Guardian*, and preparing our first "brochure", which was an A4 double-sided photocopied affair. It had a lovely Magritte bird traced on it. Our advertising slogan was: Sun, Sea, and a Sense of Community.

Because of the dreamy state I was in, I literally had no idea whether I'd written baby language or adult language. I phoned a friend and read it out to her, and was reassured that it made adult sense.

Unlike Ari who came in a hurry one month early, Chloe seemed to wait for her birth until the work was done. She was more than a week late. One day, I felt I had done enough and was sick and tired of the whole thing; the next day I went into labour. This time, I was forewarned about my speedy births, and as soon as the waters broke I called the ambulance, and gave birth soon after I got to hospital.

I was left all night on an operating table because there wasn't a bed available, but I had Chloe in a transparent cot besides me, and so was perfectly happy.

The doctors kept telling me that it was too early to tell whether she was damaged by the German measles, though it seemed clear that she could see and hear. So, the early days were quite difficult with these nagging doubts that I did and didn't believe in. Then my brother Emmet had another breakdown, and neither he nor my father could come to see us as planned. It was a difficult time, despite the wonder of having a new baby.

I used to try to communicate psychically with Chloe, to let her know how much I loved her, even if I was sad. I was also sending her psychic requests not to wake me up before I had got enough sleep; this seemed to work, and usually I got to finish my sleep. To this day, we have a deep connection that sometimes borders on the psychic between us.

When a student of mine told me that he was so busy, he was afraid he wasn't connecting enough to his new baby, I suggested that he send her psychic messages explaining what was happening and how much he loved her. He later told me that it had really worked, and that he and that daughter had a profound connection with each other.

Now that I had two babies, as I woke in the night to attend to one or the other, I realised that something had changed. When I had had one baby, I could just say about myself, "I have a baby." With two, I definitely knew I was a Mother.

And yet, at first, I didn't want the kids to call me "Mummy" or "Mum". Probably because of my own family history, I didn't trust that I could be a good enough mother, and feared being so important to them. I wanted to believe that they would somehow be mothered by a community of people, so that I wasn't the one and only mother.

So, I had them call me Dina until little Chloe at about age two simply refused to do so. She started chanting, "Ma, ma, ma, ma" as she went down the street in her pushchair. I succumbed. I think Ari was greatly relieved to be allowed to refer to me as his mother.

Sometimes when they would call me "Mummy" and expect me to know everything, solve everything, heal everything, I could feel the power of the Great Mother archetype. It was as if She stood behind me, and they were relating to this magical being, while I was still just little old me.

Luckily, I was not alone with my parenting. Greek men adore their kids, and Yannis was no exception. He had a problem at first when he tried to speak to them in English, and ended up talking politics to an infant. But as soon as I suggested that he speak to them in Greek, he knew exactly what to say and do. There was never any question that he and I were a team, offering wholehearted warm and very physical love, and that however we were getting along, the family was a good thing.

When I look at the way I parented my children, and how it compared to my family of origin, I notice this pattern: what I was conscious of missing as a child, I was determined to do differently, but what I never noticed because I took it for granted, I now repeated, for better and for worse.

What I was most aware of missing in my family when I was growing up—loving embraces, deep communication, new clothes—I made sure to give them. I adored them and I wanted them to feel it. I would wrap myself around them a lot, and tell them how much I loved them, and bought them nice clothes, and did everything I could to make sure they knew how loved they were.

And I tried to communicate so clearly that they would really know what's what, and particularly not to take my moods and my busyness personally. I would say things like, "I know you feel I'm working all the time, but I do want you to know that you are the important ones, much more important than the work." Or I'd say, "I'm sorry I'm grouchy. It's not you. It's just that I'm in a bad mood." One day, when I was particularly rushed and irritable, Ari looked at me and asked curiously, "Are you in a bad mood every day?"

I also used to make up stories that I thought would help them with what was bothering them. So, when Ari went through a patch of being quite scared, I told him a series of stories about a child who was so scared he was even afraid of going to the toilet, but he overcame his fear. I can't remember being read stories by my parents. I know my mother learned the American nursery rhymes so she could say them to us.

However, the things that went on in my family that I simply never questioned, like the fact that my mother had two jobs and was not at home when I came back from school, I continued to do, only more so. If she had two jobs, I had four. I thought being busy and out working was normal.

And yet, under the surface, I felt perpetually guilty, without really knowing it. Consciously I took for granted that I had to work. Unconsciously, perhaps no mother does. I became aware of this one morning when Yannis and the kids were all in Skyros, and I was in London about to go to work. As I walked out the door, I felt a lightness about me. I realised that this was the first time I had walked out of the house without feeling guilty. No one was peering out the windows wishing I wasn't going.

I had so taken the guilt for granted that I hadn't even noticed it.

There were also many positive things from my parental home that I carried on with in this family without my thinking much about it, such as the humanitarian values, and the lack of role playing and pretentiousness. And, like my parents, Yannis and I never used the kids in arguments between us.

Child-raising has to be seen also in the context of the parenting philosophies around at the time you are raising your kids. I was raised in a world of scheduled feeds, don't hug the children too much, that sort of thing. But when I was raising my own kids, philosophies were in flux, and there was a conflict between the "parent-centred" approach, that was seen to be more authoritarian, and the "child-centred" approach, considered more modern and democratic.

I liked neither. I thought parenting was a relationship, that was worked out in the "between", as Martin Buber[19] called it.

For example, I disliked the popular notion of "setting limits". I preferred rather that we find a way for both parents and children to get their needs met sufficiently so that we all stayed sane. I respected my kids tremendously, and never had any doubt that they were valuable people with a point of view I could learn from. But I also wanted them to respect me and my needs. I didn't want to just hand over my adulthood, just when I was learning to have a sense of myself. Where necessary, I was willing to be honest and to say, "You go to bed because I'm tired."

With two friends, I tried to start a parenting organisation called PACAP, which stood for: Parents and Children are People. Unfortunately, we were all too busy to make it happen.

I also did not agree with the whole approach to development that I had learned in psychology. The prevalent concept was— and still is—that development is a ladder which you climb, onward and upward. It seemed to me rather that at every age, rather, you gained something and you lost something, and you were lucky if you gained more than you lost.

Whatever age my kids were, I mourned the fact that they were going to grow any older. I always thought they were perfect just as they were at that moment. When they were very young, I particularly feared the moment that they would become divided against themselves rather than simply whole beings living in the absolute present. When they got older, of course this did happen, but they were perfect in a different way.

The times it was hard to see them as perfect were when they were being scared, miserable, ill, difficult or argumentative. It probably reminded me painfully of the difficulties in my own childhood, which I had wanted to spare them completely. And, more than that, it always raised the question of whether I was a good enough mother.

Indeed, when Ari developed asthma, I saw it as proof that I had failed as a mother. "Failed at what?" Yannis asked curiously. He couldn't understand what asthma had to do with my mothering. But of course, he hadn't attended my psychology classes which blamed asthma and everything else on bad mothering.

But I think the most difficult thing about mothering for me was the tug of war between the delight of welcoming these totally unexpectedly wonderful creatures who lived outside of time and space, and the need to cram them into the tiny spaces I had available for them amid all the work I was doing.

These two painful moments come to mind:

Chloe and I sit down to play mother and baby. She is about three years old. "You be the baby and I'll be the mummy," she says.

"Great." Inside I am thinking, *This is what mothers and babies are supposed to do together!*

Chloe's first words as Mummy are, "I'm going out."

Or: Ari, aged about eight, asks if he can make an appointment to see me for an hour, like my clients did.

"I know you love me," he says. "But I'm not feeling loved."

Amazing to have kids who could tell me about such feelings. Terrible that they had to.

I cancelled all my evening clients immediately. But I couldn't cancel my whole busy life. I did once ask them if they would rather have had me home more or rather have Skyros and they chose Skyros. But of course, they would have rather had both.

And yet, the kids don't always remember the worst and best of it in the same way I do. In a discussion with my friend Geoff when my kids were teenagers, Geoff asked Ari what was the worst thing about me as a mother.

He didn't hesitate. With a face full of pain, he told me what was easily the most damaging cruelty.

"You never let us have enough sweets and chocolate. You made me into a chocaholic."

CHAPTER SEVENTEEN

The Skyros centre is born

Summer 1979. Yannis and I are walking down the cobble-stone path of Skyros village carrying luggage and two babies. Ari is two years old and Chloe, three months. We are expecting fifteen people to come in three days for our first group. Yannis' father, Mitsu, will also be joining us from Athens.

The session, including accommodation, two meals, groups, and other activities, costs £45 per person if you share a large room at the centre, and £55 if you stay in village rooms. Almost all have opted to stay in the house.

We turn a corner and catch a glimpse of the centre-to-be. It has no doors or windows, and it is only half a house. The rest is a building site.

We managed to make sure that the doors and windows were on by the time the people came. The rest of the house was not finished. And this is where we would sleep, run groups, eat, and generally have a life. So, we started our first session with all of us living in half a house with a "kitchen" that was basically four un-plastered concrete walls and no roof, equipped with a two-ring gas hob and a supply of water. It eventually took the builder only a few days to finish the house, but of course he didn't get around to it until after the season was over.

In case you ever need to know, *avrio* is the Greek word for *manana*.

Yannis, the two babies, Mitsu, and I all slept in a tiny room that had just enough floor space for our mattresses. We had put a partition in the big room so that we could have this extra little bedroom. Another somewhat larger room housed the men. The largest room, which ours opened into, housed the women; as always, an inner adventure attracted more women than men.

We all shared one bathroom with two doors, one opening from the men's room and the other from the women's room—and none from our room.

The nights were hellish. I'd wake in the night because Chloe needed to be fed and changed, but I didn't dare turn on the light because if I woke Ari, he'd cry and wake everyone else up. I changed her in the dark. Shit everywhere.

Mornings weren't too good either. I'd walk into the bathroom and then someone would call me, and I'd walk out, toothbrush in one hand, baby in the other hand. The door would then shut and lock behind me because someone had gone in the other door.

Little Chloe, bless her heart, became an absolutely serene angel the moment we hit Athens. Something in her settled down in Greece. All summer she only cried when she was hungry.

Our neighbour, the *yia yia*, or grandmother, was the main babysitter, and someone used to bring Chloe into the group when she needed breastfeeding. I'd breastfeed her while continuing to run the group. Then they'd take her out again. Chloe wouldn't accept the bottle, and when she did, she would never breastfeed again. She was rather absolute.

And Ari must have had lots of people around to make a fuss over him and take care of him, because I certainly didn't have time for a great deal of mothering. I'd walk into town with the two kids, egged on by one or another of my friends, standing on the low flat roof shouting *Mama Dina, Mama Dina* as I left them. It was funny, but it was also painful.

I have said that there was no real kitchen, but also there was no real cook. We took the idea of community seriously and thought the participants would just muck in and make it all happen.

The staff, besides Yannis and me, included one other group leader. In the first session, this was my friend Silke Ziehl, who worked with me in K Polytechnic, and in the second, it was Jacques Salzer from Paris, whom I had met at the conference the previous summer.

We were also blessed with the help of a wonderful young artist named Joe Olubo who had offered his services as a gardener after seeing our little *Time Out* advert for participants. Unbelievably, we didn't actually think we needed a staff. Yannis had shrugged and said, "Come along. But there won't be much to do." This became a standing joke.

Joe was a tall, black, handsome guy with a relaxed and warm temperament, a wonderful sense of humour, and, luckily for us, a willingness and ability to do just about everything. He shopped, cooked, got the participants cooking, gardened, took people on walks, and generally worked non-stop to make the whole thing possible. Without him, I don't know how we would have survived.

I recently learned that Joe died in 1990, aged only thirty-eight. Blessings to you Joe, wherever you are. We loved you so much.

Truly, we had no idea what running the Skyros Centre would entail. There's an old Jewish story about how God went around to various tribes asking them if they wanted the Ten Commandments. As each tribe checked it out, finding perhaps that they weren't allowed to kill, or to steal, or to commit adultery, they turned it down one by one. But the Jews simply said *Na'aseh v'nishma*, which literally means, "We will do and we will listen." In other words, we agree to do it before we know what it involves.

Na'aseh V'nishma must have been engraved on our hearts.

Would we have done it if we'd known? After all, I was running Skyros on top of a full-time job, with two small children, clients, and therapy groups. Every corner of my life was spoken for, and I only rested in order to get energy to do more work.

But I was so hungry for life, and in particular for a creative, meaningful, connected life, that it never occurred to me to consider the cost of anything I thought was worth doing. This is what I later called, "soul esteem", the willingness to follow the inner voice wherever it takes you, however unworthy you feel, and at almost any price. I had no self-esteem to speak of at the time, but I did have soul esteem.

To put it another way, whoever was directing our movie had no trouble making us an offer we couldn't refuse.

The truth is that no matter how hard it got, I loved it. It was as if we'd invited people to a party on a Greek island and they all came. Most were from my Open Circle Group in London. A few came from our advert in *Time Out*. There was a whole contingent of French participants whom Jacques brought with him, many of whom could hardly speak English. They were all prepared to be pioneers, so despite the problems, it was a great party.

On the first day of the first session, Jacqueline and Maryse, two of the women from Jacques' group, arrived; they couldn't come during the second session when Jacques and the rest of his group were coming. Maryse told me she spoke almost no English. "So, you will do Silke's bodywork group?" I asked. No, she'd come for my group.

We had a Belgian participant who spoke French and English fluently and he heroically translated for us during the whole group. When Maryse took centre stage in the groupwork, all the work was conducted with a two-way translation. I'm not sure how much I understood but it seemed to work. I remember one piece of psychodrama ending with her shouting, "Maryse vit."

Somehow, as if by magic, I knew how to do this thing we had embarked upon. Although I didn't understand organisational shape and structure, I did understand the shape and structure of creating connection and meaning. I knew how to create a space where people could feel at home in themselves and with each other, often for the first time in their lives, and I had an instinct for creating the kind of communication structures and attitudes that would encourage safety, exploration, support, and truth.

Perhaps it was my soul that knew how to do it, while I was a neurotic young thing. Certainly now, more than thirty-five years later, the structure and atmosphere are still held as if by the walls of the place, even though all the staff and participants are changed, and I myself am not there most of the time.

The intention always was to create a world that heals. Holidays are a perfect way to do this, because when you temporarily leave behind your everyday life, including the people and responsibilities of that life, you can look afresh at everything safely and without commitment. Moreover, you can do it in a beautiful, warm place with beautiful, warm people. As you feel the benefits of it all, the ties to your old patterns loosen naturally, and you become open to something new.

I knew instinctively, both from my experiences and my own deep yearnings, that the alchemy of community, personal development courses, Greek island holiday, and seekers coming together from all over the world would have the power to transform lives in a matter of days.

The personal development groups seemed to be the centrepiece of the experience, and certainly were in other centres. But for me, it was the community that was the real chamber of transformation. And it was not just any old community.

It had to be one you created and let go of in two weeks. And unlike traditional communities where you got taken care of in exchange for role expectations, social control, and gossip, this was one where you could be accepted as who and what you are, and what you are becoming. I later called this kind of community a "soul community".

I used to go around in the early days asking people, "Would you rather be loved or be free" and line them up in two lines depending on the answer. I was in the "rather be free" group. But Skyros needed to be a place where you could love, be loved, *and* be free.

It had to work for people like me, the cactuses of this world, who were seeking both individuality and connectedness, and needed to have their true selves acknowledged and loved.

Nowadays there is mounting evidence that people who live in healthy communities where they are known, cared for, valued, and have a role, are generally healthier and live longer.[20] Then, we knew it intuitively because people were obviously so much happier.

To create this community quickly, people were encouraged to let go almost immediately of their normal rules of interaction and communication and invited to tell the truth to someone they hadn't met before yesterday, but might become their lifelong friend. I was used to this fairly immediate open communication in the personal development world, which was full of get-to-know you and let-go-of-your defences kind of exercises, and was an environment in which truth, intimacy, and loving support were always encouraged.

I also knew that people had to participate actively in taking care of this world, just as they would in their own home, so that they weren't passive guests but active members of the community. It was considered a rather odd idea to have people come on holiday and join work groups. Yet, I always took for granted that this needed to be part of the experience.

Years later, a BBC film director wanting to do a film about us asked me if I had been in the community-oriented Habonim camps, because he had sensed the similarity. I suddenly realised that the idea of work groups came from my summer camp experience. There we used to work in the cornfields. Here people joined work groups to help with the practical tasks around the place. The principle was the same.

It was also clear to me that building community needed to include giving people a say in their everyday lives. Hence, we held weekly community gatherings as well as a daily breakfast get-together called *Demos*, which is Greek for "the people". Again, it was rather an odd thing to have meetings on a holiday, but they did help create that unique Skyros experience of another type of society.

The normal boundaries between the experiences of staff and participants were softened. Not only would participants have an opportunity to participate in running the place, but staff would have a learning and growth experience no less powerful than that of participants. Moreover, contributing financially and culturally to the welfare of the local Greek community, as we did, was all part of it. The whole thing had to be an evolving community on all levels.

This also echoed my beliefs about how the spiritual world works.

In order to create this special world that heals, I developed a programme with an interlocking set of communication structures, from community meetings to work groups to therapy groups to one-to-one listening, to Greek island holiday experiences. It was a way to reverse the normal social rules and create newer kinder ones. Let me offer a flavour of how the programme went:

People would be greeted the first evening or morning with the introductory community gathering, where they would be encouraged to get to know each other, integrate, learn about Skyros, each other, and themselves.

I would also tell them about what I called, "the jet lag of the soul". I explained that it would take two to three days for them to arrive fully, but it they just kept participating, they would wake up one morning and feel as if they'd been there forever.

One little game we played in the early days was a great ice-breaker. People would circulate and find all the people who had their same astrology sign. They would then talk about what they had in common, and present themselves as a little group to say what characteristics they had in common and what they needed from the community. Once when there was only one other Virgo like myself, he looked at me and said glumly, "Awful, isn't it, being a Virgo?" I agreed. During the rest of the session, every time I got up to speak, he would whisper to me, "You don't have to take responsibility."

There were also two other community gatherings during the session, in the middle and at the end, where people were encouraged to have a voice, reflect on their experience, say what they liked and didn't like, solve problems together. I made up a rule: *No complaints without suggestions*.

I was so fixed on the idea of community problem solving, that when people tried to say they had no problems and just wanted to dance, I would demand that they find some. How could we solve problems if there weren't any? Eventually this boundless idealism gave way to relief when nothing problematic was raised.

Besides these special community gatherings, each morning after breakfast we had the *Demos* get-together, where we made announcements, taught Greek, asked for suggestions, gave thoughts for the day, and generally communicated about anything a community member felt was important. A different participant ran this each day.

Then there'd be work group time, which could mean helping with the cooking, cleaning the toilets, sweeping up, setting the table, and so on. Some people actually preferred cleaning the toilets. "I wanted to get into my shit," one put it. It was particularly attractive to loners who were pleased to find a job they could do on their own.

As in most organisations, what tended to transpire was that one participant would jump in and carry most of the work. Because we were into personal development, by the second week our eager beaver had worked out that this was an old role he or she didn't want to be playing any more, and would opt out. The lynch pin of the kitchen would disappear. We'd hold our breaths for a moment, but then other people always took over.

While the work groups were going on, the staff would be having a staff meeting, which always included checking in with each other emotionally, as well as talking about what was going on with participants, getting group supervision, and planning the programme. This became an important part of the day for the group leaders, who were used to working on their own in their everyday life, and loved being part of a team and learning from each other.

I remember Pulitzer prize winning novelist Alison Lurie telling me that the staff meetings were her reason for coming back to Skyros to teach again and again.

After the staff meetings, the three-hour morning courses began. That first summer, these included my Gestalt Therapy groups plus Silke's bodywork groups on the first session, and Jacques' theatre and mime groups on the second.

Afternoons after lunch were for beach going, odd workshops anyone wanted to put on, walks to various beauty spots, talk, and more talk, especially around the kitchen table. Evenings were wonderful visits to tavernas around town and by the sea. And then there were the parties and the dancing and the laughter.

If it was your birthday, everyone made a wonderful fuss over you all day. I decided that your Skyros age was made up of the first and second number of your chronological age. So if you were 58, you could be 13, or even 4. This tradition still gives people great pleasure! Some participants began to time their holidays to coincide with their birthdays.

In the midst of all the community and group work, we needed a communication structure that was one-to-one. We evolved the notion of "co-listening",[21] a safe and powerful structure for talking, or more like thinking out loud, in the presence of another person, that enabled people to recognise and resolve whatever was nagging at them below the surface.

You could see pairs of people all over the centre and village with eyes closed, speaking and listening to each other in a beautiful way. I loved it.

It all had the smell of community at its best, against the fabulous background of blue skies, whitewashed little houses, and Greeks who tended to look more ancient than they were.

Later, when I was involved in gatherings of people running growth centres around the world, including Esalen and Omega, I discovered that while other centres might have a community atmosphere for their team of young helpers, there was no attempt to create a community for administrators, teachers, and participants. We were the only ones with this approach to transformation. I was often asked how I had come up with something so unique.

When I myself taught in some of these centres, and found that I never had a chance to get together with the other staff in a meaningful way, it left me feeling a bit lonely and disappointed. I appreciated even more the structure that we had created in Skyros that kept everyone connected with each other and with the whole community.

The ethos of Skyros, based as it was on community, was never just about the personal. On a personal level, it was a hothouse for personal transformation. On a social level, it was about creating a different kind of society in which people could live together with respect and love. On a spiritual level, I saw it as one of many centres of light around the world that contributed to the spiritual fabric of the world.

It was, however, years before I used the word "spiritual" explicitly because I was so allergic to the organised religion of my childhood. A wonderful free-spirited nun convinced me that this level needed to be named.

Beyond its roots in my own personal history, Skyros was born out that beautiful enthusiasm and abundance of hope of the late sixties that was so disappointed in the seventies. We really did believe then that we could change the world. Only later did the cynicism set in.

My little contribution was to create a mini world that had some of the qualities that the world at large was missing and to hope for a ripple effect. We didn't kid ourselves that what we could do in Skyros would be equally easy to do in our everyday lives. It was a short-term holiday experience, with no future commitments weighing it down, and people were not competing for status or jobs or money. They were there to surrender to the warmth of the physical world and the community, enjoy life, and learn something new. However, it did give people a sense of community at its best, and inspired people to go home and bring something of the experience back to their everyday world.

Poet Hugo Williams called it, "A holiday to take home with you."[22] That was exactly what I hoped it would be.

We made quite a stir in the village. In particular, personal development groups could be very noisy, with people shouting at their mothers or crying desperately. The village women at first would come running asking if we had a stomach ache and could they help? No, we'd say, it's just Greek drama.

With the idea of drama in mind, Jacques created a theatre and mime performance which we all put on in Brooke Square, a village square on a hill with a view of the sea which sported a naked statue of what purported to be the English poet Rupert Brooke. Brooke is closely associated with Skyros because n April 1915, aged only twenty-seven, he died in a hospital ship off the island. His grave is in a beautiful olive grove in the southern part of Skyros island.

We all took up the challenge to perform, and I myself sang a Hebrew song, despite the fact that I can't carry a tune; I hoped people wouldn't realise since they'd never heard anything like it. All the villagers from our local area came to see us, bringing their little chairs and folding stools to sit on.

I don't think, however, they were ever really convinced we were doing Greek drama. There were stories bandied around that we were that we were a training centre for the CIA or, alternatively, a centre for mentally disturbed and backward people. It was a long time before people really understood what we were doing. But we did contribute hugely to the financial and cultural development of the town, indeed put Skyros on the cultural map, and we behaved as normally in the streets of Skyros as visitors from another culture ever do. Eventually most of the islanders accepted us and recognised our value.

Over the years, through the community meetings, which I took very seriously, and through discussion with staff, I learned a great deal about how to run a centre and especially that you need an organisation, a staff, a division of roles, some external order beyond the inner order that I understood instinctively. The practical administrative structure of Skyros has changed totally since then, or to put it more precisely, we now have one.

But the basic programme, and the spirit at the heart of it, was there from the beginning.

The Skyros Centre worked amazingly in that people did feel at home, and had wonderful times, and life changing experiences. And the staff were as transformed by the experience as the participants, and wanted to come back year after year to be part of it.

In fact, many participants said they didn't dare to go back because the first time was so magical. Thankfully, they often took the risk, and found it different, but equally wonderful.

As the years went by, I'd get more and more letters from people telling me that they now had a new group of friends, a new job, new partner, a new country. Everywhere I went in the world, someone would recognise me and tell me how Skyros had changed their lives, and they were now living where they were, or with whomever they were living, or doing what they were doing because of that turning-point moment. I'd get photos of babies whose parents had met in Skyros, or indeed who had been conceived there, with the caption, "Another Skyros baby."

Indeed, as people went home and regularly quit their jobs, I got frightened for them, and made a rule that you couldn't quit your job for forty days after coming back from Skyros. But I never met anyone who was sorry they'd taken the risk of leaving an unhappy work situation, or who didn't feel that their new life was worth it. Often people came to Skyros at a moment in their lives when they yearned for change, so Skyros was a catalyst for a long-awaited transformation.

But it didn't always work as well for me. Yes, some of my highest and most magical moments happened in Skyros. For some reason the memory picture that comes to mind is a simple one of being part of a whole group of participants and staff laughing, talking, and singing around a delicious dinner at a taverna by the sea, knowing at that very moment that this was what I had always wanted and that my life just couldn't be better.

But some of my lowest and most painful moments also happened in Skyros, when I was feeling so exhausted, weighed down by the responsibility for so much and so many. My friend Pilar once looked at me, seeing how tired and low I was, and said, "You are so good at creating environments that make people happy. But you don't get a chance to be happy yourself."

A recurring image of how it would be for me to be happy was of standing out on a balcony alone, relieved that everyone was having a good time at the party inside the house, so that I had space to rest.

And of course, when I would come home to London after being Queen of Skyros, I would return to K Polytechnic to be treated as the lowest of the low. I always felt that on some spiritual level this was good for me, in that it kept any hubris in check. I could hardly forget that I am not my role.

The most painful learning for me was that when you create a community experience because you yearn for community, everyone else has it but you.

You are backstage making it happen.

CHAPTER EIGHTEEN

A symbolic community

The first summer of the Skyros Centre was a crazy attempt to create a wonderful holiday experience in a half-finished overcrowded building site of a house. It worked because the people who came were pioneers. They loved everything, no matter how rough and tough it was, and we all worked together to create those magical times.

By the second summer, we could afford to breathe a sigh of relief. The house was finished, and everything was so much smoother. But by the second summer, people came with expectations—and complaints. We were discovering what theatre people already know about the audience on the second night of a play.

We were now running four two-week sessions. I would finish teaching at the Polytechnic one day, we would go to Skyros the next, and at the end of the eight weeks, we'd close down the Centre, and I'd start teaching the next day.

We never thought of keeping an office open in the summer months while we were in Skyros. In our minds, the Skyros Centre was simply wherever we were, so if we were on the island, we did not expect to have a presence anywhere else.

Since we rented out our house while we were away, if you phoned us you'd probably get a French or a Spanish voice answering, not knowing what you were talking about. If you hadn't booked by the time we left for the summer, you weren't going to be able to book at all. You either gave up or showed up.

So many people just turned up, despite the fact that it was a real odyssey to get there, that we had no idea how many people were coming for a session. One session, from thinking we had a near empty session, we ended with a whole influx of people who had not managed to book, and of course they were the ones who complained that the Centre was overcrowded.

On the subject of complaints, I must say that people who came to Skyros at that time did not really expect the kind of modern conveniences that they do nowadays, but still there were sometimes serious gripes. Looking back, I can certainly see why.

People would arrive at the Centre, having painfully tried to follow our minimal typewritten instructions giving approximate bus and ferry times. They'd taken a city bus from a nightmarish warren of a bus station, and then a public ferry to the island. They may or may not have been lucky enough to meet someone on the way with whom they could travel.

Occasionally they took the wrong ferry, as when Hilary and Kurt took a boat called SS Skyros which was not, however, going to Skyros, and spent three days getting to us. However, in that time they fell in love and eventually married. Sometimes a mistake is not a mistake.

When our participants finally got to the main square of Skyros, they would search desperately for the Centre. Our typewritten direction read, "Follow the main road towards the sea," so they were expecting a tarmacked road, not a cobblestone street, and you could go towards the sea in either direction. If in trouble, we told them to ask for Yannis or for one of our neighbours, Nikos or Costas. If they asked for the Skyros Centre instead, they were directed back to the village square, which was after all the centre of Skyros.

Then, when they'd finally get to us, and ask for their room, they might be told, "Yannis is sleeping right now. When he wakes up he will find you a room." And I don't mean, "Yannis will take you to your room." I mean that he literally had to find a room we could rent from among our neighbours' houses.

It really was as bad as that, and we didn't even know this wasn't okay. A slick tourist organisation we weren't. Luckily, no one really expected us to be.

But when one group created a little skit to show the importance of the moment of welcoming, we realised that no matter what the practical difficulties were, we needed to open our hearts to our new participants, and make them feel at home from the first minute.

The rooms people stayed in were very basic. Some did not have indoor bathrooms. Others had uncomfortable old beds, or were filled with the paraphernalia of the landladies, or had no real wardrobes. As one participant said of his tiny outdoor loo, "It is the only place where you can sit on the loo, take a shower, and brush your teeth without moving an inch." At the time, I thought none of this mattered. Surely the magic was worth suffering a bit of inconvenience!

And in a way, this was true. Nowadays, we meet people in Athens, take them on our chartered bus either to the airport for the small plane or to Skyros, escort them to the Centre, give them a welcome drink, and show them to their beautiful modern rooms and apartments. But I'm not sure that people complained much more about those primitive rooms than they do about one or another limitation of the vastly superior accommodation of today. It's all so relative, so dependent on our expectations, so embedded in the context of the whole experience.

I was so into being authentic that I didn't even realise I was allowed to write the speech I gave on the first evening. I thought that if it wasn't organic and spontaneous I was being phony. It was okay to structure lectures at the Polytechnic, but not here. I'd appear on the first evening, and hope for inspiration. If I was nervous enough, I might have a few glasses of wine to inspire the inspiration.

Nor did I know that you have to separate the role of therapist from things like the organisation of the kitchen or the collection of money for a coach. And since Yannis was often in London, it turned out that dealing with Greek workmen who spoke no English with my rather pathetic Greek was also part of my brief.

In the first few summers I was the centre of everything from the most mundane to the most spiritual. And, as must be apparent by now, organising the "mundane" was not my strong point. But I wanted to make sure everyone felt welcomed and at home, and thought I was the one to do it because on some level, it was our home we were inviting them to for this wonderful party.

To get me from one room to another without someone stopping me, saying "Dina, Dina", participants sometimes offered to be my "bodyguards" to guide me through.

I was basically an unreconstructed child of the sixties—or at least that's my excuse for my total lack of understanding of administration and organisation, my deep discomfort around institutions, and my overidealistic picture of creating community. The sixties, of course, were also my blessing and the inspiration for creating such an alternative world.

What fascinated me most was the evolution of our notions of community.

The community meetings were central to this evolution because this was where each session worked out its own relationship to their lives at the Centre. What one session's community meetings created, the next destroyed, until eventually we were left with a stable sense of what was important. The structure we have today is based on what we had from the very first day, developed and refined with the important learnings we gained from community meetings and staff meetings.

One community meeting that comes to mind is the time we had seven or eight rather anarchic Greeks as participants and one of them decided that he didn't want to join a work group. It was his holiday after all. He didn't just skive off work, as I'm sure many people did. He brought it to the community meeting to discuss.

The Greeks love their politics.

The question was debated at length. Should he do what he wanted, in the name of individual freedom? Or should he be told that it just wasn't fair, and that if he did this, so would everyone else and then where would we be?

I tried to steer the discussion away from moral undertones and overtones, and eventually the decision was that he should do as he chose.

As it turned out, refusing to work was not the same as being unwilling to make a contribution. He was a stage designer by profession, and on the last evening of the session he made each of us a beautiful wreath for our heads.

It felt like a gift directly from the Greek gods.

Then there was the question of what a community was. If this feels like home, participants seemed to be saying, why can't I just do what I want? Joe would buy a crate of peaches, and before the next meal came around, they were all eaten. If it was their kitchen, why couldn't they just go to the fridge and eat whatever they liked?

We discussed this at a community meeting, and people agreed that this just didn't work. But the very next day, I found people sitting around drinking the cooking wine from the kitchen, and complaining that they didn't want to have work groups. I didn't know what to do.

I went away and thought about it carefully. Maybe they were right. Why have work? And in fact, why have community meetings, particularly if people weren't going to keep to their agreements? But then without work or community gatherings, it wouldn't be a community.

And suddenly I realised that if this wasn't going to be a community, I didn't want to do it. I was not a hotel manager, and I didn't want to run a hotel with groups.

As soon as I became clear in myself, the problems stopped.

But I came to realise that the term community was confusing. Participants might be having the experience of community, but they hadn't got together to share ideas and resources to create the community together. They had simply paid us for a holiday, albeit one that looked like a community.

It was not in fact their kitchen, and if they were asked to work, it was not as a source of cheap labour, but because this was a building block of the world we were offering them.

I came up with the term "symbolic community". We were providing an educational experience of community that would be transformative, and it was built out of a series of symbolic communication structures. It was not a "real" community.

As I began to understand this, I felt freer about making more aspects of the community symbolic rather than real. Most notably, we employed a team of people who were there permanently, including a coordinator, a cook, an assistant, that sort of thing, as well as an administrator or two in London. This meant that the work was symbolic, too, rather than being essential to the running of the place.

Now, work groups did enough work to feel that they were active members of a community rather than passive guests of an institution, but they didn't need to clean toilets or cook meals. They were more likely to set tables, prepare vegetables, sweep the courtyard, or water the plants. Some were disappointed about this, others relieved. Some took the opportunity to opt out altogether.

According to Joe, participants never had been the ones who kept the place going. He said that organising the cooking group was like creating a children's work project, and it would have been easier to do it himself.

Slowly but surely, the community meetings began to make fewer and fewer major decisions. We were no longer looking to the community to create the shape of the session. The shape was there, and the decisions were relatively minor.

As the Centre grew, we began to have three personal development groups running at a time. At first, people moved as a group from one leader to another over the two-week period. That way, the group as a whole worked with all three group leaders.

Eventually, we started having people sign up for one leader one week, and another leader the second week. This introduced an element of popularity competition which I had been trying to avoid with the previous structure. I discovered that getting people to sign up for my group depended on how I was feeling that day. I'd stand up and say, "Come to my group. I do a bit of this and a bit of that." That worked when I was feeling particularly charismatic, and not otherwise.

The crunch point for me came when my friend, playwright and Gestalt therapist Max Furlaud was running a group at the same time as me. I did my casual "bit of this, bit of that" routine, and then he stood up and gave a powerful little speech. His group filled, mine was almost empty, and I had my first sleepless night ever. How was it that I couldn't attract participants in my own Centre?

In the morning, I came back to myself, realising: "Well, I've had this failure, but I'm still here." And over the week, people started to drift from his group to my group, until he himself came to sit in on my group to find out what was happening. He paid me back for my increased popularity by falling asleep in my group.

I realised, rather like when I rewrote all my lectures at the Polytechnic so that they had a clear structure, that I had to present what I was doing in a way that people could understand and feel attracted to. "A bit of this and a bit of that" wasn't quite the thing. My focus on imagery as my primary way of working became more explicit, both for me and for participants.

We also came to understand that personal development was exciting and intense but a bit one-sided. We began to offer yoga in the mornings and to have a "community facilitator" to offer creative and fun activities in the afternoons and evenings. And on the last evening, we would have a "cabaret" in which people performed in whatever way they felt inspired to perform, to an extremely appreciative audience. I often had to reassure people, "If you've been afraid of public performance, this is a place where you could fall off the stage and still be applauded."

Changes were happening also on the physical level. The wild overgrown garden became a paved courtyard with a view. Theo, a participant whose day job was architect, offered to design a second floor for our house. He stayed on for a week or two and designed the beautiful space that became our main group room. We also built another room with a glass wall through which you had a wonderful view of hills and sea. This was at first my favourite group room, and eventually became our art room.

Our brochures changed along with the Zeitgeist. After the first typewritten and photocopied brochure of one A3 page folded over, we graduated to brown and oatmeal four-page brochures, A3 size, on heavy matt textured Conqueror paper which we thought was the height of luxury.

Given Yannis' journalistic background, they were designed to look like an alternative newspaper, with the actual programme on a folded sheet inside, and they often had humorous stories, sketches and cartoons. We never wanted to be too earnest.

Even more important, we didn't want to seem too commercial. It was not until 1985 that we risked having a shiny brochure in full colour. What would people say? No one seemed to mind, so we went on with our colour brochures.

As the years went on, personal development became less popular, and we branched out into other courses. Our most successful was the writers' lab. It was a time when it was just becoming accepted that creative writing can be taught. And indeed, the writing course tutors were so inspiring that they started quite a few participants on their path to be successful writers themselves.

From the beginning, the writers' labs attracted luminaries of the writing world, including household names like Steven Berkoff, Margaret Drabble, Nell Dunn, Alisdair Gray, Alison Lurie, Hilary Mantel, Hanif Kureishi, Bernice Rubens, Arthur Smith, DM Thomas, Sue Townsend, Marina Warner, and Hugo Williams. While famous psychotherapists in general wanted to be paid at levels we couldn't dream of, famous writers seemed to be willing to come because it sounded like fun. And they loved being part of a team, and being treated in a simple open way by people rather than with the kind of famous person projections that normally limited their relationships.

The absolute importance of being treated in an honest, respectful, and loving way was true for everyone who came—participants, teaching staff, and permanent staff alike. A Skyros participant from our second summer told me that the holiday was the best she'd ever had, and that she'd laughed more than she ever did before or since, and it had also completely changed her life, including starting her on the path to become a psychotherapist. When I asked her what about Skyros had made her new life possible, she told me that when she came there, a housewife and mother with almost no qualifications, she felt herself to be of no value. She came away feeling she was someone. That was enough to change everything.

A new set of mirrors made possible a new beginning.

In the background of all this, I was finding my way through the mirror of all the powerful projections on me, for which I was completely unprepared. I was in my early thirties, but I was the mother of a community of people, some of whom were old enough to be my grandparents.

Being the founder of a world, like being the mother of a child but more so, meant that you were the "be-all and the end-all", the centre of an archetypal myth. It was rather like the Great Mother I believed my children were relating to. Whether

I smiled at someone or didn't was a major event for them. If I cried, it just proved that I was so powerful I could afford to cry in public. When there was a crisis, I was the one who had to rise to it and lead the community.

The sessions were in two-week cycles, and each fortnight was such a total experience of a world coming into being and then dissolving that it felt like a lifetime. I began to feel like an ancient being, living lifetime after lifetime.

There was a moment in a getting-to-know-each other session on the first night when I stood at the top of the stairs, and noticed that two of the new participants resembled a couple from the previous session who had met and gotten together with disastrous results. Now I saw this new pair begin to move towards each other across a crowded room.

Is this what the gods feel when history starts to repeat itself?

Faced with the demands upon me to be wonderful, I did manage to rise to the occasion, particularly at moments of crisis. The Greater Dina was a lot bigger, more powerful, and wiser than I was. But on another level, I was still an awkward, insecure, needy child.

While the adult/ancient being was taking care of everyone and everything, the child within me was left to cope on her own, desperately trying to be a good girl.

I moved through various phases of my relationship to this role I was playing. Sometimes I slipped into an altered space, feeling like an ancient queen or goddess. I had never before been the centre of so much attention, the recipient of so much overflowing love. I imagine it was like a much-adored infant's experience of being the centre of the world, an experience I never really had.

Then I'd start feeling isolated and depressed and feel it was all projection, all unreal. None of it was real love, none of it was really about me. In fact, I believed, I was completely alone, the object of envy and resentment, and I was terrified of anyone complaining or seeing my feet of clay.

I had an enormous amount of power in that little world, but I wasn't looking for power, except the creative power of being a midwife for transformation. The little girl in me just wanted to be loved.

After a wonderful high in Skyros, I'd return home and be depressed; when I was unhappy in Skyros, I came home and felt good. It was as if I was on some kind of wheel of fortune, desperately struggling to distinguish between reality and illusion.

As I managed to work my way through all this, I stopped wanting everyone to love me and began to make important distinctions. There were people who could overcome their projections and really care about me. Others could not. They could never be friends. I began to see that neither the love nor the attacks had much to do with me.

I remember my friend Sue, who was also a group leader on the staff team, saying to me, "I can't be unaffected by the fact that you are the Director here." I was devastated. Did this mean I couldn't have friends here?

"Then I give up," I said. "If you can't, who can?"

She said, "Don't give up. The point is, I'm working on it."

And for my part, I figured out that being a therapist did not mean that I wasn't allowed to have needs. There was a distinct moment when I realised that I too could reach out for help. I could feel my arms extending and had a sense that I did not need to be so alone.

Skyros eventually gave back to me what it gave to others and more, I felt valued and loved both for my contribution and for myself and I got a profound sense of contentment from the creative pleasure of this wondrous venture.

And as I learned to reach out, I found real friends, who could care for and protect me, who were not envious of me, who could accept that I was both strong and vulnerable. Many of them cared about Skyros almost as much as I did.

I was no longer alone backstage. I had my own community.

NOW AND THEN

She's moving now, is young Dina, giving birth to babies and to her first centre, soon to be followed by a second one. Even when it's hell, and it so often is, it's always a miracle.

I once heard a wonderful lecture in which a Buddhist priest said: *It is not water turning into wine that is the real miracle, but grapes turning into wine.* The grapes are turning into wine now.

So, for once, when I look back at Dina, I don't feel sorry for her. I think: "Great. Go for it!"

There are people all over the world who have been affected directly or indirectly by what she did in those years, whose lives dramatically opened up to new possibilities.

In a survey we did, about 85% of our participants found that Skyros had affected their lives, and that they were pursuing activities and connections made there. One of my colleagues told me he owes his second career, his best friends, his wife, and his new baby to Skyros. Just in the past fortnight, my body-work therapist told me that she had met her husband there, I got an email from a participant who had been inspired by the group to retire from being a medic and start the art degree she had always dreamed of, and I met someone in my neighbourhood who had started a new career as a bodywork therapist after taking a Shiatsu course in Skyros. Minutes ago, someone contacted me through my website to thank me, writing, "I feel privileged to have been around your life and work from a distance, for many years, and I'm sure there are many more like me, whom you don't even know about, who have been helped and inspired by the spirit of your vision! Thank you!"

Yet, there is younger Dina, juggling this incredibly complicated life, raising her kids in the middle of it all. Can I really tell her that she is doing a brilliant job when what she is doing is running herself into the ground? Everything she is doing is good, except what she is doing to herself.

I step inside the younger Dina and I notice:

I feel chased by monsters. It is all too much. I am amazed at the miracle of having small children. I am full of wonder about the magic of Skyros. But I feel unable to accomplish what everyone says is very ordinary—just run my everyday life.

And I say to her, "Slow down, dear Dina. Appreciate your own persistence in doing what is so difficult for you as much as your joy at doing what comes easy to you. Don't expect that it should be easy, nor think you are getting it wrong if it is not. Please recognise that you're overcoming great obstacles and limitations with enormous courage and creativity. I admire you for that. And I love you always."

Nothing prepared her for how tough it would be, with no manual, no training, and having to learn everything on the job at top speed. But equally, nothing prepared her for the wonder of having babies and of creating this world.

Then again, maybe not being prepared is a good thing. I never like it much when I go sightseeing with a guidebook. I read the description of the place and then I see it. So, what? It's a bit of an anti-climax. But when I wander through a city and come upon something completely surprising, I am entranced.

And young Dina is so often entranced at this time.

The illuminations are beginning. The children. The Centre. The spiritual experiences. The difficulties are now being counterbalanced by the highs.

And though the highs may last a lot less time than the lows, they are like fruit cast along the road to keep her on the path. They act as a lens through which she can sense the wonder of life. Not her life, no. Just Life.

Just her ever present, often tragic, but sometimes remark- able, love affair with Life.

PART IV

THE CREATIVE YEARS:
GAINS, LOSSES, AND THE
RADICAL IMAGINATION

CHAPTER NINETEEN

Emmet dies

May 1980. My brother Emmet phones me. I am juggling preparing a meal for the kids with solving some Skyros problem, so I say hello and quickly give the phone to Yannis, who chats with Emmet. I never take the phone back, just say goodbye through Yannis. Too busy, as usual.

Yannis went to Skyros the next day and then three days later, my father phoned to tell me that Emmet had jumped off his balcony and killed himself. He was probably psychotic at the time, so I never knew if he was trying to fly or planning to kill himself.

Have I ever fully forgiven myself for that phone call when I wasn't listening to what may have been a cry for help?

When I got the news, I secluded myself with the kids and didn't phone anyone except Yannis. It was too fresh a wound, too hard to admit to the world that this terrible thing had happened.

My friend Sheila Rossan, a fellow American psychologist and one of the other PhD students of my professor, happened to phone me to invite me to a barbecue. I burst into tears when I answered the phone, so I was forced to tell her what had happened and how I was feeling. She started talking fast, saying whatever she could think of to soothe the pain and the guilt.

I wailed, "I was the person he was closest to and I let him down just before he died. I might have been able to save him." She said, "You must have done something good to be the one who was closest to him."

She said many other things, but this is what stuck with me and made a difference.

I didn't say a word to my kids, Ari and Chloe, who were then only four and two years old respectively. But Ari developed a fear of death during that period. It may well be that he unconsciously picked up what was so carefully left unsaid.

Two days later I ran one of my Open Circle weekend groups. It didn't occur to me to cancel it, nor did I tell the group that my brother had just died. The truth is that I felt I had to hide the fact that I had a mentally ill brother who killed himself. After all, in my mind, being a therapist meant that I should be a healthy person with a healthy family. Otherwise, how could I be trusted?

And I also feared that they would think I was too distressed to take care of them. I was a professional, and they had paid me to be there for them one hundred percent.

It is not the only time I have kept silent about a fresh tragedy or trauma when I was being a professional. It was my practice, until I learned better. Now, while I wouldn't normally share my everyday problems with a group or a client, if something traumatic has just happened, I will either cancel the session or tell them about it, albeit briefly.

But at that moment, I was still thinking that my role of therapist required me to be Superwoman, and I didn't dare break the spell. My memory of that group is of simple unalloyed pain covered up with a professional helping mode.

How much of our professional helping is like this? And do the clients usually know on some level, pick up on our pain, just as my son Ari did, and perhaps think it is their own pain they are feeling and not ours? In my experience, they often do.

My father had Emmet cremated, but there was no funeral. I was shocked at this, but I think he just couldn't bear it or deal with it. Later, after my father's own death, I was to find Emmet's ashes in a tin in his wardrobe.

But my father did what he could. He arranged an evening in Emmet's memory to which he invited friends and family. He wrote a long beautiful poem to him. And then he came to London to mourn with me. There was a lot to mourn, including not only Emmet's premature death but his painful life.

His name, Emmet, is the Hebrew word for truth, and his middle name Shalom means peace. In fact, he was secretive and as a young child had a raging temper. But on another level, he was a seeker after ultimate truth and peace. Unfortunately, his life was too short and troubled for him to find it, except for moments.

Emmet was my older brother by two years, but because of all his problems, had never quite been a big brother to me. He was a one-year old when my sister Ora died and my mother retreated into a shell but turned to overprotect him. Much later I read that schizophrenia is more common in children who are overprotected because of the fear of death in the family. My father was probably unavailable emotionally, as was my sister Shira. Then I came along when he was almost two.

Emmet later told me how hard it was for him to be in a family of strong women, with no strong male father figure to model himself on. My father was insecure and anxious at the best of times, but I think Ora's death made it all much worse, and I used to think of him as the most anxious person I knew. We children believed my father was weak and my mother was the strong one, though in fact his strength was on another level.

When Emmet went to Israel for a while as a teenager, he came back enthusiastic about the warmth of the Eastern Jewish families, which he so missed in ours.

Emmet and I were close, going to the same school, experiencing the same family from a roughly similar point of view.

Yet we didn't speak of what was happening to us on the inside or how we felt about the family. Probably, neither of us had the words, and it was not something people did then, certainly not in our family.

I did once try to talk to him of my inner world and met his blank cold refusal to join in. He must have closed himself behind his defensive walls quite early. According to my father, he and my mother realised that there was something wrong by the time Emmet was three. I think that at that time they focussed on him and I, already neglected, further lost the attention of my parents.

My father went out of his way to help Emmet make friends, and used to take him to museums and events with a group of neighbouring boys his age. I tagged along, the only girl among the boys. I remember the birthday party I had when I had no friends of my own and could only invite his.

I have since seen a similar pattern in families where one child has a problem; the other child is thought to be okay and not to need anything.

Emmet and I always had a complicated relationship. Though we loved each other very much and had this underlying closeness between us, he would often treat me badly, hit me, betray my confidences, and make fun of me. I can picture him running around the room around the table after me in front of his friends, making fun of me because I stammered. He had stammered when he was younger, but had by now stopped and I had started; it was if we were taking turns. I had no idea what to do when he taunted me.

I did finally deal with getting hit all the time. At first, I complained to my mother endlessly and I was always told he would lose pocket money, which seemed to do no good. One day, I turned around and hit him back. That was the end of the hitting.

I have very few happy memories of my childhood, but one is of me riding on Emmet's back, playing as if I were riding a

170

horse to market. I suppose this kind of game is a normal event for many siblings. I remember it as a one-off for me.

Another memory picture: my parents and I are going off to see friends of the family and Emmet refuses to go. We turn around and see his sad little face in the window. My mother says she feels bad leaving him. I feel puzzled: after all, he was the one who had decided to stay home.

When we were in high school, Emmet and I both went to the same speech therapist at Brooklyn College, one who was more interested in psychotherapy than in speech. The therapist began to open out, and give words to, what was going on in my family. Talking about such things was completely outside my experience. I felt as if I was in a film.

But it was ground breaking. I discovered that there was a surface and a below the surface, there was a language for what went on below the surface, and if there was a language, it meant feelings were human and you could talk about them and find your way through. This probably was the first step towards my becoming a psychotherapist. For Emmet? I don't know. Emmet and I never talked of it, but we both looked at each other one day and he said, "It's weird, isn't it?" I agreed.

He was sometimes bullied by friends and classmates who sensed his vulnerability. Once or twice I was there, and I moved in to protect him. Of course, I wished he could have protected me sometimes and been a proper big brother.

Along with his vulnerabilities, Emmet was enormously bright, funny and creative, as well as deeply spiritual and truth-seeking. He was also a real rebel in my orthodox Jewish school, something I never dared to be. He grew a beard when the school forbade it, and was threatened with expulsion. He even had a picture of Christ in his room, which was a real taboo-breaking statement in a Jewish household.

And my friend Debby told me years later that when he came to visit me in Michigan, he walked her home one night, and

171

when some guys in the street were threatening, he put his arm around her and protected her.

He began to go psychotic in his teens and was in and out of mental hospitals, diagnosed as schizophrenic. Unfortunately, it was before there were adequate medication and treatments that might have helped him. He also experimented with marijuana, and possibly other drugs, to give him the kind of spiritual highs he was looking for. But this was very dangerous for him and probably sent him into further psychotic states.

Once he came through England from Israel, thinking he was God, and throwing money around with abandon. Another visit, when he was more in contact, he told me that he felt very guilty about his treatment of me, and that he had always been jealous of me.

He paid me a lovely visit after Ari was born, quite sane at that time, and told me to tell Ari about the adventures of his uncle, the Great Emmet, as he used to call himself sometimes.

But the psychotic episodes continued. At one point, not long before he died, he told me that he'd bought a guitar but didn't need to learn how to play it because he could do it naturally. To me, this signified that he had lost the will to put in the effort needed to make life work. I had been trying all this time to write to him and to help, but at this point, I kind of gave up on him ever getting better and I closed my heart a bit. I felt there was nothing more I could do.

I was very wrong. He still needed me very much, though not in the old way.

Interestingly, Elisabeth Kübler-Ross, the expert on death and dying I had met at that conference in Geneva in 1978, was always pointing out that doctors close down when a patient has gone beyond their ability to cure them and is now dying. Her whole approach to working with the dying was based on showing health workers how they could be immensely helpful to dying people by not closing down, but just being there, fully present, helping them finish unfinished business, and assisting

172

in whatever way possible in the dying process. The hospice movement is based on this principle.

If I'd understood that I needed to switch from rescuing to being fully present with my brother, perhaps I would have taken that phone call from him. Maybe it wasn't just being busy that stopped me.

All the years that he was suffering, I had feelings of what is now called survivor guilt. Why was I doing better than he was? And did he want me to be happy if that meant I was okay when he wasn't? Then of course, when he died, there was more guilt.

Much later, I was visiting my friend Max and we went to visit some standing stones in Brittany where he lived. I touched one of the stones, and this message flashed out at me: *Keep Emmet in your heart and he will live forever.*

I reflected long and hard on what this might mean. It came to me finally:

The guilt stops the love.

As long as I felt guilty every time I thought of him, I couldn't really hold him in my heart. And he needed me to do so. I decided to give up the guilt and love him wholeheartedly.

I began to talk to him in my mind, and even try to heal him in the other dimension. I felt him closer and closer to me and I had a sense that he was indeed healing and developing.

Years later, after Yannis and I had separated, I was having a relationship with a man who was charismatic and fun but rather unkind, and we eventually split up. On the day I moved out from living with him, I lay in bed, and it was as if Emmet's presence suddenly appeared, and he said to me:

Thank God you got rid of that awful man.

I was so touched by his protectiveness.

My big brother, after all.

CHAPTER TWENTY

Just imagine

"You've turned psychosis into an art form," my friend Julie McNamara once told me.

That art form is what I call Imagework. Where you find the golden threads in the tapestry of my life, you will find the world of the imagination, which has always been my true home.

Some of my earliest memories are of my disappointment when imagination came face to face with reality. There was the time I was skipped from kindergarten to first grade in the middle of the year. I sat there in my new classroom where children sat in rows rather than in a lovely big circle, and I learned to write my name. I showed the girl next to me that the D was like a mouth if you turned it around. I was excited about it. She was profoundly uninterested. My little heart sank.

Then, in the early days of television, I hung on our new television and somehow managed to break the screen. There were no people inside, only grey. I can still remember the dull emptiness I felt. I never much liked television after that.

Sometimes, I strayed too far for my own comfort into the world of the imagination, and then yanked myself back when it felt dangerous to me. I tended to see it as a stark either/or kind of paradigm—either the inner or the outer world. Each time, I chose the outer world; it must have seemed safer, saner.

There was for example the story of Charlie and the magic box. I was about six years old, and going to a little Jewish school called Kinneret. The anthem of that school was a traditional Hebrew song about a boy who studied Torah on the banks of the Kinneret, or the Sea of Galilee, directly from the mouth of the Prophet Elijah. So, in my mind there was already some magic in that school.

It was miles away from my house, and I was going there because my mother wanted us to be familiar with her culture, though she was not religious. This was before I switched to the much bigger and more Orthodox Yeshivah of Flatbush because it was closer to home but never as close to my heart.

Each day I was picked up in a station wagon, or estate car, and driven to and from school. The driver was named Charlie, and I so desperately wanted him to like me that I sat quiet as a mouse in the back. I knew absolutely that one day the doorbell would ring, and I would come to the door to find Charlie standing there with a box in his hand, a present for me for being such a good girl. Inside the box would be a magic wand, and every wish I wished would come true.

Later I decided it should only grant every wish that was good for me.

With this wand, I could create other wands and give them to my friends. But their wands wouldn't be able to create new wands—only my original big one could.

One morning I sat up in bed with a start and thought: *But that's magic and I don't believe in magic*. And that was the end of the magic box, at least until I created a kind of magic box with my Imagework world.

Then there was the time when I was at Brandeis University, and we were asked by my psychology professor to hand in a dream diary. The trick was to wake up but keep our eyes closed, or close them rapidly, then write down the dreams that were clinging onto us. This was an extraordinary exercise, because

I began to remember more and more of my dreams, indeed to live with them more and more.

One day I wondered why people took for granted that the world of everyday life was more real than the world of dreams. After all, I spent hours of my life dreaming, and the only difference seemed to be that there was less continuity in the world of dreams—you didn't go back to the same place as you did in everyday reality.

I'd never heard of the philosopher who wondered if he was a philosopher dreaming he was a butterfly, or a butterfly dreaming he was a philosopher. I just knew that this was a crazy view of reality. I got frightened, and I gave up the dream diary, as suddenly and absolutely as I had given up the magic box.

I made a similar decision to abandon the inner world in favour of the "real world" when I was in my third year of college, studying at the Hebrew University in Jerusalem as part of what was called my "Junior Year Abroad". I was taking a course in the Kabbalah, the Jewish mystic tradition, and at the same time reading a book by Oscar Lewis, *Children of Sanchez*,[23] about the culture of poverty in Mexico.

I told myself, "Either this—the esoteric mystical world—is true, or that—the reality of poverty—is true." I chose the reality of poverty and gave up the Kabbalah.

And remember, my given name Zohar is the name of the main book of the Kabbalah.

Perhaps I knew I was at risk, because of course it did come to pass that I slipped into the world of the unconscious imagination, was declared psychotic, and it took a few months and a few pills and a great sea voyage to return to the world of everyday reality.

However, after that brief period of madness, when I landed back in everyday reality, and decided firmly to stay sane, I began to realise that there was a way to live safely and sanely with the magical imagination.

Essentially it involved holding the outer world of everyday reality and the inner world of the imagination separate enough so that I knew which was which, and then using the inner world to illuminate the outer world, and the outer world to feed back into the inner world.

Sometimes the philosopher is dreaming he is a butterfly, and sometimes the butterfly is dreaming he is a philosopher. There is no need to choose. Both are real, and both are important, and they reflect each other in beautiful ways.

But they mustn't be confused. That way madness lies.

This conscious work with the inner world of the imagination is what I came to call Imagework. I prefer the term "Imagework" because the more common word "visualisation" implies that you must see visual images. I don't see images fully, nor do many other people. I sense them, feel my way into them, hear what they have to say to me. But I don't know the colour of my Egyptian Queen guide's dress, or how tall she is. I just recognise her by her presence.

I began to learn about imagery from many different traditions, including Jungian Active Imagination, Gestalt Therapy, Neuro-Linguistic Programming, Silva Mind Control, Creative Visualisation, Laws of Manifestation, self-hypnosis techniques, Shamanic practices, and the Arcane School. I also made up many of my own exercises as and when I needed them, and then eventually systematised them so they could be used in therapy and groupwork, or become part of an everyday toolbox.

At first, my work with images evolved because I was desperate to work my way through and out of the thoughts and feelings that were causing me pain, and to keep clearing and clearing until I found an inner wisdom that would enable me to rest securely in my own body, heart, and soul.

But it was not just a form of self-therapy. It was also a serious part of my endless search for truth. It was a way to burrow under the symbols and language of the culture, and find those that came from my deepest imagination. I came to call this level of truth the *radical imagination*, or the *genius imagination*. It couldn't show me the ultimate truth, but it could reveal to me my own authentic truth, which was usually miles away from the conventional wisdom and imagination.

I believed that the truth would indeed set me free. I think it did.

I began to use imagery regularly until it seeped into the pores of my existence and eventually made it possible for me to live rather than survive painfully. My understandings, my sense of direction, my planning, my will to achieve, my will to stop achieving, my inner joy and outer adventure were all shot through with my adventures with imagery. You'll see examples of it everywhere in this book.

It was as if someone gave me an extra brain with which to run my life.

I came to see the images as building blocks of the project of understanding ourselves and guiding our lives, as well as connecting with that which is beyond us, re-imagining ourselves and life, and making positive changes. I couldn't conceive of a life without them.

The diaries from the Chrysalis Years were shot through with imagery—a combination of the fairy stories about the little girl who lived by the sea which seemed to be metaphors for my life and my possibilities and tended to end happily, and those awful attacking conversations between me as adult and me as child. Slowly but surely, the conversations became more loving and the fairy tales closer to reality. It was all part of my healing.

But the imagery work wasn't confined to my diaries. If you peeped into my home, you would often see me in the sitting room with my eyes closed, a cup of tea within reach, moving between my arm chair and all the various seats in the room.

I might, for example, in typical Gestalt Therapy fashion, be carrying on a conversation with someone I was angry at or hurt by. I'd imagine him on an empty seat opposite me, and tell him all my feelings and thoughts. Then I'd switch seats, and become him. I'd slip into his body, and try to see the world from his perspective, and then respond. There might be a third seat for someone who could love, understand, and respect both of us, and could say things like, "You both need to …" This would continue until I reached some resolution.

Or I might have come up, either through an imagery session or from a dream, with an image which was a metaphor for some aspect of my life. For example, after my first summer in Skyros, when there were so many demands on me to which I felt unable to say no, I had an image of being an apple tree with bare branches and no fruit. As I asked the tree about its past, it said that it had had apples, but people had torn away the fruit, and even pulled the bark off, and it no longer wanted to fruit.

I worked with the image, viewing it from the point of view of a bird on the tree, and the sun shining on it, thus giving it other perspectives, and asked what was its next step. The tree eventually decided that from now on, it would allow itself to have apples but no one would be allowed to pull them off its branches. The tree could offer them if it wanted to.

Something shifted in me about my ability to choose how and what I give others.

Or I might be talking to my own inner child who has been hurt by someone's unkind comment, and then further hurt when I started to attack myself. I'd switch back and forth between child and adult. One of my most powerful discoveries was that every time I attacked myself, the child suffered. That made me want to be kinder. I didn't like the thought of causing pain to a child.

Once I was lying on my bed, feeling my energy had gone, listening to music, and suddenly I got a memory image of being a little girl lying on my bed in Brooklyn. I asked the little girl: *Do you know what music is?* She didn't. There had never been music in the house in Brooklyn. *Do you know what love is?* She didn't. Love was not really spoken of in the family.

I realised that while I was having all these experiences, she was still back in Brooklyn. I started to tell her about music, and about love, and all about my life. She was fascinated and delighted. The energy streamed back, as if my life was now feeding her too.

And from then on, when I went to Greece, I'd whisper to her. *Now we're going to a foreign country. It's called Greece.* And I'd tell her all about it. Odd feelings I had had whenever I went to Skyros disappeared. She was with me on my trip.

It turns out that the inner child needs not just emotional care, but information and explanations about things the adult part of us knows but the child doesn't. We have such separate centres of consciousness in our minds, that unless we set up communication lines between them, we will literally find that the right hand doesn't know what the left is doing.

It was all part of understanding that my perspective at any moment is not the whole story, and that I have access to so many other perspectives within me if I just take the time to find them and communicate them to other parts of me.

I had an array of inner advisors, who could range from Dr Jones, my inner financial and practical consultant, to Hathor, the Egyptian goddess of love and healing, to detectives Miss Marple and Hercule Poirot of the Agatha Christie mystery stories.

We'd all sit around as if it at a board meeting, and I'd move from chair to chair in my sitting room to get all their points of view, until I could reach an inner conclusion. I discovered that the times I was in most trouble, the Board was being run by the child, and she had fallen asleep on the job.

Going shopping for clothes, I was never alone. One of my Egyptian goddesses always told me whether the dress was great or I should leave it in the shop.

Sometimes only a conversation with God, or rather my inner version of God, would do. Once when I was in a lot of pain, but was just beginning to get the feeling that I didn't always have to be this unhappy, I called out to God to help. God sent a messenger in a boat. I rejected the messenger and said, "No, I want to speak to God." God sent another messenger in a bigger boat, and I rejected that one too. Finally, God came. I knew it was God this time because I experienced the boat as winter, summer, spring, fall, and past, present, and future all at once.

When I saw God at the helm I said, "I demand better conditions for the troops."

God cried and then said softly, "I'm so happy that you've decided not to be a victim."

I discovered another wonderful way to get wisdom and healing when I created the "Houses". I started with the House of Truth, where my consultant was Ma'at, the Egyptian goddess of truth, and discovered that I could explore any House I wanted—Sexuality, or Love, or Money, or Time, or Health, or indeed any area where I needed wisdom and healing. I'd invite an image of the House to emerge, have a conversation with the House itself, discover a consultant and a healer, get a gift, and leave with great gratitude.

One of the visits that comes to mind now is the one to the House of Time. I am one of those people that doesn't have a sense of time built into their system. I am happy with timelessness, and in many ways I have good timing, but clock time has always been a problem for me.

Indeed, my feeling had always been that Time was like a frightening stranger chasing after me, so that I was always late, always running, and there was never enough time, and I could never do enough.

Yet it turned out that my House of Time was a beautiful grand cathedral. As I met Father Time, I almost wept to realise that he had been there since the beginning of time, and was not just some scary stranger. He told me that it couldn't possibly be that I don't have enough time, since I *am* time. Time is the days of my life.

I needed to stop trying to play hide and seek with time, and simply decide how I wanted to spend my time or energy, open that file on the desktop of the imagination, and it would naturally get done. It was a wonderful discovery for me.

Rachel, one of my students, visited the House of Time, and asked her Consultant what to do about the fact that she never had enough time. Rachel paused, and suddenly said with wonder, "Oh, I see. I just need to do things more slowly." I loved that too.

Another major aspect of my use of imagery was to decide what I wanted and to go for it. It was my way back to the magic box. You did it not by looking forward and deciding what you wanted, but by actually going into a future in which you were happy, and then looking back to see how you got there. Moreover, if you went into a future in which you were unhappy, you could look back and see what not to do.

You could use hindsight before you began. And then you could go for the future you chose with wisdom and will.

The whole process of visioning the future, and then putting my will behind it to make me happen did function a bit like a magic wand to open a direction or a path that I could then travel down successfully. And my insight as a child that I had better also include the caveat that the wand would only give me what was good for me was totally valid.

The popular visualisation literature was suggesting—and still does– that you "create the life you want", by deciding what you want, visualising it, and making it happen. But how do you know if this was what you truly want? Maybe you simply haven't rethought the programming from family or peer group, and you are going for what you think you should want.

I came to feel that it was not enough to make my dreams come true. I needed to know what my true dreams were. I needed to consult my radical imagination.

One method I developed was to take trips in a space-and-time ship, leaving the earth and going into two possible futures, one where I was happy because I had honoured my true self, and one where I was unhappy because I had betrayed or neglected my true self. After experiencing them both, and seeing how I got to each, and the difference between them, I would choose one, and then come back to set an intention for the future.

I discovered, working with myself and then with others, that there was always a pull towards choosing the negative future. Why? It was familiar and it was safe and you didn't have to do much. In fact, people generally said that the way to get to your most feared future was just to do what you were doing already.

Choosing the positive future always involved upping your game.

I loved also to use the image of a crossroads when I had a decision to make. I'd walk down the path of my life, come to a crossroads and follow each of the possible paths in turn. I'd go forward five years, ten years, twenty-five years, then look back and send a message to the present me. Then I'd come back to the crossroads and choose one path.

There was the time, for example, that I tried the Path of Power. I discovered as I walked on this path that I was very successful, my courses were oversubscribed, and my students were serious acolytes. I thought it was pretty good. Why hadn't I tried this before?

Then I came to the moment of death, and discovered I was empty. I had nothing to face death with. I gave it up, and chose the path of Being Me.

Sometimes the image didn't need to be imagined, but was a real life object or plant or photo or sculpture that I could talk to and sense the answer. You might see me standing in front of a great Buddha statue, or it might be a lamp post, or a flower, or a rubbish bin, and I'd be rather quietly having a conversation and asking for their insights.

"I'm half-full," the rubbish bin might say. "You look full up. If you don't go and dump some of that rubbish soon, you'll be in trouble."

My friends kind of got used to this; "That flower wants to speak to you," my friend Ilene would say.

There was the evening when I was visiting a couple I didn't know well for dinner and I was drawn irresistibly to her Teletubby toy complete with antennae. It seemed to be trying to communicate with me. I stopped and tuned in. I found myself saying to her, "The Teletubby toy says that John has a problem with commitment, and this is upsetting you. Is that right?"

It was. I wasn't invited back.

One of my most powerful methods has been something I call "tuning in". It involves, with permission, sending out my antenna to someone to get a sense of what is going on for them under the surface and what they need to do about it. It is as if I can reach into the image of the world they are having, but haven't quite been able to name and make sense of, and ask also what is the way forward.

I discovered that friends and family who hated when I tried to give them advice loved the tune-in, because they sensed I was just telling them what they themselves knew unconsciously, rather than imposing my views on them.

I have also taught a few of my friends and family to tune into me. It's a bit like that old joke about the two psychiatrists meeting, and one says to the other, "How am I?" But it works, and I am always grateful for the gift.

As one of my students put it, the images and tune-ins are a way of finding out what we know but haven't told ourselves.

Imagework became not just my life, but my work. I learned that if an image structure worked for me, it worked for other people too, and the results were dramatic. It seemed that the deep structure of our imagination, like the deep structure of language, was shared. This was very exciting.

At first, I just added imagery into my "a bit of this and a bit of that" workshops. Then, we started Atsitsa, and because it was not meant to be a personal development but a holistic health centre, I looked to offer a course that was not therapy. I reasoned that I was interested in consciousness, imagery and symbol, and decided to specialise in what I was good at.

I created a five-session course called Visualisation and Life Choices. This was the most popular course I had ever taught. The sessions, in which I used all the exercises I had created for myself over the years, might be called *Image as Life Metaphor*, *Relationships*, *The Inner Child*, *The Inner Male and Female*, *Visioning the Future*. We started with a metaphor for the present, then got a sense of the history that was frozen or blocking us, and then moved onto the future, and then made some decisions. When it was a two-week course, I'd add in more exercises, including the Houses, or talking to plants, animals and objects in nature, or tuning into each other.

I created a new method of taking the whole group through an image structure. Normally, group leaders invited participants to lie down, be guided through an imagery session, and then sit up and share with a partner or with the group. I preferred a much more active, lively, interactional approach. Participants would "become" the image by standing up, breathing into it, moving around, making sounds, and sharing from within the image world. In this way, it is as if as a group, we are sharing our dreams while in the midst of them. It is a profound experience.

In a typical group, I might do an imagery exercise for the whole group, then divide them into twos and threes to work further, then work with one person in the middle of the group, with the group members helping to work with the image. This meant that participants were immersed in the imagery non-stop. The intensity of the work amazed people, who were sometimes expecting a week of pretty pictures, and not the profound understandings that emerged not just from their own work but those of others. Many took the work home and incorporated imagery into their everyday life.

And after a session, sometimes even years after, I would meet my participants by chance, or get emails or letters from them, and they'd tell me that they had started a new career, a new relationship, a new way of living after the workshop. One of the most extraordinary stories is Dorothy's. Beginning with her image of being a parrot in a cage, and managing to leave the cage and to fly freely, she ended up overcoming her anorexia and becoming a distinguished woman pilot. She did indeed want to fly.

Sometimes what emerged wasn't exactly new, as Anna wrote me, "Interestingly, I did not discover anything new about myself, I just rediscovered many of the things I felt I had lost, given away or forgotten. It's like readmission to a language I had forgotten I was able to speak. It has restored and affirmed my faith in myself and in people in general."

Imagery and tuning in eventually became my best methods of helping people quickly without being too intrusive or therapeutic. Years later at our Atsitsa Centre in Skyros I created a structure called "On the Bench" whereby people would come to me for help, sitting on a park bench next to me for only ten minutes. Tuning in was the best and quickest way I found to show them where they were in their minds and hearts and what was the way forward.

After the Atsitsa course, I created a more expanded imagery training course over five Sundays in London, and prepared a handout for each session. These handouts turned into a manual, and this then morphed into my first book *Life Choices, Life Changes*.[24] Two further books followed, *The Joy of Burnout*[25] and *You Are What You Imagine*,[26] both featuring the use of imagery.

Then came the more advanced training courses, now over five weekends, and then my students created The Imagework Association and made me Honorary President, and put out a quarterly newsletter which continued for ten years. At each point, I was pulled along by students asking for more.

Eventually the students started to teach the Imagework. I seemed to have transcended that old magic box restriction that the wands I gave away couldn't make other wands. When my then student Deborah Plummer published her first book, *Walking on the Magic Mountain*,[27] on Imagework for children, I felt like an Imagework grandmother.

Perhaps the biggest thrill was when I ran an Imagework Practitioners course in Skyros, and had the surrealistic experience of seeing people in pairs dotted around a Greek village, sitting on rocks or benches or in cafes, and guiding each other through their Houses of Truth, or onto a space-and-time ship to go into the future and see themselves at eighty years old.

It was as if I'd created an esoteric university of the soul.

Could I have taken my journey to the centre of my life without Imagework? Hard to tell. But I do know this: Imagework was my carriage of wisdom and transformation. Without it, I would have had a very long and dusty walk.

CHAPTER TWENTY-ONE

An insight a day

Spring 1984. We are organising the next summer at the Skyros Centre and planning to open our new centre, Atsitsa. We are knee deep in creating a brochure, hiring staff, and getting Atsitsa ready. We have also just moved house. Chloe and Ari are now five and seven years old respectively.

The original plan was for me to quit my day job once we started the Skyros Centre. It hasn't worked out like that. I have kept the day job, the clients and the workshops, and just added in the Skyros Centre and Atsitsa and a new home. I need an insight a day just to cope with all this pressure.

One morning, I sit bolt upright in my bed with a great insight that looks like a solution to all my problems, namely: *There only needs to be two of me.*

This particular insight was not, I must admit, my most helpful one. I enquired into cloning, a phenomenon I had vaguely heard of. When I was told that it would take time, and indeed, hadn't yet been done on humans, I was very disappointed.

In retrospect, what *is* useful about this insight is that it shows how desperate I must have been to think this was a solution. And at the time, I was so-called sane.

One evening, I stopped at a department store on the way home for work so that I could shop for the kids' clothes. I caught sight of a woman in the mirror who looked back at me with such an exhausted face that it took me a moment to realise who it was. I put the clothes down and went home. If I hadn't seen myself in the mirror, I wouldn't have noticed that I was tired.

Every night, I'd go to bed feeling a failure because I hadn't done everything I had to do. I berated myself for every moment I wasted. My life was geared around doing, and resting as much as I needed to so that I could do more.

It was obvious to the naked eye that I was completely beyond my limits. When I look back at all the things I was doing, I become tired just listing them. But I had no idea that what I was doing was hard. In my mind, someone else could do it all, and why couldn't I?

How about my dental technician, a single mother with small children, who told me that when she got home she didn't dare to sit down because that would be dangerous? Why did I have to sit down?

A professor who came to Skyros ran a biochemistry department, and he told me about the dinner parties he and his wife held. Why wasn't I able to hold dinner parties too? It didn't occur to me that he wasn't doing all of this himself, that he had a wife, a PA, and a whole team of assistants.

I used to read the "Day in a Life" diaries in Sunday papers to see how other people manage their lives. They always seemed to get up at six am. I tried that but after a few days I got ill.

I told myself that if only I had more energy, I could do all this. I must have an energy problem. I searched desperately in science fiction books to see if I could find an answer from the future. My childhood belief in the reality of my children's stories was still there under the surface.

In one science fiction novel, an inventor found a way to get energy from the other dimension by waving your arms around in a particular way. I stood in the bedroom practising. When it didn't work, I'd go back to the book to see if there were any more precise instructions.

When I was a kid I used to practice flying by jumping down from a chair. One day, I believed I had stayed up in the air for an extra moment and I thought I was finally on my way. It was a bit like that.

Now, indeed, I was having dreams about flying. I dreamt that I was flying, and even in the dream I knew that being able to fly is quite amazing. I was hoping for some admiration, but no one seemed impressed or even took any notice. Wasn't flying good enough?

To be honest, I myself didn't know the word "enough". I only knew "not enough".

It came to me that I was like the goose with the golden eggs. I had always taken care of the golden eggs. What about the goose? You can't get too excited about a goose, I believed. It's the golden eggs that are important.

Later I discovered that this was a typical attitude of people who eventually burn out.

One night, I lay awake worrying about how I could manage everything, and the more I lay awake worrying, the more I worried that on top of everything else, I wouldn't get enough sleep to get the work done, and of course that would be my fault for keeping myself awake worrying.

I kept thinking there must be something I was meant to learn. What was it? If there was an insight in the haystack, I'd find it. My whole being always lit up at the thought of learning something new.

Sure enough, as I tossed in my bed, looking for the wisdom that would get me through, this image came to me: *There's a magician inside me, getting the work done. As in any magic show, it looks impossible to the audience. But actually, it's easy once you know how. The magician is going to do whatever needs doing. It's the audience that is waking me up disbelieving.*

I looked back and saw that all my life I had actually delivered, done what I had to do, no matter how much inner struggle I was having. The work would get done. I didn't need to be anxious. The magician would do it. I just needed to give up the doubts.

Then I also remembered what I was always teaching others to do: to create a vision of the future and find out what it looked like. I was particularly concerned about the mechanics of setting up our new centre, Atsitsa, so I chose to go three months into the future to see what it would look like. I discovered that by that time, we had appointed most of the staff and all the main tasks were in hand.

Given that we were putting out a brochure before we quite knew what Atsitsa would be, and certainly before we had a staff, this visioning enabled me to go ahead without anxiety. I knew with my whole being that I wouldn't fail. After all, I'd seen it.

It was the beginning of a new kind of trust in myself and in life.

But magicians do have to practise, practise, practise. Until then, I had used my anxiety to whip me into action. If I let go of anxiety, what would I use instead?

I realised that I needed not a whip but a will. If I was going to trust myself, I needed to be trustworthy. And trustworthy meant: you do what you say you are going to do.

I began to train my will. I decided that I would commit to sitting at my desk every day at the same time for three hours unless I was out teaching at the Polytechnic. It didn't matter what else I had to do that day. And it didn't matter what I accomplished. Whatever happened, there was no get-out clause. I was going to sit there.

It worked. The anxiety dropped some more.

The next insight had to do with that thing so dreaded by this child of the sixties—systems. It came during one of those middle-of-the-night sessions when I woke in a panic worrying about all the scribbled notes to myself on my desk which represented applications for an important office position.

I had spoken to everyone who applied on the phone, explained to each what the role was, asked them about their experience, and taken notes. But with bits of paper everywhere, I couldn't be sure what I had forgotten, and how I would make it all work.

I suddenly saw that I was like an animal without a skeleton trying to hold up my bulk by will power. I needed a spinal column.

How do businesses do it? They must have some system that doesn't rely on panic. In the morning, I phoned my friend Gaie Houston who had done a lot of consultancy for businesses. "Tell me what they do in businesses when they advertise a post?" Gaie talked about preparing a job description, putting out applications, having a deadline, and not opening the applications until the deadline came.

The idea that you could wait until you had a neat pile and then open everything at once was a revelation.

Trust, will, and systems. And now a new concept emerged. In the tiny spaces that now began to appear between the work, I began to discover that amazing thing I hadn't really known for many years—rest.

When I first met astrologer Darby Costello, she told me: "When you are eighty years old, you will want to look back and know that you rested." I cried. It seemed then to be an impossible dream. Now it wasn't.

As I discovered rest, I began to inch my way towards another turning point. This came in the form of a getting-dressed-after-a-bath insight moment.

I had an image of myself beating a donkey, saying, "Work, damn you, work." I realised that this was one of my most basic underlying attitudes to myself. But what if the donkey is really okay and not some wicked obstinate being? What if I supported it to do what it had to do rather than beating it?

The thought was revolutionary.

If I was tired, I didn't need to figure out why I was so tired and whether it was justified. I just had to rest. If I had a phone call to make but felt I couldn't do another thing, I didn't.

No need to attack myself for not doing it. And indeed, when the energy flowed back, I would find myself walking over to the phone naturally. After all, it was what I wanted to do and I would do it when the time was right.

Remembering those terrible conversations in the diary trying to get myself to work, I realised how far I'd come. All that time, my own creativity had become my persecutor—criticising me, driving me, and frightening me, implying that whatever I did was never going to be good enough. Now, I was finally beginning to trust my own view of the situation, decide what I did or didn't want to do, and then trust myself to do it. It all sounds rather simple now.

Finally, I made an inner decision that may have been a small step forward for mankind but was a giant step forward for me:

Take care of yourself first and everything else second.

It's like they tell you on an air flights about how in case of loss of pressure, adults should put their own mask on first, and then their children's masks. I had seen this already with my kids. If I woke up in the morning and went straight to doing what my kids needed, I just felt pushed around. But if I got up early enough to meditate, focus on myself, and get to my own centre, I could deal with them with energy and love.

Hungry, tired and irritable was the same. If my blood sugar fell, I felt awful, and was in no shape to be nice to my kids. When I fed myself first, they might have to wait a little longer, but then they got not only food but my wholeheartedness.

Deciding to take care of myself first now took a new tangible form. Each morning when I was working at home, I ran out the house before Penny, my administrator, whose office was our dining room, could grab me to ask all the questions that had mounted up on the days I was at my college teaching.

I went straight to the café to have my breakfast.

It was before cafes became so popular. I would go to what was the only local cafe, Charlotte's. The cafe was connected to Charlotte's bed and breakfast rooms. It had tables with chess boards painted on them, and was quite funky looking, but it was definitely not one of your modern trendy affairs. Although open to the public, it was used mainly as the dining room of the bed and breakfast residents. I was probably the only one who actually had a home around the corner, and chose to come out for breakfast at a cafe. It was not done then.

Most of the bed and breakfast residents were homeless people in the process of being housed by the local authority, and some of them had mental health problems. Every now and then, one or another would start talking to themselves or shouting. I felt very much at home.

For me, having breakfast in a café was like being on holiday every morning. Later, I was to remember that period of over-work not as torture, but as a time of pleasure.

I had made a little room for myself in my own life.

It was also the beginning of my love affair with cafes. With it opened up a whole new world of caffeine addiction, notes written in little notebooks, and that intense pleasure that cafe goers know, best described by a Viennese poster I saw advertising cafes:

For people who enjoy having their solitude in company.

CHAPTER TWENTY-TWO

Atsitsa is born

Prince Charles is present at the birth of our second centre, Atsitsa. He is not aware of this.

Yannis is sitting in Skyros reading a newspaper account of Prince Charles' famous speech on complementary medicine. As far as we know, it is the first time a member of the British royal family has expressed an interest in the alternative health world. As Yannis reads about the balance of mind, body, and spirit, he keeps feeling that this is familiar to him in a way that all our psychological work is not. It sounds almost Greek.

But of course, it *is* Greek. It is the ancient Greek approach to health.

While most people know only about the alternative health principles originating in the East, the Western roots of the holistic approach lie in Ancient Greece. And it turns out that what we have been creating in Skyros is remarkably in tune with the Ancient Greek approach.

According to this Ancient Greek approach, not only do mind, body, and spirit need to be in balance with each other, but we also need a healthy relationship with the natural world and the social and political world. You can't have good health without a good relationship to nature. And you can't have good health without good politics.

To put it another way, you can't be truly healthy in a sick world.

And there we were, doing our best to create a healthy community life with a good social and political structure in a beautiful rather unspoilt natural Greek environment. Ancient Greece meets modern Greek holistic holiday.

Yannis and my friend Silke Ziehl, who was at the very first Skyros session, had become interested in making use of a beautiful piece of land nine miles from the village, between the pine trees and the sea, to create an educational centre. Silke eventually dropped out, realising how challenging it could be to negotiate such a project on a Greek island.

Yannis turned to me, of course. Would I help him start a second centre with the principle of holistic health? No, I wouldn't. Enough was enough.

Fatefully, one of the participants, Clark, seeing how exhausted I was, offered to take care of my kids while I went over to Atsitsa to rest for a few days. I camped on a concrete slab in front of the taverna. Didn't they have rooms? I didn't think to ask. Pay for a room? I still hadn't left my sixties mentality behind.

I was so very worn out that my image of myself was of a tree reaching down into the parched earth, unable to reach water.

There also happened to be an infestation of wasps that summer. I'd try to eat a watermelon and it'd be covered with wasps. I felt as if I was being chased by the furies. I just didn't have the energy to deal with them.

After two days in Atsitsa, I had a profound sense of the healing spirit of the earth and sea. By the third morning, I could sense that the roots of that inner tree had pushed down and had finally reached water. As I looked at the wasps now, I was no longer frightened. After all, I was bigger than they were.

Returning to the Skyros Centre refreshed, and a bit in love with Atsitsa, I began to take Yannis' idea seriously. I sensed the possibility that Atsitsa would attract people who were not in my rarefied psychological world, and yet could benefit from the healing environment, the community spirit and the courses that we had to offer. And as always, I wanted Yannis to be happy. I agreed to do it.

When we had started Skyros Centre, I had a kind of unconscious template in mind, coming as it did out of psychology and community traditions I knew well. This time we were trying to start a holistic centre, without fully knowing what "holistic" meant, and what we were about to do. The concept of holistic medicine was just beginning to become known, and we were trying to do something even more unheard of—to create a holistic way of living.

Once again, we were pioneers and didn't know it.

We never considered doing market research to see if this was what people wanted. How can you ask people if they want something, when that something is evolving, and needs time to become what it is meant to become? Instead, we assumed that you need to get a sense of what you feel inspired to offer, find out more about it, and then put it out there. You hope others will get on board. More than that, you assume they will.

You just need to let them know how to find you.

On New Year's Eve, 1983, we invited everyone who had ever been to Skyros to an all-night party at our new home. The house was packed, and parking was a serious problem, but it was a great success and the first of many.

Then we put out our first Atsitsa brochure, calling it the Atsitsa Club. This was the last year of our brown and oatmeal newspaper type brochure, before we turned to colour, and it had the spoof headline: "No war games? Count me out," says President Reagan.

Some people actually took it seriously and were horrified that we'd invited Reagan even though he wasn't coming! We took fright and replaced it with Holistic Health and Fitness on Fabled Greek Isle—not half as good, of course. Another headline was: "If only Achilles had never left Skyros ... he might still be alive," weeps his sea goddess mother.

I was to spend our first summer in Atsitsa trying to discover what Atsitsa was meant to be, and how to construct a programme that would make that happen. I say "discover" because with a few new factors—the holistic focus, the location by the sea rather than in the village, the potential size—a rather different world might emerge than at the Skyros Centre, and we had to find out what that world would look like.

Summer 1984, and Atsitsa was launched.

Atsitsa was in an undeveloped bay, and people stayed in bamboo huts or in the house, mainly in shared accommodation, minutes from the sea, but miles from the village. There were two tavernas and a few houses nearby, but that was it. We didn't even have a telephone and it took ages to get allocated one. To make a phone call, you had to go to one of the tavernas, and sit in a queue to wait to use the phone presided over by the rather ancient Kyria Anna who spoke no English and sat there watching you speak as she banged her big fly swatter on the table.

Not surprisingly, given our way of doing things, we had extraordinary teachers, great food, a seriously committed and helpful staff, and an amazing programme, but the place itself was nowhere near ready. The first session was completely crazy, with rooms and huts in the process of being completed, and people being moved from room to room as the work got done.

Did the participants complain? No, they thought they were in paradise.

To my mind, their delight was totally to be expected. After all, they were in a beautiful bay, between pine trees and sea, enjoying the company of wonderful people, taking courses from world-class teachers, eating delicious meals, and having exciting conversations, parties, and midnight swims. Of course, they were happy.

What I didn't see was that once again, the first session was attracting pioneering types who love to come to a new venture, and are willing to put up with inconveniences and constant moves because the spirit of the place makes it worth it. Not everyone would feel the same way.

Our beginners luck had ended at the Skyros Centre in the second summer. Here it ended by the second session. Things were so improved that we expected a delightfully happy group. Then they arrived and we heard shocked whispers that it wasn't what they expected. We waited to hear how this beautiful place was so much more than they had hoped. But, no.

"Where are the tennis courts?" they asked.

It was our fault, I guess, given that in our desire to sound trendy, we had called it the Atsitsa Club.

Same beautiful bay, same wonderful courses and participants, same midnight swims, very different group.

The group split into the faithful pro-Atsitsa zealots, and the anti-Atsitsa zealots. The arguments continued until the very last day of the session. Not paradise, no. But this passionate debate contributed as much to Atsitsa as the halcyon first session.

Some complaints inspired wonderful debates in *Demos* breakfast meetings. People who had thought that living in nature would be quiet and peaceful complained about all the animal noises. The big question in *Demos* became: "What should we do about the cockerels that wake people in the morning?"

"Get rid of them," said one group.

"They belong here and it is up to us to get used to them," said the other.

"If you want to get rid of them, then you should be willing to kill them yourselves," argued a third group.

Eventually we rounded the cockerels up and sent them on a holiday to a neighbour who was happy to have them for the summer.

It was not just the lack of tennis courts and the presence of cockerels that were the problem in our paradise. The natural world, so beautiful and so healing, was our biggest asset at Atsitsa, but it was also our biggest challenge.

Atsitsa was an exciting and joyful place from the beginning, with the same potential for transforming people's lives as the Skyros Centre. We knew how to create that wonderful atmosphere. But we didn't understand the new difficulties we were going to face in the lap of nature. Put simply, when you are not in a village or a town, you have to provide everything from water to electricity to a sewage system.

Yannis and I, used as we were to New York, Athens, and London, were not prepared for this.

We discovered that every machine you have can go wrong—and will, particularly if your handyman neglects to put in oil, or proceeds to dismantle it and lay the bits out in neat rows without the slightest idea of how to fix it, as was sometimes the case in the early days.

Most important, we relied on a generator to run the place, including pumping water from the well, so that when it occasionally broke down, everything from electricity to running water came to a standstill. People improvised with devices constructed from buckets or whatever they could find to create showers for themselves. Some loved it. Others, of course, did not.

We began to need a large permanent staff. The days of my being the first port of call were long gone now, and we seriously needed a structure to meet all the needs of the site as well as of the participants and staff. Managers like Niko Sikkes, Pam Chaplin, Julian Colborn, and Pete Webb were brilliant at taking charge of this sprawling monster, a feat that was completely beyond my understanding. We also created a team of "work scholars", young people who came to work as well as take courses and be part of the community.

Being in a rather isolated world as we were, if someone became ill or became mentally unstable, we were thrown back on our own resources, at least until we could get to the clinic in town. At first, every alternative practitioner in the place would crowd around and prescribe something different. Eventually we decided to have a nurse who took charge of physical illness.

Where the illness was emotional, it was usually the therapist on site who was consulted. But not always. Writer Sue Townsend talked to me about what she did when a group member, who became quite paranoid, was disrupting the group with his accusations and suspicions. With her usual panache she confided in him that she had a crime that needed solving and sent him off to Athens to do some research. By the time he returned, he was much improved.

One memorable session in the early days, Dudley, a massage therapist from Germany, brought a whole group of German clients with him. He hadn't dared tell them what sort of place it was, so they thought they were coming to a luxurious hotel.

When we saw their beautiful leather suitcases lying piled up by the buses, a ripple of fear went through us. And indeed their first reaction was shock, particularly when they realised they'd be staying in a hut or sharing a room. Many wanted to leave straight away.

At that moment, I realised that it was never going to work to try to please Dudley and the group, as was my wont to do when I feared disapproval. I had to take care of them, a rather different attitude. We won them over, took care of their needs as best we could, and this session was eventually one of our most profound and exciting sessions.

I remember the language difficulties of one of the German women in my Visualisation and Life Choices class. She was having everything translated by her friend because she spoke no English, or so she said. Then on the last day, we did an exercise in which you visualised two cinema screens, the first showing how you are now, and the second, how you will be after your desired life change. The change she wanted was to be more confident.

As she stepped into her second screen, becoming the confident person she could see on the screen, she opened her mouth and English came out. We were all stunned. She explained that with confidence, she could speak English quite well.

Some years later, inspired by our success with the German group, we gave bursaries to a group of Russians. This time we were not as lucky, or we were just badly informed. Russia was now pretty capitalist, and it turned out most of them were incredibly rich, took taxis to Skyros, and bought all the gold jewellery in town. Most were horrified by our simple life style and largely vegetarian food, and left as soon as they could.

The ones that stayed were great. One loved to play the violin with local musicians, so that we had loads of impromptu concerts. Writer DM Thomas, who was offering a course in Atsitsa, read his translation of Pushkin poetry, had it translated back to Russian by the visitors, and retrieved his long forgotten Russian to have fascinating conversations with them.

Another group of Russians had flights that meant they would arrive and leave late. When the session was over, and we needed them to vacate their rooms and huts to make way for the next group, they staged a sit-in and refused to go. Pam, our manager then, even offered to pay for them to have rooms at the local taverna; they still refused to move. Somehow or other she managed to convince them to stop their demonstrations and move to the taverna. That was our last group of bursary supported Russians.

As time went on, we became clearer in communicating what people could expect, and more reliable in providing it. But it was interesting to discover that there would always be appreciations and complaints, no matter how smooth the operation. I noticed, for example, that when it rained a lot, complaints of all kinds increased, often seemingly nothing to do with the weather. And this was also true when they were unhappy for any other reason.

When I feel disconnected, I become critical. The same must be true for groups.

But there was quite a big difference between the level of the early complaints and the later ones. When people moaned that the seats at the meal tables were too hard, rather than that they had no electricity or water, I considered this a victory and breathed a sigh of relief.

I sometimes felt as if Atsitsa challenged us every inch of the way. There was one physical problem after another, and each time it seemed insoluble. Even shopping was difficult. Shopkeepers saw that we were a potentially big market and their way of getting our business was to threaten us that if we didn't buy our food for Atsitsa from them, they wouldn't supply Skyros Centre, or they wouldn't give us the empty gas bottles which we needed to fill with gas for cooking. One shop-keeper offered us a discount instead of threats and we bought from him for many years.

Nor did the neighbours always welcome us. In fact, land disputes are the stuff of Greek life, and since it was quite cheap to take people to court, we ended up embroiled in quite a few court cases. We always won, but they added another layer of difficulty, travel, and expense.

Atsitsa certainly toughened me up, and this was all to the good. The endless problems became easier when I stopped fearing that there would be a problem, and started assuming that there would always be at least one, and just asked, "Which problem?"

I discovered another little trick that helped me—I inserted the dimension of time into every problem. With time, either the problem would be resolved, or we would forget about it. No need for panic or despair. Life will flow on.

Something I had learned during my spiritual awakening stood me in good stead all this time: *The important things are meant to be and the unimportant things are unimportant.*

Through all the difficulties and the obstacles, we knew the important thing was the spirit of the place and the good it did for people. All the rest was detail.

One evening, looking at Atsitsa from outside the gate, I remembered the time I was in Israel back in 1964, aged nineteen, and had come across a Club Med holiday for the first time. I had stood outside admiring it, amazed to see people sitting at outdoor tables drinking wine with their meals, something I'd never seen in my home or my friends' homes in Brooklyn. Despite the obvious camping type situation, I thought it was all incredibly glamorous and French, which were probably synonymous in my mind.

Now I saw how similar Atsitsa looked to the Club Med I had gazed at longingly all those years ago. We even served wine with the meals—Retsina, to be more precise.

My friend Max Furlaud had once dubbed Skyros, "The Club Med of the Soul."

I secretly loved that.

CHAPTER TWENTY-THREE

Growing up

Our intention in Atsitsa, just as in Skyros Centre, was to create a world that heals. As always, I knew this needed to begin with a sense of community. We had the community meetings, the courses, and the co-listening, as well as the *Demos* and work groups in the morning, swimming and sunbathing in the afternoon, and evenings of parties, special events, and cabarets.

And yet Atsitsa was obviously quite a different animal than the Skyros Centre. This was not a personal development holiday but a holistic holiday which was intended to address the health of the whole person—mind, emotion, body, and spirit. To this end, we had a very wide range of courses, from windsurfing and swimming, to yoga and tai chi, from theatre, music, art and voicework, to meditation and psychological courses.

Rather than taking one main course for two weeks, plus various drop-in activities, in Atsitsa you had three courses a day, and you could change them each week. You could be doing early morning yoga or tai chi, late morning windsurfing, and late afternoon music in the first week, and early morning meditation, late morning personal development, and late afternoon theatre improvisation the second week. Or you could skip it all and hang around in the sun. Few people did, because the courses were so enticing. But by the second week people often opted for fewer courses and more sunbathing and chatting with their new friends.

All the courses were focused not just on that particular skill, but on the development of the whole person. And there was no telling which was the best route of transformation for whom.

Sometimes we went too far on the holistic focus. In the early days, when we taught windsurfing, we invited teaching staff who had expertise in what is called: "The Inner Game", an approach to learning sport from the inside out.[28] Unfortunately, the people we had invited to teach the inner game of windsurfing at Atsitsa had a great approach to teaching, but very little idea how to windsurf.

Some of the participants loved it. Others got incredibly frustrated, saying that they just wanted to be taught how to turn the windsurf board around.

As usual, I couldn't at first understand why you would care if you could turn a windsurf board around when this inner approach is so much more interesting. Eventually, even I got the point. We began to invite teachers who could actually windsurf. We started having wonderful windsurfing teachers, especially Windy Bob, as Bob Shelley was called, who were great with people but most definitely knew how to teach people how to get themselves back to shore.

Because people took a number of different courses with different group members, they got to know more people, but they didn't have a stable connection with one group as in the Skyros Centre. We evolved the *Oekos* or home group, *oekos* being Greek for home. It was a bit like co-listening in a group, and it served as a safety net in the community, as well as being a way to focus with a small consistent group of people on what was important.

When we had a meeting in London asking people what in Skyros could most help them in life back in their own towns, they named *Oekos* as the best social invention of all, which they could bring home to their friends, community, their work.

I myself eventually started an *Oekos* group with friends and colleagues in my Hastings neighbourhood and it had a profound effect on all of our lives.

The wide range of courses to dip into meant that people could ostensibly come for one thing and end up doing another. A typical comment, particularly from the men, was, "I only came for the windsurfing." The fact that they ended up doing meditation in the morning and self-esteem development in the afternoon was a bonus, and probably could be kept secret from their friends back home.

I used to advise people to take one course that was their sort of thing, one that definitely wasn't and would take them outside their comfort zone, and one that they found themselves choosing when they walked up to the course board. This meant that people not only stretched themselves beyond their normal limits, but were able to experience something completely new. Often a particular course would surprise someone and inspire them to follow through back home. Quite a few new careers started with a wildly unexpected course choice.

For me, it was the more physical sports that were more challenging, and a greater learning experience. I don't mind getting up in a group and showing all my feelings. This feels quite comfortable and normal to me. Standing up on a windsurf board is another matter. Just to believe that I am the kind of person who can windsurf requires an identity transformation.

I got as far in windsurfing as to have a photo taken of me standing up on the board to impress my kids. I wouldn't say I ever became a windsurfer.

I even tried out abseiling, though I was terrified and almost went right back down the way I came up rather than step off the cliff as everyone else was doing. Once I did it, I found how amazing an experience it was to walk down a rock face as if you were horizontal, held safely by ropes tied to the earth and to your teacher. I immediately translated the experience into a psychological metaphor I could use in my courses. But after that one short course, I was glad never to have to abseil again. No new career there.

It was learning how to swim that made the biggest difference in my life. For one whole summer, I attended every swimming class, until by the end of the summer I could do the breaststroke well enough to get somewhere. As I swam around the promontory of Atsitsa towards the shore, I experienced the kind of exhilaration that I would previously have associated with a profound spiritual experience.

Indeed, it *was* a profound spiritual experience.

And nowadays when I am in Atsitsa, my swim to what I call Emerald Isle, a little rock island in the bay, is a daily practice; if I haven't done it, I haven't had a day.

While the backdrop of Skyros Centre was Greek village life, here it was the beautiful and rather wild natural world. We ate three meals together in the open-air dining room. Courses were normally held in the big outdoor circles with views of the mountains and the sea. But they might also be held in the threshing circle, or in a cave, or in a fishermen's chapel by the sea, or on the promontory, or in the sea.

Another wonderful outcome for me of the way Atsitsa worked was that I created my Visualisation and Life Choices course which became the basis for all my future imagery trainings. I usually held these courses in what we called the Magic Circle, a beautiful large outdoor circle with magnificent views all around. From the start, these courses were very popular, so we might have thirty people doing deep and dramatic work all at the same time, either in pairs or singly, or watching one person enact their image and helping them find their way through. It was something between therapy and theatre.

I remember one group I had in which everyone seemed to burst into tears at the drop of a hat. I began to say, "I'd like you to allow to emerge an image of someone with whom you have unfinished business ..." and before I finished my sentence they were all in floods of tears. I stood there thinking, "What have

I done?" But when the exercise was over, they wiped away their tears and went off, very happy, having resolved something important. All was well. It looked a bit like the end of a Shakespeare play when the curtain comes down and the players move off the stage. Yet it was powerfully real and had real effects.

With such a big group, it was important to keep things safe, and we had clear rules about confidentiality and about people letting me know if they had a problem and not just leaving the group. Yet participants did not seem to mind the odd participant passing by the circle and seeing them doing this deep work. This was probably because I didn't mind. It was all part of the open community life.

The same was true when I would counsel people on a park bench not far from the dining area, using the second bench as the "waiting room". As long as others couldn't hear what they were saying, they felt it was okay. I loved working in this open way on a park bench rather than in traditional therapy contexts. The inspiration actually came from a Peanuts cartoon in which Lucy put up a stand with the sign: "Psychiatric Help, 5 cents. The doctor is IN."

Recently I was very moved to read about elderly Zimbabwean women in Harare being trained to sit on park benches to offer therapy in the community. This Friendship Bench project,[29] set up in a country where one in four suffer from mental illness and there are only thirteen psychiatrists, has transformed thousands of lives.

At Atsitsa, we lived what was by and large an outdoor life with no village to spill out into. We'd go to town once a week or even once a fortnight to visit the local shops, eat at tavernas, and be part of everyday Greek life. Mostly, we hung out together and there was a lot of excitement and partying along with the serious work on the courses. And then there was the wonderful food made of fresh ingredients by our great chefs. Indeed, some people claimed they returned mainly for the food.

211

The evening activities emerged, suggested by staff or participants. There was the pea fair, where people set up stalls, and offered services paid for by peas. These stalls were intensely creative and varied. There were witches offering prophecies (I was one along with fellow group leaders Hazel and Lisehanne), complementary practitioners offering "complimentary therapy" where you got three compliments in exchange for a pea, masseurs offering face massages, or a poet offering haikus written on the spot.

There were also the "passion evenings" which were actually gatherings where people talked inspiringly of what they loved, from bee-keeping to surfing to map making to crisp new sheets on the bed. And on the last night there was always a hilarious cabaret, which gave people a chance to sing for the first time in their lives in public, or to make fun of the teachers or of Atsitsa traditions in little skits, or to choreograph dances, write songs, or show films they had made.

Sometimes these cabarets changed peoples' lives. Comedian Jimmy Carr told the *Sunday Times* that he'd had one life-changing holiday, and that was Atsitsa. He came to Atsitsa after giving up his job in Shell, found that people kept telling him he was very funny and should try becoming a comedian, and so he did. He has since become a household name in England as stand-up comedian, writer, and media star.

In their spare time, people would sometimes hire cars or motorcycles and explore the beautiful unspoilt island. I seldom managed to get away but I do remember a wonderful excursion in my friend Pam's yellow VW camper which she called Bryony, visiting a church up in the hills with our friends Julie and Hazel. Pam was at that time co-manager of Atsitsa, and Julie and Hazel were facilitators.

Julie sang a song to Bryony, and then we lay on our backs on the roof of the church, seeing the beehives, smelling the herbs, feeling we were on the top of the world, and singing *I've got the whole world in my hands*. As we watched the clouds, we imagined that they were still, and we were moving. It was one of those magical afternoons.

Participants and staff alike fell in love with the beauty of the place and the warmth of the atmosphere. Many people have told me than when they are imagining going to a beautiful and safe space in their meditations, they find themselves sitting on the promontory of Atsitsa, looking out at the sea.

Indeed, Atsitsa became a second home for many participants and staff. They'd come back year and after year, one participant actually reserving a hut for the same weeks of August each year. Or they'd come on their birthday to be sure of a great day. Or they'd come once or twice and then thirty years later. Couples who'd met in Skyros sometimes returned to have their marriage ceremonies on the promontory. I remember a speech Yannis gave at one of these weddings, "Many marriages end on the rocks. This one is starting on the rocks."

There's a lovely story about a participant from Chicago who brought his son and daughter, both single. That session, there was a wonderful group of work scholars from Frome, Somerset, who dyed their hair red, and wandered around painting murals and beautiful designs on the stone circles in their spare time. The brother and sister participants fell in love with two of these work scholars. A double wedding ensued.

Years later, a young woman came to visit and told us she was the daughter of one of these couples. She could even say which hut she had been conceived in.

And at the other end of life, a number of participants and staff have asked for their ashes to be sprinkled in Atsitsa. I find this very moving.

The two centres were a bit like two competing neighbouring tribes. We used to have visits between Skyros Centre and Atsitsa, some walking and some going by coach, and participants of each centre thought their own was the best by far.

Each centre's participants thought the other centre was claustrophobic. The Atsitsa people thought Skyros Centre was claustrophobic because everything happened on that small terrace while Atsitsa had the big outdoors. The Skyros Centre thought Atsitsa was claustrophobic because they were together all day in the same location, rather than spilling out into the village.

Atsitsa people thought Skyros Centre people cried all day. The Skyros Centre people thought Atsitsa people were superficial. And so it went.

And if you moved back and forth between the two, as I did, but also many other staff and participants did, you seemed to adopt the point of the tribe you were in and forget how much you loved the other one.

At one point, someone suggested that when one group visited the other we should bring gifts as if to placate the neighbouring tribe. Someone else came up with the idea of washing the feet of the Skyros Centre participants who had walked to Atsitsa, and this became our ritual for a while. Occasionally, also, we had wonderful dramas played out between the two centres. One was the heroic battle between the Trojans and the Greeks, a drama introduced and master-minded by therapist and writer Gaie Houston. Another great cross-island adventure, complete with Odysseus, Greek gods, terrible temptations, and a wise Sphinx, was created and staged by psychologist and writer Richard Stevens.

Despite all the differences between the centres, on the last day, when people wrote their evaluation forms, their descriptions of what was important to them about the experience were almost identical. I have always believed that this was because it was the nature of the community that was the real healer.

The Skyros experience started to be the basis of television programmes, books, novels, short stories, and poems, as well as press. The Yorkshire Television series, *First Tuesday* did an hour-long documentary about us, saying it was "almost like living your life in a fortnight". Writer DM Thomas wrote a book called *Lady with a Laptop*[30] which was a spoof of Skyros.

He kindly named the mad bumbling holiday centre in his book Skagathos Holidays and made clear that the Skyros Centre on a nearby island was the real thing, and Ruth Rendell was teaching there (which unfortunately, she never did). Sue Townsend wrote a little Adrian Mole piece as an introduction to my book *Life Choices, Life Changes*.[31] Jane Salvage wrote a history of the Skyros Holidays called *Skyros: Island of Dreams*.[32] I began to hear of published poems[33] and short stories, including in the New Yorker magazine, which referred to our holidays or were inspired by them.

We had found ourselves a place on the cultural map.

Meanwhile, because I needed to hang around in Atsitsa all summer the first year, to fathom what was this beast we had created, I could not also be directing the Skyros Centre sessions. Clearly my spiritual powers hadn't enabled me to be in two places at once.

A bit like becoming mother of two, I was now having to learn to organise on a new level. I saw that each session needed an acting Director to take care of the emotional life of the community, because it couldn't always be me anymore.

This device of having a different Director each session was, I think, quite unique in Skyros, and kept each session alive and creative. Whether I personally was there or not, each session was the focus of someone's creative attention and direction.

I have seen how centres where the founding visionary leader is absent can deteriorate into bureaucracy, power struggle, or worse. In fact, this is what I had experienced when I worked at the Henderson Hospital after the founder Maxwell Jones had left. From being a revolutionary establishment, it was now conservative and stuck. One nurse, arguing in a staff meeting against making a change, literally said, "If it was good enough for Maxwell Jones, it's good enough for me."

I invited different teaching staff members whom I felt I could trust to run the centres to be the Directors. Skyros Centre

Directors were by and large psychotherapists, but Atsitsa was a holistic centre. Who was best suited to direct?

My friend and fellow group leader Stewart Mitchell, naturopath and yoga teacher, told me one day as we hung around in the kitchen, that I was the wrong person to be Director. You needed body-oriented people. I was rather shocked but obediently tried giving up my role and invited some of our body-work practitioners to be Directors.

It didn't work all that well because they often didn't have an instinct for community. I took back my role on the sessions when I was in Atsitsa. People did say that when I was there, it gave a sense of depth and history that was important for them. But in general, it turned out that while psychotherapists could be great Atsitsa Directors, often it was the Directors with theatre experience who emerged as stars. Atsitsa was after all a great piece of street theatre.

At first, each Director came to my kitchen and I went through everything they needed to know. Then it occurred to me that I could write it all down, and the Directors' Notes were born. And with this movement from the oral to the written tradition, came a clarity about the fact that this was a stable institution with standard processes that happened each session, even though on some level it felt completely new each time.

I began to see the sessions as being like enactments of an ancient Greek drama. The general storyline was given, as were the roles of the actors. But within this, the director and the actors had room to create their own version, improvising in line with whom they were, but still recreating the spirit of the ancient story.

Inviting people to be Directors of sessions was not always easy for me. It was a bit like that mother of two letting a new child minder take care of her beloved older child. Yes, the child minder has all the credentials and references and seems to know and like children. But will she do it in exactly the right way, in other words, in the way that the mother herself would do it?

Perhaps worse even than this, would she do it so well, and be so loved, that the mother would no longer be needed?

Each time I came over from Atsitsa to the Skyros Centre to visit, I would barrage the Director and staff with ideas of how they could do things better. Surely, they needed me.

I heard later that the staff used to dread these helpful visits.

One day, when I was visiting the Skyros Centre, I was walking along the village street with my friend Tom Feldberg, who was at that time the Director of the Skyros Centre. He said goodbye, because he was going to the staff meeting.

"I'm coming too," I said.

"No, you're not," he answered.

At first, I was shocked and outraged. Kicked out of the staff meeting in my own centre?

I met Tom recently and reminded him of this story. He smiled and said, "You should have fired me." But, at the time, I didn't insist. After my flash of anger, the thought suddenly came to me. *Why am I giving myself more work?*

I said goodbye, turned around on my heels and went for a coffee in the local *kafenion*. And as I sat there, I had the profound realisation that my contribution and value did not lie in being needed, but rather in having set up a structure and employed a staff that were so good that I was not needed.

A structure? A staff?

Was the wild child of the sixties growing up?

CHAPTER TWENTY-FOUR

Faking an orgasm before God

A t the heart of the inner project I was engaged in all this time was the attempt to become my own person, to live from the centre of my own life. I had come a long way in this project. But there were still a lot of deeply held, childhood fantasies about myself that had to go.

The "good girl" was probably the worst. I date the birth of the good girl to a moment in my childhood when I was about six years old and standing on my doorstep in Brooklyn, having a disagreement with my mother. She looked at me in a tone that combined anger, hurt, and disappointment, saying:

"I thought you were the good girl."

I answered angrily that I was not the good girl. But I was not angry enough. I took on the role. I would become a good girl, if that's what it took to feel loved.

All these years later, all those miles away, and underneath there was still a good girl trying to get out. Embarrassing but true. Wasn't I a bit old for being a good girl? Unfortunately, not. Deep down inside, that six year old was still yearning to feel loved.

I am reminded of a retired physics professor in his seventies, a participant of my Open Circle groups, telling us that all the years he was a professor, he thought he was just a little boy making believe he was a professor. "When I retired," he confided, "they couldn't find anyone they thought was good enough to take my place. I must have been pretty good. But I never knew it."

Running the Skyros holidays in those early years was a real testing ground for a good girl. When I walked around being wonderful to everyone, I would almost glow, imagining myself as the classic good girl from one of my childhood stories—a little girl with a white nightgown walking up the stairs angelically with a candle in her hand.

As I glowed, I'd leak so much energy and get so exhausted that I could hardly do the angelic things that were required.

Anyway, the glow never lasted too long before I'd notice that someone else was better than me, or more giving, or that I had acted in a way that looked selfish. I'd wake up early, tossing and turning, ruminating for hours, trying to prove to myself that I really was good, but knowing that I was so bad.

And if I was actually accused of being selfish, or demanding, or greedy, even by implication, I would go into overdrive, practically hurl myself against a metaphoric wall, to prove I would do anything for anybody and nothing for me.

The night I stayed awake worrying if I could pay the printers for the Skyros brochure, I was secretly relieved. Since the business was obviously making a loss, nobody could possibly say I was exploiting them. I really, really was a very good girl.

Unfortunately, this was not all just in my head. In the alternative world in Britain, and perhaps in Europe in general, there was at that time a deeply held assumption that if you did something worthwhile and good, you should do it for free. Otherwise it wasn't really good.

Because Skyros was so successful at creating a loving community atmosphere and it felt rather Garden of Edenish, some people began to feel that if this is how life should be, it was their natural inheritance. Why should they pay for mother love?

People would actually come up to me and ask if they could see the account books to make sure we weren't making any money. If we were, we'd be exploiting them. I heard that in Atsitsa one of the *Oekos* groups spent their time working out how much it cost to run Atsitsa and how much money we must be making. Amazing to be concerned with this when you are having a great holiday.

The funny thing was that their calculation was based on the cost of food and the cost of the staff. They neglected to include the costs of running an office, printing and posting a brochure, building and maintaining a site, and all the other business costs that people who run small businesses know about. In their picture of Atsitsa, it seems, this magic world emerged full blown each summer from the sea.

We were running a vulnerable small business in a time of recession. They thought we were earning millions.

Once, when I was running a group in the UK, a participant told me how resentful she was of me because she thought I was rich and a "snazzy dresser". It transpired that she had come to Atsitsa and she had had her best holiday ever and it had changed her life. So why wasn't she appreciative, instead of competitive and resentful?

As we looked at it in the group, it seemed to be something to do with her own thwarted ambition. When she owned her own power, she stopped being angry at me. This helped me a bit to understand what was going on.

Americans who came to Skyros had a totally different approach. They would march in and say: "I love this place. I hope you are making money because I want this business to survive."

One German participant saw the situation and told me about two bookshops in his neighbourhood in Berlin, a conventional one and an alternative one. People were always complaining to the people running the alternative bookshop that they were making too much money and asking to see their accounts. The conventional bookshop was supposed to make money, so it was okay.

I wonder if it was also something to do with a woman being the face of a successful venture.

My personal "good girl" story came to a crisis point when I developed a serious case of intestinal bleeding and was admitted to hospital. It happened right after Yannis got some bad news. *He* was having problems, and *I* ended up in hospital. I had developed the same kind of intestinal bleeding when I had a rejection which I considered to be a failure experience in my PhD programme at the University of Michigan.

On some level, I perceived Yannis' problems as my failure to rescue him. The good girl hadn't managed to be good enough.

I secretly loved being ill enough to lie in that hospital bed with crisp white sheets. After all, I must have done my best if I'd worked so hard and worried so much that I had landed up there. Now I could take a rest while the world moved on around me. Later, when I studied burnout, I discovered that many burnt out people have this same desire for those crisp white hospital sheets.

And as I looked around my ward at the hospital, I could see the emotional issues of each person. As I talked to the woman with repeated heart attacks about what she was doing with her heart on an emotional rather than physical level, she told me I was like an angel come to help her. All were treated only with drugs, including sleeping pills for the young teenager.

When I got out of hospital this time, my energy simply didn't return for months. My consultant was surprised that I wasn't getting better. Although he had made clear to me when I was in hospital that in his view stress had nothing to do with illness, he now said surprisingly, "It must be something to do with the spirit."

I searched and searched deep inside to find out what was stopping me from getting well. I finally came upon Beth, a character from one of my childhood books, *Little Women*.[34] Beth was the good girl who never thought of herself and never had a sense of the future, and she dripped around being angelic until she died young.

Most girls admired her sister Jo, the interesting wild one who became a writer. I am always embarrassed to reveal that I identified with Beth.

The good girl is neither sexual nor assertive nor, indeed, an adult. She lives in the haze of approval rather than in her own light. It is a terrible waste of life.

I now made what was for me an incredibly difficult decision:

I'd rather be healthy than good.

My energy streamed back the very next day.

It's a good thing I decided that. Good girls do die young. The pattern of pushing myself beyond my limits until I got ill was no joke, particularly as I got older and the illnesses became more serious.

I still had a long way to go to give up the self-attack about not being a good enough girl. One day, standing in the middle of the bathroom, toothbrush full of toothpaste in my hand, and tormenting myself for one or another way I had failed to be good, I suddenly thought:

I am just faking an orgasm before God.

What's the point of trying to prove I'm good? Either I am or I am not. And if I'm not, I'll just have to live with it.

It is hard to convey how dramatic this understanding was for me.

I'd never faked an orgasm in the usual sense of the word. I was too much into authenticity. I was a "what you see is what you get" sort of girl. How could I approve of faking an orgasm before God, or to be more precise, before my inner judge and jury?

I dared now to look honestly at my personal qualities. Being good was not top of the list. I was interesting, challenging, insightful, loving, but I was just not that "good". Not a good girl after all?

I told my friend Peter about this and he asked curiously, whom I thought was good. "Mother Theresa," I answered. I was puzzled when he laughed.

Of course, I *was* actually a good enough human being. My childhood desire to be a good girl was, as is so often the case with these illusions, the distorted expression of a real underlying soul reality. I had to let it go before my authentic goodness could shine forth.

I began to notice that proving I was good was not my only attempt to fake an orgasm before God. There was so many other ways I was trying to prove to myself that I was what I was supposed to be—an ideal something or other, good enough to have a right to be here.

Let's take the rather mundane example of packing my bag to go away—and I was doing a lot of travelling and a lot of packing. I didn't just figure out what I would need or want and how much I could carry, and then pack in the most effective way. No, I was looking down on myself, as if from above, to check if I was getting it right, doing it perfectly.

People used to say when they saw my struggle, "Don't worry. You can always buy anything when you get there." They had no idea how irrelevant that was.

I would have a critical commentary going on non-stop not just while I was packing but when I got to the airport. If I felt I'd done it right, I'd feel proud. But this never lasted long. Everyone I met with a smaller or lighter bag was proof that I was this clunky boring uncool person who can't travel light. Anyone with a bigger bag made me suspect that I must have forgotten something they knew was important, and, on some child level, I felt I'd burn in hell for the mistake.

Once I got where I was going and unpacked it was not over. Each time the weather was too hot for a cardigan I had brought with me, or cold enough that I should have brought that other pullover I left home, I'd attack myself. In the almost impossible case that I'd needed everything I had brought, and not anything I didn't bring, I'd be very proud. Until next time.

Falling short of being whatever I thought I should be was incredibly painful. These difficult feelings tended to come up when I saw someone else doing something I thought I should have been able to do, or succeeding at something I should have been able to succeed at. It wasn't exactly envy. It wasn't even competition in the sense of a spur to be better than someone else. It was simply a comparison—and an underlying perfectionism—that put me in my place.

Why hadn't I done it? Why was I so bad?

In fact, saying I was so bad doesn't quite capture the feeling. It was worse than that. It was the sense that my life simply vanished, became so worthless, that I had nothing and was nothing.

And it was so easy to evoke this devastating feeling. My friend Geoff told me he always kept his desk clear. I couldn't conceive of having a desk not covered with papers. I lay in my bed, consumed by the awful feeling that nothing I had ever done in my life was of any value because I didn't have a clear desk.

I never felt that way when it was something I knew I could never have achieved. If someone had a glittering career as a musician, that was fine. I was never going to be a musician, so it was not my fault that I wasn't.

These feelings were so extreme that I tried to understand what they were really about. They were obviously coming from some very early experience. I came to believe that babies who are lucky enough to have the full focus of their mother's or father's attention and love, for at least a short period, do get the feeling that they are the most wonderful beings on earth. Later they reciprocate by believing their mother or father is the most wonderful in the world.

Neglected as I was as a baby, it was this feeling I was now yearning for, this sense that I was the centre of the world, the apple of my mother's or father's eye, completely and utterly loved and loveable.

As an adult, in the world of everyday comparison, being so special that I was the best I could possibly be, even the best in the whole wide world, was the equivalent of this infant feeling. It meant that the light of love was shining on me. If someone else was better, I was thrown into darkness. I was nowhere and nothing, unloved and unlovable.

No wonder I so needed to be the good girl, the best little good girl in the world.

Faking an orgasm before God, or before your inner self, is an exhausting process. The inner gathering of evidence for and against the prosecution, and the constant self-attack or threat of self-attack, is non-stop and debilitating. The drive to prove that you are this thing you believe you should be can indeed lead you to burnout. And you are always guilty until proved innocent.

Until you give it up, you don't realise how much it has dominated your life, pushed you in the wrong directions, and stopped you from enjoying the simple pleasure of doing your thing. Compared to this, faking an orgasm in bed is child's play.

At least men want to be convinced.

Somehow or other, each time I gave up faking an orgasm before God, gave up trying to have what I had never had as an infant, I could relax into the reality of being a good enough, wise enough, loving enough and loved enough adult in a world of adults.

This insight was not quite the end of my good girl illusion, but it was at least the beginning of seeing that it is indeed an illusion. Illusions are like weeds. I would uproot the good girl weed from one part of my life, and before long it would appear somewhere else, completely unlabelled. I'd glow with pride saying: "I've been so wonderfully good to so and so." And then I'd realise that it was that good girl weed again, and if

I didn't get rid of it quickly it would destroy all the seeds I'd planted.

So, there were still lots of mornings to wake up worrying about what I had done or not done, and lots of depressed feelings when someone had indicated I was less than good, or when someone had done better than I had, and lots of bending over backwards to rescue others who didn't necessarily want to be rescued. But each time I realised that it was the good girl again, I could let go of it.

Sometimes I found that instead of just pointing out the illusion to myself, I had to reach in and love the real little girl underneath so she knew she didn't need to prove herself. After all, if the little girl in me had got enough attention, had felt loved enough, she wouldn't ever have needed to prove that she had a right to be here.

I discovered this when my aunt Esther died, and I went into the usual self-attack about all the things I had or hadn't done which it was too late now to redeem. As I lay in bed unable to sleep, feeling I was so very bad, I said to myself, "How would it be if you were the kind of little girl whose mother said, 'Oh what a wonderful girl you are'."

I considered this possibility, and let this feeling of being a wonderful little girl sink in. I realised that I were that girl, I'd just say, "Aunt Esther, I'm so sorry you've gone."

And with that, I fell into a deep and satisfying sleep.

Best of all, my mother, who was in a sense also the mother of the good girl myth, gave me a hand in demolishing it. One day, I was leading an Imagework course in Skyros doing an exercise about resolving "unfinished business". As always, I did the exercise quietly while everyone was doing theirs, and asked for an image to emerge of someone or something with whom I had unfinished business.

An image of my mother emerged, though she had died more than twenty years before and I hadn't been aware of thinking about her for some time.

The "unfinished business" exercise involves talking to whomever emerges, and then switching roles and becoming the person and responding. When I saw my mother, I found myself pleading with her, "Please come back. I still can't stand the fact that you are dead." It was rather like in that psychodrama of death I had done so many years before.

But this time, when I switched roles and stood in the place of my mother, I found myself saying to Dina rather brutally, "I'm not coming back. And neither are you. So, you better not spend your life being a phony good girl and then think you will stand up at judgment day and be looked upon with grace and favour. This is it!"

I realised that I was still holding myself back from daring to be fully myself, unconsciously believing that someday all my self-sacrifice—which was in fact the sacrifice of my true self—would be rewarded. Indeed, I was even using beliefs about the eternal life of the soul to protect me from the tragedy of not being here now.

I had to face the truth. Whatever the future of the soul, however many incarnations my soul may or may not pass through, I, Dina Glouberman, am not coming back. There will be no opportunity to make up for the damage to myself that I am perpetrating right now. There is no day of judgment that will prove the point and reward me once and for all. There is no glorious future for that good girl.

This is it. I better believe it.

CHAPTER TWENTY-FIVE

The case of the disappearing self

In the background of my public life, but in the foreground of my consciousness, was a constant struggle with that amazing relationship called marriage. Marriage was probably the deepest testing ground of the process of becoming myself. It was as if I needed to lose myself for years in order to find a stronger, healthier self. Eventually, the marriage didn't survive, but we both did.

I am not being overly dramatic when I say that I could have died of marriage, or rather of my response to it. That death might have been physical, or it might have been a psychic annihilation. It was that serious. Not only my ulcers, but my subsequent burnout, were directly related to that relationship. Indeed, probably my madness was in part, though not wholly of course, my response to what was and wasn't happening in that relationship.

I know that I am not alone in this. I have met too many women, and to a lesser extent men, who could tell similar stories. This is not to say that the other person in the relationship was to blame, rather that until we ourselves transform, we are at risk. What the other person needs to do is another story.

The disappearing self, the inability to honour yourself and your own experience, even to know what is in your own highest best interest, is, in my understanding, a phenomenon that regularly precipitates burnouts, breakdowns, abuse, even life-threatening illnesses.

As in a traditional shamanic initiation, if you don't heal, transform, transcend, grow up, your survival is not guaranteed. In fact, I later came to believe that on some level, my own subsequent burnout was a kind of shamanic initiation.

It is difficult to write about my marriage sensibly, partly because it is all so shrouded in mysterious unconscious forces, and partly because I don't want to tell stories that are not mine alone to tell. I am not pointing a finger at either Yannis or myself for the difficulties between us, as I might have done when I was still enthralled by the story of whose fault it was—who was the victim, who the rescuer, who the persecutor.

I am simply looking at my own story, and at what I can learn not just for myself but for others who have shared similar experiences. And I am seeking to understand what shift in my sense of myself would have allowed me to feel safe and happy about myself no matter what was happening in my relationship. Indeed, even being able to conceive of such a scenario is a major part of my healing.

Here are, so to speak, just a few of the exhibits in the Case of the Disappearing Self.

I check the daily horoscope in the papers every day, and I always start with Capricorn, Yannis' sign. Will he be okay? My own sign, Virgo, I consult only as an afterthought. After all, if he's all right, I'll manage.

I am giving birth to my first child, Ari. Yannis is in the delivery room. At the height of my labour pains, I ask him anxiously, "Are you all right?"

We have a bad fight. My friend Naomi who happens to be visiting, sees how upset I am and says, "Now, what do we need to do for you to feel better?" I think I've misheard her. Surely, she means, "What do we need to do for him *to feel better?"*

He is angry at me for leaving the office early to go to therapy. He looks at me accusingly as if I have betrayed him. I resist and leave,

230

but not before I have hung around the office long enough to make myself late. Then I take the train to my usual station, turn down the wrong street, and get completely lost on the way, though I have been there many times. I turn up late, shocked, confused, lost. My therapist takes one look at me, hears my story, and says firmly, "Those are his feelings. They have nothing to do with you." "But he's angry at me!" I protest. She repeats, "Those are his feelings. They have nothing to do with you." I don't really understand.

What is absolutely stunning to me is that as a young girl I was fully committed not so much to my present self as to the self I would be when I got where I was going. I left good relationships to make sure I had that future self I believed was possible.

Then came this new phenomenon, commitment to another, sharing a life, sharing a future, and I fell headlong into an illusion that took me more than twenty-five years to fight my way out of. I gave myself away, and the self I took back to care for consisted of him first and me a poor last.

What was the illusion? It was, I think, the belief that even if you ignored the whisperings of your own heart and soul, as long as you did everything humanly possible to make someone else happy, however *they* themselves defined happy, you would end up happy, loved, and loveable.

This song I learned in summer camp in my childhood comes to mind: *I want to be a friend of yours ... mmm and a little bit more. I want to be a pal of yours ... mmm and a little bit more. I want to be the little flower sitting at your door. I want to be your grandmother, grandfather, father, mother, sister, brother ... mmm and a little bit more.*

It was a bit like that.

I had a client whose very wonderful and loving husband died suddenly. It was a terrible loss. But a year or two later, she took a trip to California, and, she told me, "It was the first time I looked at the world through my own eyes." This is what I mean when I talk of the disappearing self.

And incidentally, after her husband's death, and her increased responsibilities, my client was able to leave behind her persistent and debilitating neurotic illness, the one she came to see me for, and to become far more competent and active in the world.

Indeed, time and again I have noticed that when a much-loved husband to whom a woman has been devoted dies, despite the pain and loss, she charges ahead with wonderful new energy to get an education or a career or do whatever she feels called to do.

Coming back to my own marriage, there is no doubt that powerful compelling forces brought us together and kept us together, and the full story is beyond my comprehension. Rather like my response to the psychiatrist in the Middlesex Hospital about the reasons for my breakdown, "It depends on your theory."

My theories about my marriage, of which I had hundreds over the years until the question itself receded into the background, have spanned the biological to the psychological to the spiritual and back again. Indeed, I doubt whether it is only this lifetime's business, whether because it includes my own past and future lifetimes, or the past and future generations of men and women generally.

Did I marry the missing patriarch, the one my father wasn't? Or even the man my Mediterranean mother would have chosen had she stayed in her culture? Did I get together with a man with a powerful will so that eventually I could find my own will to stand up to his? Did I choose, as I so often did, that which was both most creative and also most dangerous, and was most likely to push me out to the farthest edge of my resources and beyond? And did I then, as usual, feel completely surprised when the shit hit the fan?

All of the above and more.

There was a great deal about my marriage that was profoundly life enhancing. We loved and respected each other and were totally committed to each other. We created a little self-contained world and made it beautiful. We had a powerful creative partnership, creating not only a good family life, but also healthy spirit-filled environments like Skyros that have lasted long after the relationship ended. A great many lives were changed for the better because of our partnership. And we had some wonderful times together.

But at the heart of the relationship, something was very wrong.

It is hard to pinpoint what was the essence of the problem, if indeed there was only one essence. But if I am to begin somewhere, one important aspect of this was my overwhelming need to rescue Yannis and make him happy at any price.

Like many Greeks of his generation who suffered during the years of the Greek dictatorship, Yannis spent a lot of those years feeling angry, frustrated, and depressed about the fact that the political future he had pictured for himself had become impossible and nothing else would do.

These feelings were at their worst in the mid-seventies when it was impossible for him to find work and he became very depressed. Being a resourceful, creative man, he eventually set about creating an alternative future, including joining the Greek newspaper *Eleftherotypia*, starting Skyros holidays with me, later launching *i-to-i* magazine with my support, and writing one book after another. So, things definitely got much better. But he was never fully reconciled to the loss of his childhood plans for the future.

Naturally, I helped as much as I could, and in every possible way. I loved him and was grateful to him for having stood by me when I was having my breakdown. He tells me now how grateful he himself is for the way I stood by him and helped him during his difficult years. All good. If I'd looked after myself alone, I could not forgive myself for abandoning someone I loved.

Unfortunately, I didn't know how to look after both of us, so I abandoned myself instead.

Since in my mind we shared a future, whenever he felt hopeless, there was no hope for me either. But while my own problems were in my hands to solve or come to terms with, his were not. Still, I took responsibility and blamed myself if it didn't go well.

No wonder I ended up in hospital when he had a problem he couldn't solve. In my mind, that was my failure, not his, because it was my job to make it okay. Later, I was to burn out because I agreed to help launch a magazine that was important to him, but at the worst possible time for me.

I was willing to hand over my health, my happiness, even my life force if that helped. It's as if I was saying: *You have it. It's no use to me if you are not okay.* Sometimes I decided simply to give up on this life and look forward to my next. Maybe then it would all be okay.

Nowadays they call this loving too much or co-dependence. But then it was just called loving your husband till death do you part. Nobody ever told me it was too much. It seemed as if most women I knew at that time were doing something similar, though perhaps less extreme.

Loving too much is actually a misnomer. You can't love too much. I may well choose out of love to do what someone else wants rather than what I want. I may even sacrifice my life for the other. But it must be a real choice from my highest and my best self, not a reaction born of fear or guilt or shame or any other sort of desperation.

What was really happening was not too much love but rather the sacrifice of my true self to please or rescue someone else.

What does this mean, I wonder, this sacrifice of my true self?

It is something to do with reacting automatically to what is going on with someone else, whether it is a partner, a parent, or a boss, and taking on their point of view, neglecting to come back to yourself and listen to how it is for you and decide how you want to respond. It is making the choice to have no choice.

You live in someone else's force field, and react, rather than having a space around you, and responding independently. Their will, not yours, defines the situation. Their view is the last word. But you both lose, because you can't truly meet.

If Yannis was angry, for example, I was automatically frightened or guilty. It didn't occur to me I could simply acknowledge his feelings, stay peaceful in my own space, and then choose to act in a way that was loving to both of us. "Those are his feelings and have nothing to do with you," my therapist had said. Impossible. His feelings and mine were two sides of the same coin.

I was helplessly swinging with someone else's psyche, and I didn't know there was any other way.

My marriage wasn't the only place I was unable to step out of someone else's force field, even when I tried my best to do so. One rather amusing story comes to mind. I took a minicab, and, feeling that the driver had overcharged me, I decided against giving him a tip. I could feel the driver open the door for me suggestively, willing me to give him that tip. I stood my ground.

Later that evening, I discovered that my wallet was gone. After various phone calls to locate it, I realised that at the moment I felt the will of the driver try to dominate mine and I opposed him, I became completely unconscious of what I was doing, and had no idea what happened to the wallet. I was well and truly hypnotised.

The next day, after I cancelled my credit cards, Yannis phoned and said, "You owe me £10. That's the tip I gave the minicab driver when he brought your wallet back. You dropped it when you left the cab."

I had to laugh. That driver got his tip after all. But then again, so did I.

I think that in the marriage, there was the added fact that my self-esteem and sense of being loved came from the relationship and I thought I had to make the relationship work to get it. I was like a little girl taking care of her mother, hoping that mother would then mother her. I was probably doing that with my mother in the womb.

How are you?

Well, he … But, once he is okay, he will care for me like that good mother I so desperately need.

On the face of it, it looks as if this strategy could work, except for some simple facts:

I was not a little girl.

I wasn't really saving his life, but his ego, and egos never mother you.

In any case, men are not mothers.

And I was so out of touch with myself that I was ignoring all the information I was getting from my own body, heart and soul that would have helped me to figure out what was going on. No matter what finally happened, I would have slipped, for all intents and purposes, down the drain.

Don't forget also that I was sensitized in my family to thinking that men are dangerously vulnerable and need to be protected. I didn't want a repeat of what happened to my brother. Yannis' feelings were very different from those of my brother, but my programming was not that specific. A man is a man is a man.

It wasn't that way when I cared for my kids. I took a view about how they were feeling and what was the best thing to do. I also took a view about how I was feeling and what would work for me. I knew they were young and needed me to do this, and that it was part of a developmental process. Doing this in a relationship with an adult was, it seems, a very different matter.

I must add here that, despite all this, I probably didn't look like a lot like a doormat, and I doubt that Yannis or anyone else would have ever seen me that way. I was always being considered powerful by others, even when I felt so helpless and vulnerable myself. Indeed, if I had been able to fully understand who and what I was in the eyes of others, things might have been different.

Astrologer Darby Costello once told me that the *koan* of my existence, the central paradox, was the need to merge and the need to fight to establish my individuality. This exactly described our relationship. I've been writing about the merging, but I have left out the way I came out fighting. I may have fought to lose, but I did fight. Indeed, we both merged and we both fought.

My pain was not just about his pain. It was also about what I wasn't getting in the relationship. I desperately needed caring, attentiveness, sensitivity, communication, cherishing as a woman. I was crying out for the kind of intimacy that was not really on offer. As the years went on, we seldom held hands, smiled at each other lovingly, put our arms around each other. We were more likely to spar, challenge, and argue, hiding our mutual hurt behind a humour that made us both laugh. And when he felt wounded, he could withdraw so completely that he never said, "Good morning" or "How are you?"

When we were splitting up, one of the things I said to him was, "You never made me feel beautiful." He looked at me amazed. "But you are beautiful," he said, as if that was so obvious it never needed saying. Or perhaps he believed he'd said it once and that was enough.

It was the distance and lack of affection between us that worried me in relation to the children. We never used the children in our battles, but they also didn't get the best model of how an affectionate happy relationship can be. Once, when we had an awful fight, we stopped speaking to each other for days except for the most mundane practical arrangements. The kids didn't seem to notice. Not a good sign.

On another level, our personal story was really a story of cultural difference. I didn't marry what they nowadays call "a New Man", and I didn't have the tools to understand his version of maleness or his expectations of his wife. To comprehend the differences between us, you only need to sit in a Greek village taverna and watch the Greek men sitting there in their power—shouting in their loud deep voices as if they own the world, and pleasing themselves in any way they see fit as long as they know that when they get home it is their wives' domain.

Compare this to Woody Allen, for example.

But who looked? As usual, I ignored the context and bounced in doing what I thought was right. I wanted men to be what I wanted them to be, indeed what I thought they truly should be. If they weren't, I thought I must be doing something wrong, and just tried harder.

In my defence, in the psychological world of the States in the fifties and sixties, the personal psychological world was all-important; culture and class were never mentioned. Had I grown up in Europe, I certainly wouldn't have been so clueless about our cultural differences.

Luckily, Yannis was not a classic archetypal warrior. Like many Greek men, he supported my being a successful professional, indeed put his energy behind it. The Greek wife doesn't just do the housework and childcare. She also runs the shop. This is what I did, though it was a rather glorified kind of shop, and one which gave me an enormous amount, both professionally and personally.

While other women were getting their husband's slippers, I was, for similar reasons but to much better effect for me, setting up pioneering centres and managing them. As a result, in the world, I became more and more competent, powerful, loved, and valued. But for a very long time, when I was with him, I unconsciously reverted to being a submissive little girl, with all the dangers this entailed.

So, I did have to find my true self and my central will, and start to chart my own course both in my relationships and in life. Indeed, in my view, the nature of your relationship with your partner is, also your relationship to life. All those awful conversations with myself about the work I *had* to get done were about me simply submitting to what I thought life expected of me.

I didn't realise that in my relationship, and in life more generally, it was up to me to consult my most enlightened self, choose what to put on my plate, and achieve only what was possible and desirable from my point of view. Moreover, this is not a selfish choice. There is a wonderful saying from the Hawaiian Kahuna religion, "If it is in your highest best interest, it is in the highest best interest of everyone around."

Or, to quote Rabbi Hillel, "If I am not for myself, who will be for me? If I am only for myself, what am I?" It sounds even better in Hebrew.

All the inner work I did in my life, some of which is described in this book, was directed towards this process of coming back to myself and finding and honouring what was in my highest best interest and that of others. In this, I was aided and abetted by the fact that my growing confidence and power in my work life began to make it less and less tenable to give it all away.

Our shared project thus carried within it the seeds of the destruction of our old relationship. Unfortunately, we didn't manage to transcend the old patterns to create a new one that fit the people we were becoming.

An image I had in the middle of all this is a wonderful expression of my unconscious conflict, one that started long before I met Yannis. I was running a small Imagework group in Vienna, and the group members encouraged me to take a turn having an image and being guided through it by them. This is what emerged:

I am a rhinoceros walking back and forth in an electrified zone, constantly receiving electric shocks. I can't leave the electrified zone

239

because I can hear a baby crying. I let my spirit rise above and looking down I see that there is no baby crying but only the tape recording of a baby played by a little boy to arouse my mothering instincts. Even knowing this, I still keep pacing, unable to walk out.

One of the participants, a man who strangely enough reminds me of Yannis, says: "What are you doing? You look pathetic. Remember that you are a proud rhinoceros."

At first, I am angry. Why doesn't he understand? Then I think again.

I draw myself up to my full height and walk right out of the electrified zone.

Daring to be that proud rhinoceros was a central struggle of my married life, indeed of my entire life.

Since then, this rather stunning realisation came to me: I was not the only one who gave myself away. Yes, I gave myself away to the man, as women often do. But he gave himself away to his role and career, as men often do.

Neither of us knew that we were perfect as we were and that we had a right to rest.

CHAPTER TWENTY-SIX

My father dies

November 1988. My sister phones me in the middle of the night to tell me that my father Isaac is in hospital and it is serious. "He may not ..." She doesn't finish the sentence.

I lie in bed trying to tune into him to heal him. Suddenly I feel as if he has turned over and gone still. Has he healed or died? I telephone the hospital and the surgeon comes to the phone almost immediately. Isaac has just died. His heart gave way during an operation for stomach cancer.

My father was always in such a hurry. I could imagine him saying to himself, a bit like a New York Jewish version of the white rabbit: "Boy oh boy, I'm in trouble. I'd better be going quickly. They probably need my place," and then scooting along to the other dimension in a bit of a panic, worried all the while that he'd forgotten something important.

Oh daddy, why couldn't you slow down for once?

I had been talking to him on the phone just the day before. He was worried about his health, and wanted to go for another diagnosis. He sounded so distressed. "I had to take the bus to work yesterday instead of walking!" I remember this as a wail.

He didn't miss a day of work. He'd gone to work Friday, gone into hospital on Sunday, and died early Monday morning.

As luck or grace would have it, I had just spent two weeks with him in Israel, travelling together just the two of us for the first—and the last—time.

I do think it was more grace than luck. It had come about when I had decided to go with him to the airport, which I didn't usually do, because of course I was always too busy. As we sat there together I found myself saying, out of the blue, "Should we go to Israel together?" Without a moment's hesitation, he said, "Yes."

Though we didn't know it at the time, he was already suffering from stomach cancer. Had we known, our little odyssey would never have happened.

He didn't seem to have any symptoms at that time. He did say that he had lost his appetite. But since my father didn't like spending money eating out, I just thought he was being stingy with himself. He was generous with us, happy to fund our private education and later my analysis, and to help me financially at those moments in the early days of Skyros when we ran out of money. But he was almost constitutionally unable to spend money on the everyday pleasures that he considered unimportant, even wasteful.

That trip was a kind of epiphany for both of us. We'd probably never spent so much concentrated time together, certainly not since I had become an adult. And since both of us were rather shy about contacting the family who were living in Israel, we didn't have much socialising to fall back on.

But we did have wonderful conversations with strangers.

I did quite a lot of imaging to keep myself going with my usual insight a day. Then I developed the principle of "a miracle a day". Each day I looked for the miracle, and each day brought a new conversation, a new coincidence, a new understanding. My father particularly loved my willingness to talk openly with the Arabs we met, which was a new experience for him.

At one point, he said to me in his humble, self-denigrating way, "Why do you want to be travelling around with an old man like me?" I answered truthfully, "There's no one else in the world I'd rather be with."

This seemed to him to be an amazing thought, and something in him came to rest.

After his death, whenever I worried that I had failed him in my life, I would go over that moment, feeling so grateful that I had risen to the occasion and conveyed to him how important he was to me and how much I loved him.

When he got home to New York, he went around giving little lectures called, "Travels with my Daughter."

Once before I had made a conscious effort to communicate to him that I loved him. Remembering all the psychodramas I had guided in which people were wishing that they'd told their parents that they loved them before they had died, I said to my father, "I just want to say this, because I'm not sure I've said it before—I love you." He was embarrassed, mumbled, "I know" and quickly changed the subject. I now felt embarrassed about having brought it up.

Later, however, he wrote this poem and sent it to me:

> *I never said "I love you"*
> *But the love was there*
> *Stuck in my throat*
> *Imprisoned in my breast*
> *It was there through all the years*
> *of sorrow and of joy*
> *It has a touch of holiness*
> *And you saw it in my eyes*
> *Although I never said a word*[35]

I assumed at the time that the "I" in the poem was me. But maybe he was also talking of himself.

Did we know he was going to die soon? We had no idea he was even ill. Yet, in the last few years, I had reasoned to myself that since he was in his mid and then late seventies, which at that time seemed very old to me, I needed to live our relationship as if each time might be the last time I saw him.

I decided that whenever he stayed with me, we'd go out every day to the local Turkish burger shop, called Jennie's Burgers, and have cups of tea together and a chance to talk. We would sit there in the booth and I would imagine that sometime that seat opposite me would be empty.

Now it would be.

It seems such a small thing, to say that I would spend up to an hour with my father every day, just the two of us, when he'd come all the way from New York to see me, just as it seems shameful to admit that going with him to the airport was not just a normal event. But, sad to say, it was in the nature of the life I led—or perhaps my driven attitude to that life—that these spaces in my life were so hard won.

I wonder if he himself sensed his death was near. Looking at the cards he wrote just before he died, one card was dated December, while he died on November 15th, and another put the year as 00. And his last words in his last card to me were this little poem:

> *My love flows on*
> *Past rocks and reefs*
> *And waters turbulent*
> *To shallow streams*
> *Gurgling in the sun*
> *And then to foam filled seas*
> *Spraying sea gulls in the wind*
> *At last to dive*
> *To depths unknown*
> *Where currents moan and moan*
> *To shake the water overhead*

And on where?
Who knows?
I only know it flows
And flows and flows[36]

Is there a good way for people you love to die? If he had died slowly of the cancer, we would have had time to say goodbye, but what about the wasting away and the pain? And at that time, I felt I couldn't bear the idea of knowing that he knew that he was going to die. It was too real, too inconceivably painful.

He would have been okay with it, I'm sure. And now I would be too.

Everyone in my immediate family had died in a hurry. I was not present at my mother's death from a heart attack nor my brother's death after he jumped from his balcony. The suddenness of their death was particularly hard because there was so much unfinished between us. The healing had to be done by talking to them in my mind after they died. Luckily my father had lived long enough for us to heal our relationship and to feel that the regrets were few and the gratitude was great.

But still, I am very sad that I didn't have a chance to be present at his dying, to hold his hand and say: "Goodbye and thank you and my love goes with you on your journey." I hope he knew that, despite the distance, I was right here with him at the moment of death, and, perhaps, even after.

Let me backtrack a bit:

My father Isaac, or Casey as my mother called him, was born in New York in 1910 to Solomon and Sophie Glouberman. I never knew Sophie, who became mentally ill and died young, but Solomon, a charismatic anti-religious Russian communist Jewish dentist, came every Friday night to our home, told Jewish jokes with Yiddish punch lines that I never understood, and wouldn't have a word said against the Soviet Union.

245

The story went that my father's older sister, my aunt Esther, was their father's favourite, and his younger brother Roland was their mother's favourite, but Isaac was no one's favourite. As a child he was bright, hyperactive, and rather neglected. As an adult, he became an adult educator, a pioneer in his field, and loved creating innovative programmes for senior citizens and for the visually challenged. In his spare time, he led walking tours around New York.

He met my mother, Sara, when she was his student in his evening classes in English as a second language. They were married until her death in 1967. Though they had a deep commitment to each other, their relationship was a rather matter of fact one; I never even saw them touch each other. Both were outsiders, and had rebelled against their family, but still, they were culturally strange to each other. The cultures they came from were so different—she from a traditional religious Syrian Jewish family living in Jerusalem, and he from an antireligious Russian Communist family living in New York—that they couldn't fully understand or appreciate each other.

Is this beginning to sound like *my* marriage?

While we were growing up, we didn't have a lot of respect for my father. His social skills, from table manners to small talk, were awful. My mother would criticise him for this quite a lot and he didn't stand up for himself. Then there were also the broken chairs mended with a rope, or the cheap appliances that broke almost immediately and then gathered dust in the basement in case they could be fixed. He was also a hopeless and messy cook, and I have a memory of him preparing hamburgers badly, his fingers dripping with water, and me feeling sick to see this. I am ashamed to say that I remember changing words in songs from "dear old pop" to "dear old mom".

It was only later I came to understand and deeply respect him. An eternal seeker, a poet of everyday life, and a whimsical free spirit, he was a man who loved humanity more than he loved anything in the material world. He struggled with the heavy weight of madness and early death in his family, and yet still managed to survive and grow, to learn, and to teach.

He worked hard and creatively as an adult educator, as well as filling the gaps when my mother was out working two jobs, and trying to mother us as best he could. Although he seemed weak to us, in the end, it was he who was the survivor, perhaps because ultimately he was willing to be vulnerable and to seek solutions to his problems.

This is not to say that anyone in my family talked about feelings, and that included my father. When I asked him what he was feeling, he'd say, "I feel that ..." and give a thought, or more precisely, a defensive rationalisation about the feelings he didn't want to be having. Yet he yearned for a more open and transparent way of life where he could be himself more fully. In this yearning, as in many other things, I took after him.

In so many ways ahead of his times, he used to attend workshops at the National Training Laboratory in Bethel Maine, which pioneered the very early group and leadership trainings. He embraced the very newest movements of psychology, psychotherapy, and adult education, not just for his own development but also for his work with adults and the aged. He told me later that he wanted my mother to come with him to a couples' workshop, but he didn't dare ask her. To be fair, I cannot imagine her saying *yes*.

One day he took me to the old age home where he was teaching. He was using the latest personal development techniques to create an amazing teaching environment. His students crowded around me telling me, "We love your father."

I was astounded. How was this possible? I had never heard anyone talk of him with this degree of love and gratitude.

He introduced me first to humanistic psychology and then to alternative therapies and personal development approaches. I even chose my college, Brandeis, because my father loved Abraham Maslow, founder of humanistic psychology, and Maslow was teaching there.

Then I returned the favour by creating a world in Skyros based on these principles, and in so doing, offering him a place where he could find joy and fulfillment. My father loved Skyros. He used to attend all the groups, put on little skits with the children, and generally delight in being able to talk honestly with people without the small talk he could never manage. He particularly wanted to feel he could be of service to the people he met there, bringing his wisdom, his humour, his kindness, and his poetry. And he loved the therapy and the intimacy and the transformation. He felt it was possible in Skyros to be seen for whom he really was.

However, being one of the oldest people there, as he was in all the personal development groups he ever attended, he was usually selected to play the roles of father and grandfather. "Why can't they see that I'm just a little boy?" He'd complain.

It was the perfect environment for him and he flourished. People appreciated his virtues there in a way that didn't happen as much at home, perhaps much the way the residents of the old age home had done. Often, when he went home he would write to me about various illnesses, but in Skyros he always seemed incredibly healthy.

My Aunt Esther once told me that my move to England and to Europe was a gift to him. She once said, "The best thing that happened to your father was that you went abroad. That forced him to leave his armchair and see the world."

I asked him one day if he felt bad about not fully expressing his vast potential. He answered, "No, because you created Skyros, which is was what I would have wanted to do." Was I fulfilling his secret dreams rather than my own when I created Skyros, as so many children do? Or did our dreams so closely coincide?

Our relationship grew and matured as we ourselves matured. Once, when we were in Skyros, he said something that really upset me, and I went for a long walk, furious and disappointed in him. It came to me that the problem was that he was not fulfilling my idea of what a father should be.

I now said to him in my mind: "Thank you for being one of the people who has chosen to befriend me on this life's path." And as I said this, my expectations melted away, and I could just appreciate all he had given me. It was the beginning of a new relationship.

Coming back now to my father's death:

After getting the news, I travelled to the States on my own, and Yannis followed, because his father Mitsu was staying with us and he couldn't leave immediately. Strangely enough his father had also been diagnosed with stomach cancer. It didn't occur to us to bring the children, though later they told me how hard it was to hear of his death and then be left behind.

On the plane, every time I closed my eyes I would see what looked almost like a real-time video of what was happening to my father after death. I say "real-time" because when I opened my eyes to attend to something else, it seemed to go on without me, so I would miss a bit.

I saw him walking alone on a pathway. It all seemed incredibly painful. The pain, it transpired, was the pain of transformation—of having to change all one's molecules into a different state of being, and to face an unknown path alone. I felt I needed to focus with him on this painful path.

He was now trudging up a hill with a sack on his back, full of the memories and feelings that tied him to life. Though it was heavy, he didn't want to let go of it. He would put it down for a moment, and then pick it up again. He was exhausted.

Finally, he put the sack down and started to sift through it. It turned out that it was full of all his resentments and bitterness and "if only" feelings about life—all the things he wasn't happy about. The happy memories were not in the sack; these did not weigh him down or keep him attached to life.

He had to go through each of these resentments, and say each time, "So be it."

I was surprised that even my gentle loving father had enough resentments to keep him tied to life.

When he'd emptied the sack, he put it down, and started walking towards the light. Four angels came to greet him. Always a modest man, he could hardly believe it. "This feels like heaven. Why are they doing all this for me?" He seemed to be marvelling.

I laughed and whispered to him, "This *is* heaven." Soon after, he was surrounded by the angels massaging him with light and love.

I was very moved by this massage of the angels. Like so many older people, he had so little opportunity for touch. We had almost never touched since I was a child. Indeed, the trip to Israel was the very first time I could remember kissing him good night, and even that came from a conscious decision to break our usual rules.

Now that he was in the hands of the angels, we said goodbye to each other, and there were no more images. I felt miraculously peaceful for a week or two after this.

When I got to NYC and went to view his body, I thought this was the hardest thing I'd ever had to do. I was relieved when the undertakers said we couldn't go in yet. A few days later when we could, it felt more natural, and as I looked at him, it seemed as if he had seen God before he died.

The undertaker claimed the credit for how good he looked. I'm not sure that was the whole story.

We decided to hold a funeral without a Rabbi, and people just came and talked of their memories of him. I told the story about what I saw on the plane. One of my friends came up to me and said, "So you're still taking care of him even after death!"

In the days after he died, I was of course doing my imaging. I went into the House of Health to ask about healing myself. There I met a consultant/healer who told me: *You have a choice.*

You can go into the House of Health or the House of Healing. If you want to go the House of Health you need to give up guilt. If you don't want to do that, go into the House of Healing, go through the whole process, and you'll get to the same place in the end. It will just take a lot longer. Which do you want?

I chose to give up guilt and go to the House of Health. Although there was much I could have felt guilty about, I just didn't. I mourned him simply and sincerely.

There was a terrible moment when I opened my father's wardrobe and found in it the ashes of my brother, my uncle, and my grandfather, all in their original tin cans. My father had not known how to deal with their deaths, and they were still literally in the closet.

We now had the ashes of three generations of Glouberman men to dispose of.

Yannis suggested we sprinkle my father's ashes in Skyros, because he had loved it so much. I thought it sounded like a really lovely idea. At that moment, the image of a boat came to me, with Apollo and Aphrodite sitting on it. This was one of those rare times when an image comes to me totally unbidden, so I took it even more seriously than usual.

Apollo and Aphrodite told me that this disposal of ashes was outside my culture and my experience, given that the traditional Jewish approach is burial, and it was just too hard. I must simply do it the easiest way possible.

It seemed I still needed a visitation of a god and goddess from the other dimension to tell me what I was doing was too hard.

My sister and I sprinkled all the ashes in the East River. That was hard enough.

My mother was the only one in my family to be buried and, as I saw it, to reign in glory on her little plot of land. But I had never seen her grave because I left New York soon after her death, and she was buried in a massive graveyard far out of town, impossible to get to without a car. Neither my sister nor I could drive.

We didn't even know where it was. It was the undertaker for my father's funeral who told us how to find it.

Then a friend of my sister offered to drive us to my mother's grave. I was nervous. This was not because of any feelings about confronting my mother's death. No, it was that I was prepared to be embarrassed on behalf of my mother when I saw the gravestone, which by Jewish tradition is put up on the grave a year after the funeral. My father had such a tendency to botch things up because he was trying to save money. What gravestone had he bought on the cheap?

But my mother's stone was exactly the same as everyone else's. They looked as if they all came from the same shop. They probably did. The sheer anonymity was a great relief. We planted a tree to show that Sara did have visitors who cared, even if it had taken twenty years.

It was a completely soulless graveyard, and I didn't sense my mother's presence anywhere. She'd probably got bored and gone to Florida, the place she had hoped to retire to before she died.

But as I stood at the grave, I suddenly realised that my problems with my mother would have been resolved had my mother lived long enough. She was a fascinating human being but, unfortunately, I never truly got to know her because she never spoke of her deep feelings and then died young. My father and I were lucky enough to have adult years together, in which I forgave him for my rather poor early parenting, and appreciated him for his wonderful humanity and love. The same would have been possible if my mother had lived. At that moment, I completely forgave my mother for all I felt I hadn't received, and gave her my full unconditional love. I hope she got my loving message.

I returned to London from the funeral to do the next Skyros brochure with Yannis.

We wrote to Skyros people to let them know of my father's death, and to invite them to a memorial for him. We included this poem of his on the invitation:

> I shall be seeking ever
> Even until I die
> And when the last moment comes to me
> I shall be asking "why?"
> And a still small voice
> Shall say to me
> "All living things must die"
>
> I shall be seeking ever
> Until my last breath and sigh
> And on that fatal day
> I'll say "Teach me how to die"
> And the self same voice shall say to me
> "Having learned to live, you've also learned to die."[37]

The gathering was touching, and the love in the room was simple and deep. He had made himself a place in the hearts of Skyros people.

Finally, when it was all over, I mourned and mourned the loss of my father's unique light from this earth.

The period of mourning my father took nine months. Perhaps preparation for welcoming a baby into life and preparation for letting go of a loved one into death have a similar rhythm.

During that time, I managed to seclude myself and write my first book *Life Choices, Life Changes*[38] about my Imagework approach. The writing was pure pleasure, and I was sorry when it was over.

Then, a somewhat belated twenty-seven years after my father's death at age seventy-eight, and just in time for my own seventieth birthday, I put together and self-published a little book of his poetry, called *A Poem Is Anything That Sings*,[39] which is the first line of one of his poems.

A natural poet, he was always writing poems about what he experienced in Skyros, or about the people he met. They expressed not only his soul journey, but also his deep love and appreciation for others. He seemed to write poems at the drop of a hat, on any scrap of paper to hand, inspired by other people, by his own inner quest, by the groups in Skyros, by love, pain, and the wonder of life. He might be chatting to someone, or even think of them, write a poem, and then give it to them.

He never managed to complete the PhD or the books he had begun, and I wanted to give him this. He didn't believe in the hereafter, but since I do, I hope that in whatever dimension he now resides, he is gaining suitable pleasure and pride from seeing his name on the cover of a lovely book.

NOW AND THEN

I'm sitting here in my study in London, looking back at the younger Dina going through those years of gains and losses. It all seems unrelenting. An insight a day is not quite enough to carry her safely through. The deaths, the difficult marriage, moving house, creating a new centre in Skyros and keeping the old, writing her first book—all packed in together. Whether gains or losses, they all cost so much.

"Dear Dina," I say, "My heart goes out to you. You are still a young thing, and this is hard. I'm also incredibly proud of you. You still have this wonderful persistence that enables you to survive difficulties and keep going, keep examining your own inner attitudes, keep transforming. In that, yes, you are like your father, whose difficulties were immense, but whose spirit was bigger than the difficulties. It is lovely that you were able to care for your brother as much as you could, both in this life and after death, and then to provide a spiritual home for your dad, and a magical trip that blessed your life together.

And of course, there are all your achievements, setting up Atsitsa, writing your first book, doing your inner work. I don't think you realise how amazing this all is. Nor do you think about how much it costs you, and whether it is wise to be going at such a pace. It all seems to have a momentum that you can't or won't stop.

I am always trying so hard to help you, but to be honest, this time I don't know how. I can see that you are doing your absolute best and that you are simply spread too thin. Talk to me. Tell me what you are feeling and what you need."

She says: *Thank you for coming. Knowing you are there visiting me does somehow lighten the load. It's not so much that I feel alone, but that I am stunned by what I am meant to be doing and dealing with, and I don't think of myself as a super-competent person. My back aches with the stress and the hurt. Maybe just give me a hug and tell me you love me.*

I look at her and I realise she is at the end of her tether, still going, but only just. I give her a big hug and I whisper to her:

"I love you Dina. Rest. Please let yourself rest."

And she whispers back.

Thank you. I love you too. Rest? That sounds so wonderful. It makes me want to cry with relief. It is time. It is my time.

PART V

FROM BURNOUT TO NEBBISH WISDOM

CHAPTER TWENTY-SEVEN

Dismantling

Spring 1989. Writing my first book, *Life Choices, Life Changes*[40] is the last of my creative projects for quite a long time. When I finish writing, I lie down on my bed exhausted. I am forty-three. It feels as if the first half of my life has been all struggle. I don't want the second half to be the same.

It is indeed time to rest.

The summer before, I had been sitting in a Skyros *kafenion* talking to my friend Max Furlaud, who was teaching with me at the Skyros Centre that session. I told him about my need to go within to find a new place in myself, and my fear that if I retreated too much, no one would be there for me when I emerged. He reassured me that people do come to find you, as they had come to find him when he had retreated.

He also told me that in traditional Indian society, at a certain age the householder is expected to retire from worldly life, and there is a word in Sanskrit for what happens when the householder does not hand over the keys to the household to the younger generation at that time. I later came to believe that in English that word is burnout.

In one of my imagery sessions, this message came to me: *All your life you have given to the community, and in so doing you got more than you gave. Now it is time to receive. You must receive, and receive and receive and receive until like a river it overflows its boundaries and then you will find a new form of giving.*

I decided to leave my lecturing job. While I still loved the teaching, the bureaucracy was getting worse and worse. The old head of department who used to swoop down and mess us up, but left us alone otherwise, was succeeded by a new one who was a more efficient and controlling bureaucrat. I still had the reputation of being a renegade so I was always going to be a prime target for control. Time to go.

Despite all the horrors, working in an institution had offered a lot. I got a pay cheque whatever happened. I got pregnancy leave and sick leave. I managed to teach a lot of wonderful students, yet still find time to do my PhD and then Skyros. And it conferred upon me a recognised social identity. I was officially a responsible citizen and a professional.

Now my social identity would come only from my own creative world. That was scary.

Leaving my job was only the first step in a plan to simplify my life. I was determined to let go not only of my college work, but also, as I put it to myself, of "all the institutions in which I was a necessary cog". I began to pull out of the day-to-day running of Skyros. I started the process of letting go of my clients. And of course, my kids were older and did not need me so constantly anymore.

This kind of dismantling is something I have done more than once in my life—a bit like pruning a tree so that it can grow straight. It doesn't always feel great. This was a particularly tough one.

I remember how one morning, I sat in my local café feeling depressed, wondering where is that "happily ever after" life I was going to have when I took a break from all the pressures. I found myself writing this note:

You stopped working to be yourself. This is yourself. Take it or leave it.

It was definitely hard to take. The anchors that had kept me part of the institutional world were now gone. I was determined to find some way back to myself that didn't depend on these. But to do this, I needed once again to face the monsters of worthlessness, pointlessness, helplessness, and loneliness.

There was an image that summed up my fear, the image of ending up in the streets with no name. I think it came from a dream. These streets with no name are back streets of an unknown place in which I wander alone and afraid, with no sense of direction and no hope of finding a map that could guide me. I have nowhere to go and no one to go with and I don't know where I am. And to add to the horror, it is my fault I ended up there. Had I made a different choice, I would have ended up in paradise.

In retrospect, I can see that it was a courageous thing to do, to cut all my moorings, and to look for a new harbour. But I always took it for granted that you would risk everything to get closer to the truth of who you are.

I lay down in bed one day, feeling I was no longer needed, that if I walked out of my life right now I'd be missed, yes, but everything would continue more or less as before. While that was what I was trying to do, at that moment I couldn't see the point of my going on. I had a sense that my spirit had left my body. I was like a living dead person with no feeling in my body. I couldn't move a muscle.

And then I heard, or sensed, a whisper calling me to come back.

"Why should I come back?" I asked.

Because you have work to do.

"No, I'm not coming back to do more work," I answered.

So that you can love your body from the inside.

And hearing that, my spirit popped back into my body.

I started to live again, but this time with a sense that it was my time of flowering. I had a wonderful book launch for my first book, *Life Choices, Life* Changes.[41] I had a great forty-fourth birthday. Everyone was saying how beautiful and relaxed I looked. A doctor examining me for a health check told me I was in glowing health, and even started to flirt with me.

I was looking good and cruising for a bruising.

The gods don't let you get away with half measures, much less three-quarter measures.

All those years when I was completely overcommitted and didn't think I had a choice, I may have been exhausted all the time but I was more or less okay and healthy because I was doing what I thought was right and necessary. People would look at me and say, "I don't know how you do it." I believed I could do even more if only I slept less, had more energy, or wasted less time.

But now that I began to sense deep in my heart that there was another way, I was at risk. Racing forward when you are divided against yourself is a dangerous thing.

So, beware of insights. They can seriously endanger your health. If you hear the whispers of the heart and soul, and don't follow, you are in trouble.

Just when I prepared to go inward, Yannis wanted me to help him start a new magazine. I said yes when I needed to say no. I knew how important this was to him, and after all, it was such a good idea. Perhaps I was still too eager to please, to do the right thing, to be a very good girl.

I was being presented with a challenge that was dripping with everything I was addicted to. I ignored my soul's whispering and murmured to myself, "Just this one last time."

Only later did I realise that this sequence is the classic recipe for burnout or worse.

We found an office for the magazine, but until it was ready, my home was full of people sitting at desks, computers in front of them and telephones by their side. There were people in the entrance hall, people in the office, people in the sitting room, people in my private study, and of course people in the loo. There were also decorators in my bedroom repairing the effects of subsidence. The only place I could go to be private was the bathroom, and even that had two doors, one of which didn't lock.

It was so much like those early days of Skyros—including the bathroom with the two doors—but this was my home, and I was no longer pioneering. I had been ready to rest on my laurels for a bit and have a quiet life.

Every time I walked out of the house people asked cheerfully where I was going. They were just being friendly. But I dreaded telling them I was going swimming. After all, shouldn't I be working like they were?

We took out an enormous mortgage to finance this, and we were losing money hand over fist. I started thinking people on the television were moving too slowly. The medical test for this mortgage showed my blood pressure had gone up. The doctor wasn't flirting this time. He looked concerned.

In the run-up to the decision to launch the magazine, I'd been having dreams in which people were selling things in my front room and I couldn't ask them to go home because, I told myself, perhaps their own house wasn't as nice.

Now I really did have people selling advertising in my front room.

One young woman said to me, "You're very assertive." I looked at her, knowing how many people had thought that about me because they saw my direct New York Jewish style and assertiveness about everyday things, and missed my willingness to give myself away. I asked, "If I were assertive, do you think I'd be having this going on in my home?"

And one day I walked out of the house and couldn't come back until the people working in the office that had been my home left for the day. It felt as if there were workmen drilling in my head. I stood in the middle of Piccadilly Circus, unable to bear the sound of the traffic, and I took refuge inside a cinema. I saw the new film Shirley Valentine, and I dreamed her dreams.

After that day, I could not make a decision, write an email, make a business phone call. Whenever I tried, my mind just ground to a halt. I was well and truly cooked.

That was the start of a seven-year health breakdown which I realised much later was burnout, and eventually became the subject of my second book, *The Joy of Burnout*.[42] At the time, my doctor just said, "You need a holiday, not on the National Health I'm afraid," and a homeopathic doctor I consulted said, "My dear, your heart is tired."

Of necessity, now, I shed all the rest of the administrative work. I could run groups, just about, as long as I could retire after into my room and shut myself off in the dark. When I took my turn in my group to give my image, it was of a ghost in the attic. No one noticed because, as usual, I was using all my energy to do my work, and collapsing later in secret. When I told my group months later how bad I had been feeling, they were shocked. How could I have looked so energetic when I was in such trouble?

I was now forced to continue the dismantling that I had started, because I had no choice. Eventually, the last institution to go was to be my marriage.

And, strange to tell, it is as if this life crisis was foretold.

Twenty-three years previously, at the age of twenty-one, my college professor asked us to write our obituary. This was probably my first experience of an Imagework exercise by another name. Keen as ever, I had written ten typewritten pages about my life and death.

The story I told had many parallels with what really came to pass. In the obituary, I left America and lived in another country (Israel, rather than England), and married a man from a third country (a Frenchman rather than a Greek). I also wrote a book about bringing psychotherapy into the educational process. At the time, I couldn't understand what this meant. After all, I was going to be a psychotherapist. Yet turning therapy into a practice that you can educate people to do for themselves became one of the basic principles of Imagework and of the book *Life Choices, Life Changes*,[43] that I had just published.

Ten years after my health breakdown, when I realised that that it was a burnout, and was writing about it, I went back to the obituary again to find out when I had died. I was stunned to discover that I died October 27th 1989, aged forty-four.

October 27th was my brother's birthday; I couldn't have known then consciously that he would have an early death. But more to the point, it was exactly when I burnt out, if not to the day, since I don't remember the date, but close to it.

It was as if destiny had offered me an option, a kind of shamanic initiation challenge:

Transform or Die.

If the burnout hadn't stopped me, I could certainly have died of a heart attack or stroke. It was as if I was the "death seat" passenger in a speeding car, and had thrown myself out before the car crashed.

I had met what the esoteric writers call "the dweller on the threshold"—that shadow figure standing between us and the light which represents all that we have been placating, denying, fighting, repressing, but never truly meeting. We are warned that when we do meet our dweller on the threshold, we are lucky to get off with just a physical illness.

Who or what was my dweller on the threshold? No, it was not Yannis asking the impossible of me. It was my own need to please at any price.

In the space the burnout offered me, I had no choice but to transform.

CHAPTER TWENTY-EIGHT

Alone

The story of that post-burnout transformation is given in my book *The Joy of Burnout*.[44] But what I didn't write about there is that a few years after my burnout, Yannis and I split up, and I was officially alone.

The level of illness, stress, and depression was too much traffic for the once sturdy bridge between us to bear, and it broke. The story is complex, but the outcome perhaps inevitable.

I won't go into the ins and outs of that deep wounding to my life pattern, except to say that in the pain of separation I had to confront everything I ever believed about myself and about my relationships and about men. I had to untangle the skein to work out what was mine and what was not mine. I needed to find out who I was now, which is not the person I was before I got married, nor the one I was while I was married, but a new person, a composite of the old plus something else—a new molecular organisation.

And I had to understand what it was to be alone.

Alone is an interesting word. Of course, I was not alone. I had my kids, my friends, my sister, my community of students and colleagues, my spiritual life, and a raft of imagery friends and guides to counsel me and comfort me.

Alone typically means: without a sexual partner to whom you are committed and probably living with. One of my friends talked of her fear of splitting up with her partner. "I don't want to grow old alone," she said. She has so very many people who care about her. But she would still be alone.

And aside from the reality of living on your own, and feeling lonely, especially when confronted with the world of couples, there is also the sense of failure. If a woman is alone, she is a failure, or she is past it.

One day it occurred to me that this was a bit crazy. How was it a failure to be on my own? No. I was a success. I could have a viable life without relying on a man.

True, but the doubt remained under the surface. A friend came to stay with her husband and children and I noticed I was feeling ashamed. She had a life, while I was living unhappily in splendid isolation.

At first, I thought that I'd just find another man. But the first man I was attracted to after Yannis and I split up was suspiciously like Yannis. And the second, suspiciously the opposite. I took a good hard look at my past relationships with men.

It was as if for the most part, I'd been involved with two kinds of men—the more macho, charismatic, often dismissive, and the more open, loving, adoring, and vulnerable. I knew both loved me, but I didn't always feel loved. With the first, I felt challenged and eager to please, and I gave myself away; with the second, I felt cared for and cherished but also more complacent, and I never fully surrendered. Either way, I often saw it as my task to rescue them, though this rescuing took different forms.

Given a choice, I tended to go for the first. But neither worked out. Each relationship had within it the seeds of its own destruction.

I got a new slant on my two kinds of men when some years later, I met a handsome young sexy Frenchman at a workshop, who to my surprise and delight told me I was his sexual ideal woman. He said, "You come here with all your colours; you are a sun woman." The French, he told me, had this concept of *femme de soleil*.

"But men like moon women." I said sadly.

He explained that I needed to find a moon man, but one who had found his power. Sun men had to find their heart, and moon men their power. That made a lot of sense.

But as I reflected further, I asked myself: "Only two kinds of men? Two kinds of relationships? How is this possible?" I remembered the Jewish professor in the Woody Allen film, *Love and Death*, who talked about how the Jews took a bold leap of the imagination to conceive of a monotheistic God, and then this God asked Abraham to sacrifice his oldest son. Why?

Because this was the best they were able to imagine.

This was true of my relationships with men. This was the best I had been able to imagine. I needed to learn to imagine better.

I realised that the imagining was not just in my head but in the shape of being me. I began to think of it rather like being an amoeba, with certain indentations and protuberances. This amoeba fits with the indentations and protuberances of another amoeba. We are a pair.

When we split up, we float away from each other but we keep the same shapes. A new amoeba that floats towards me is only going to fit if it has the same shape as my last partner, or exactly the opposite.

Either way, I don't escape my fate. My shape is still the same and imprisons my potential for imagining a new kind of relationship.

I had to hold off on new relationships long enough to find my own shape. That maybe I could be attracted to someone who fit my new shape. If I still wanted to, of course.

It was the same as with my work. I had to stop. Wait. Suffer the depression. And then slowly my own natural energy would emerge. I could begin to find out what I really want to do.

In the service of learning to imagine better, I undertook a small personal research project into what men were like. It was based on flirting. I'd learned from my friend David, who had wanted to prepare me for a single life, that flirting was play. It needn't lead anywhere. I decided to have a few months of playful flirtations with different men which, as I made clear to them from the beginning, were not going to lead to a relationship. With all the stress taken out in this way, I could relax and find out more.

I discovered, of course, that there were many more than two kinds of men. I also found out that the men that looked attractive or charismatic to me were often men who, at base, didn't like women, while those that didn't have that magnetic sheen could often be more fun, loving, and respectful.

I learned to stop looking and evaluating the men in the old way, but rather to ask myself: "How do I feel in the presence of this man?" If he looked wonderful, but I felt awful, needy, rejected, eager to run after him and please him, I knew I needed to turn around and walk the other way.

I was still not ready to actually embark on a relationship. I realised what a high level of fear I carried in relation to men whom I might have a relationship with. I was afraid *of* them and *for* them. I was terrified of rejection or domination, yet desperate to rescue them and please them. And I was angry and hurt, and couldn't understand why it was so hard to feel happy, loved, and understood in a relationship.

I'm not sure it was always that way. Looking back at my relationships before I came to England, I notice a lovely casual quality, an easy intimacy. After all, in camp and on campus we shared a life and an openness to the future. The community held us. We didn't have two histories to bring together, and we were not defending ourselves from the pain of all our ex-relationships. We hadn't been told there is a battle between the sexes. We hoped for the best. It all felt unlimited.

Perhaps also the kind of young Jewish American men I met in my Habonim camps and at Brandeis were easier for me to

270

rub along with because they were simply more like me, with similar expectations of men, women, and relationships. I wasn't crossing a chasm to meet them.

I think, too, there was less at stake because the one thing I wasn't willing to share then was my future. I was always poised to leave any relationship. I knew that to choose a man was to choose a life, and I wasn't ready. I hadn't yet got where I was going.

Now it was different. But I needed to get back to that ease, that trust, that sharing.

One morning I woke early and lay awake for a long time, sensing that I was on the verge of some new insight. Finally, it came to me simply. I don't *need* men.

I needed a mother, but men are not mothers. I needed confirmation as a woman, but men are not my mirror. I needed to be needed, but men are not my children.

My neediness was part and parcel of my hurt and anger. I had to let it go to find my softness, my receptiveness, my femininity, my kindness. I remembered Martin Buber's phrase: "All real living is meeting."[45] Could I truly meet men? And what part of me will rise up to meet them?

There is a place inside me that is like a heat-seeking device propelling itself through space, or even like a suicide bomber on a self-destruct mission. This is not a mission to kill. It is to make you love me, or to make you happy, or to get this right, or to have the love of my life, or to do what men and women do.

There is another place in me that is not like that at all. There I stand alone as a woman with a space around me, knowing that it is my relationship with life that is important, and men are one aspect of that. This is a place from which I can look at men, as at women, or children, or flowers, or trees, or panthers and say: *Thank you for being there. I so enjoy you.*

In the first place, I am contracted, have been swept off my feet, am flying through the air or doing a crash landing, am completely off my rocker. In the second, I am expanded and stand my ground. Yet it is the first that pop songs consider normal, while the second is rather out of the ordinary, not quite the done thing.

I wonder if the first place comes from the wounding inherent in living in a patriarchal world, and the second belongs in a gentler, more feminine world.

Then there is a kind of vision in the background somewhere like a dream memory, which has another quality to it altogether. It is that of a man and a woman, who were once boy and girl, and who will one day be old man and woman, like dream images that continually shift.

It is not always the same boy/man/old man but the story continues and develops. It is about meeting the Other.

It as if there is a long-term relationship between me as female and this male, one that powers the earth with its creative fire. This creative fire varies from love to sexuality to baby making to creativity to parenting to love again, but it is always potent and always makes babies of some sort. Both the sexual juices and the creative juices flow. Sometimes we merge and then we also emerge, and something has transformed either in us or in the world when we do. And always, we are equal in value, and willing to live truthfully and meet truthfully.

I knew I couldn't have this yet, if ever, and I didn't want to move straight back into the kind of addictive situation I'd stepped out of. But that did mean that I had to face being alone.

This view was confirmed when I did an Imagework exploration when I was with my friend Naomi in her camper van. I got a clear message that I was never going to have the kind of relationship that I had wanted and needed when I was twenty. It was too late for that, and it was no longer relevant. A relationship, yes. But not that all embracing one I always dreamed of "Why?" I asked.

Because you're going to dance with God.

This understanding sustained me through many difficult moments of being without a relationship.

I had spent much of my life dealing with the monsters of worthlessness, helplessness, and pointlessness and I felt I was winning. I did have a sense that I was of value, that I could take charge of my life, and that I had a purpose. But now I had to deal with the mother monster of them all: Loneliness.

I sometimes felt it in my dreams, a deep, haunting, piercing, heart hurting loneliness. The dreams might be situated at conferences, or in social situations where I believed everyone else was having a good time, or in courses I was running where I was meeting everyone else's needs but my own. And whatever I tried to do in the dreams to overcome the loneliness, and however many people I tried to surround myself, nothing ever helped. I just felt lonelier and more alienated. For example:

I am wandering around at lunchtime in school. I am an adult and school is actually a conference or a course. I feel lonely and have no one to eat with, so I sit down with some people I know, but I am not interested in them or their conversation and I feel even more lonely. I know that this terrible loneliness will come every weekday lunchtime. I am terrified. I long for the weekend so I can escape this torture.

The profound loneliness in my dreams and images probably went beyond my normal conscious everyday feelings. The only time that came close to it in my waking life was on Sundays and holidays, particularly when the streets were empty and the shops closed, and everyone seemed to be with their family and friends.

Easter Sunday: I have decided to sit home and work. The weekend before I was in Paris with my kids, and the following weekend I am going away to Scotland to stay with friends. I am not exactly a social isolate. Yet I can't escape the terrible feeling of loneliness. In my heart of hearts I know that everyone else is at a barbecue but me.

I suddenly see that this loneliness cannot be a real need for people. I have enough people in my life. It must be to do with being shut out of the social world, with the sense that everyone else has a life but me. What is this social world I am shut out of?

I can only guess that on some primitive level, it must be Mother. As an infant and young child, Mother is the social world.

I imagine being the baby, and I wonder: *Where is mother? Why do I feel so bad? There must be something wrong with me. If I fix myself up, make myself okay, I will never be lonely, lost or helpless again.*

As the adult, I see how the baby has taken on all the responsibility for the fact that mother is far away, and she is lonely.

"Call her," I say to the child.

As the child, I call out. *Where are you Mommy?*

Just calling out helps. I am connected. I don't feel I am on a planet all by myself.

Mommy answers: *I'm here, and I'm busy, and I'm sorry, and I do love you, and this is the best I can do.*

How many times have we said that to our children?

After Mother, life at school became the next enveloping social world. I felt there was a world out there with rules I didn't understand, and because of that, I could never belong. I assumed everyone else knew what they were doing, and were happy doing it, and I just had to struggle to catch up and to be where the action is, to have a life.

An image of life I once had was that I'd been thrown into a play in which I didn't know the plot or my role, and just told, "Act, damn you, act." All I could do was copy everyone else and hope for the best.

I finally saw that there was no point rushing around trying to have a life. No point searching for a partner so I don't have to confront that pain of being alone without a partner. After all, I had had a husband, and a family and all that for more than twenty-five years. I had had what to all intents and purposes looked like a socially successful life. It didn't stop the loneliness.

274

The only answer to the loneliness was to be alone. I needed to create a safe haven with a space around me, and have a life, just for me, just by my own rules. Maybe once I am at home with my solitude, I can reach out to people out of love rather than desperation. Maybe not. But this came first.

I reach in to the baby inside me and say: "I'm here, and I love you, and I have time for you because I'm not busy or running around trying to be with people."

Then I call out to all those imaginary people who are having a wonderful time and I say, "We're here, and we're okay, and we're open to being with you, but we do, very definitely, already have a life."

I have a new kind of dream: *I'm at a conference and feeling terribly lonely. I return to my own room and I discover that the party is on my floor. It turns out that my room is where the action is.*

I wake up, so touched by my dream. Easter Sunday is coming around again, and I have the courage to phone a friend and say, "What are you doing this Easter Sunday?" It's okay to ask, because if she is busy, I'll still be okay.

She says she's free. Maybe we will have a barbecue.

CHAPTER TWENTY-NINE

Socrates and the pig

Let's fast forward to one sunny afternoon about two years after I split up with Yannis. I am still single, except for occasional short-lived relationships, but I am finding my way. I am sitting in my garden in London feeling that life is good, and I have accomplished whatever I set out to do today.

I am at peace for a glorious moment.

Suddenly the thought comes to me: *Why am I not in a hut by a rice paddy in Malaysia?*

Translation: *Since I left my country anyway, why have I ended up in this boring old garden in boring old England? Why didn't I do the exotic thing properly and live my life to the full?*

You understand, perhaps, that I didn't know what rice paddies looked like, had never been to Malaysia or consciously thought about it, and I would be unlikely to last long living in a hut.

It was like the time I had had a really good day, which once again meant achieving what I had set out to do, and went to bed happy with my accomplishment. I woke up to the sound of my radio alarm belting out opera, and my first thought was: *I've got it all wrong. I should be going to the opera.*

I wasn't particularly interested in opera.

My mother once joked when I got a ninety-seven on my exam, "What happened to the other three points" Except, in my thinking, it was probably, "What happened to the other six points?"

This time fate was kind enough to cooperate in my learning. The next summer one of my students in Skyros invited a few of us to stay with her over Christmas and New Year in her house next to a rice paddy in Thailand. I was thrilled. Heart's desire coming true, I thought.

But for a variety of reasons that had nothing to do with Thailand and rice paddies, the trip was not a success, and I was very relieved to go home. Heart's desire did not make me happy after all.

The story continued. On the plane, there was an empty seat next to me so that I could stretch out and hopefully sleep. I was pleased with myself until I saw a young man near me who had two empty seats next to his, and was lying there comfortably fast asleep.

At this point, for some reason I decided to feel really hard done by, and to have a serious conversation with Life. I put Life into that empty chair next to me (no chance of sleep now) and I launched straight into attack.

"Life, why is it that you give me everything but what I really want?"

I switched seats to become Life and the response was immediate:

Why is it that whatever I give you, you are still complaining?

I had to laugh. As we continued the conversation, Life made clear to me that it was no good sitting in my garden looking at my life and attacking myself saying, "Why did I choose this life and not some other one?" My life is the physical manifestation, almost the sedimentation of me. It is me, or rather me as I was until a moment ago. My choices emerged from the person I was, and my life now is a result of those choices.

As I change, so will my life. There will inevitably be a time gap between the new choice and the manifestation of that choice but it will happen. I just need to stop complaining, give up those punishing perfectionist standards, and get to work making those new choices.

Perhaps even more important, Life pointed out to me that I took the good things in life for granted just because I had them already. My relationship with my children was a case in point. Instead of noticing what was missing, why wasn't I celebrating what I had already created at great cost and with great struggle—and with such success?

Something came home to me. I spent a few months of pure delight in my everyday life, and in particular adored the time I spent with my kids.

Everything felt extraordinary. I went to visit family and friends in America, and one day my friend Naomi was apologetic about the fact that it was raining and she was afraid it would spoil the day in her camper van. I found myself saying contentedly:

"Even a rainy day is a day."

This period came and went, and I duly rediscovered self-attack and complaint. But I am still grateful for the pleasure I found in that precious time with my kids, particularly because it was not long after that they left home to create their own adult lives. I would have missed that period completely if I hadn't been told in no uncertain terms to stop and appreciate it.

Then the point was pressed home to me when I was having an Imagework conversation with God and the Angels. As one does.

As I hope is clear by now, this means that I would talk to an image of God and the Angels, and then I would switch places to respond. I was neither prophet nor madwoman.

But nevertheless, it was an important moment.

They said to me: *If you make your life into a* hechal (the Hebrew word meaning palace and temple) *for us, we want only the best.*

I laughed. They were telling me that if they were going to live there, they were going to make sure it was great.

But I guessed there was a catch.

"What do I have to do to make my life into your *hechal*?" I asked.

They answered immediately. *You have to give up thinking that there is anything you need in order to be happy that you don't already have.*

It was almost more than I could imagine. "The good life" had always been somewhere else, almost by definition. My feeling of being "all wrong" and of my life being all wrong was a leitmotif of my daily existence.

I looked deeply into that background feeling of "all wrongness" that had haunted me, and realised that it was just that—a feeling. It had probably been there since my birth or before. Perhaps I was all wrong because I was not my sister Ora, who was dead and was never coming back, or perhaps I had ingested my mother's guilt at not getting Ora to the hospital on time.

Perhaps and perhaps, but whatever the reason is, the point is that it is just a feeling, not a Truth about my life. Could I give up now on insisting that I have all those things I believed were necessary to the good life and consider my life complete as it was? Could I live happily ever after if I never met the Prince?

God and the Angels were still waiting for an answer.

I fought with the idea, but I knew they were right. The good life couldn't be somewhere else. The good life was an experience of all-rightness, of being in love with life, and I knew that nothing out there could give it to me in a lasting way.

I finally agreed. And I gave such a deep sigh of relief.

Of course, I didn't give up forever that belief that if I only had X, then I'd be happy. It's a bit like being brilliant at giving up smoking because you've done it so many times. I've had to get very good at giving it up, because I've needed to do it again and again.

But each time it gets a bit easier. It is as if each time I have more self to do it with.

And I guess that is what the whole thing has been about—getting more and more self, or Self, so that I can have an equal relationship with Life.

If I don't want to shrink Life into a small box of daily pettiness, I need to grow to meet its full grandeur.

And yet, this determination to have a good life was not all bad. If as a child I had felt that I didn't need anything to make me happy that I didn't already have, would I ever have left Brooklyn and done all the things I've done and become all that I've become? And would that have been okay, and just a different life story? Of would I have missed my destiny?

As a child, I used to think: *The worst thing in the world would be to live and die in Brooklyn.* Now Brooklyn is very, very cool. My sister, who still lives in Brooklyn, is definitely in the middle of the action, and my daughter Chloe has left London to live in Brooklyn.

But I suspect it's a case of T S Eliot's, "We shall not cease from exploration, and the end of all our exploring will be to arrive where we started and know the place for the first time."[46] I had to travel all that way to discover that my backyard was perfect as it was. Indeed, as a child, my backyard bordered on the subway tracks, and now I live in London just by the railway tracks, and love it for that.

The process of discovering and rediscovering the flavour of being me took me through failures and madness as well as sanity, success, love, and creativity. It took me around the world and back. It led to beautiful creations and terrible losses.

The biggest surprise and delight was in how the creations, ranging from my kids to Skyros to my Imagework community, grew up, took on their own dynamic, and went on to bear their own fruit. It is so miraculous that I still haven't fully grasped it.

As writer Ken Kesey said in a lecture I once attended, "Remember, you can count the seeds in an apple, but you can't count the apples in a seed."

That little baby I was, shorter than a forearm's length, had within her the potential to create worlds, and those worlds created other worlds. How can you not fall in love with Life?

And then, sitting in a café one afternoon preparing a lecture on "Living Truthfully" that I was about to give for the Alternatives programme at St James Church in Piccadilly, an old problem that was set us by my philosophy professor back at Brandeis University popped into my mind.

Is it better to be an unhappy Socrates or a happy pig?

In my college days, I used to muse over this question. I so much wanted to be happy. But on the other hand, would I give up being the wise and wonderful Socrates to be a happy pig?

But this time, at the moment the question came to me, so did the solution.

Obviously, it is better for Socrates to be Socrates and the pig to be a pig. Happy doesn't come into it.

CHAPTER THIRTY

Nebbish wisdom

As they say, the end is in the beginning. Let's go back to observe.

I am conceived in December 1944, in a moment I imagine as an explosion of pure light and joy. Within a week or two, my sister Ora dies of gastroenteritis and my mother is in shock and mourning, feeling guilt, indeed suffering all the desperate feelings attending the death of a child. The womb becomes a terrible place to be. I imagine that moment in my life as a contraction, a despair, a sense of being all wrong and unwanted, having made a mistake, having been a mistake, kicked out of my place.

Are these moments the original model for the swings between deep happiness and deep unhappiness, shining light and terrible darkness, all-rightness and all-wrongness, creativity, and depression, that were to dominate my life?

Then the moment of birth, another chance for light and hope. I propel myself out of my womb world, with my natural innocence shining through, delighted to be invited into this new world and looking forward to a warm welcome.

Instead … nothing.

Oh you're here. Stick around. You might be useful.

Not lack of love, but definitely not much loving there. How could there be, when they look at me and see Ora.

The story is not quite as it seems. *You might be useful* is what it feels like, but it is probably more like: *We might get used to you.* Such subtleties can be missed in an infant's translation.

But whatever way you look at it, it is not a great welcome.

Did my mother really want me? Maybe not. Not at that moment, anyway. It was pretty bad timing. No blame.

This unfortunate beginning launches me on a lifetime's course of misplaced workaholic effort, trying to please all the people I depend on as well as all the theatre critics inside my head, hoping against slender hope that I will finally be welcomed and truly loved.

I nearly die trying.

In the meantime, as a young child, I had no mirror in my mother's face to reflect me, no one even to point to me in a mirror and say lovingly, "Who's that?" They loved me, but they couldn't see me. I felt completely invisible.

I was at least seven or eight years old when I walked in my school playground and suddenly realised that other people saw and recognised me just as I saw and recognised them. It simply hadn't occurred to me until then. But what did I look like? I had no idea.

I went home that night and studied myself in the mirror trying to memorise my face. I wanted to make sure that if I met myself in the street I would recognise myself.

Even by my thirties, when I did a "video feedback" session in which I watched myself live, I was amazed that I didn't disappear when I wasn't talking or doing anything.

I not only felt invisible, but on some level, I also felt empty, shapeless, or in Jewish terms, a *nebbish*. For those not initiated into the Jewish world of insults, the *nebbish* is a blob, a nothing, a loser, a pathetic pitiful character.

There's also the *schlemiel* and the *schlamazel*. The *schlemiel* is the one who manages to spill the soup at a fancy dinner party. The *schlamazel* is the one he spills it on.

Not great. But at least they are noticed enough to be laughed at.

The *nebbish* is the one who when they walk into the room it is as if someone has just walked out.

When I was growing up in Brooklyn, Hallmark cards had a range of *nebbish* cards. A typical *nebbish* birthday card had an amoeba-like being on the front cover, and inside it said, *Nu, so you're older*.

Nu is a kind of Jewish nudge with a range of meanings. In this case it means something like: "Well, big deal."

Nebbish was how I felt inside as a kid, in that empty space right at the centre of me. I assumed that everyone else was completely full—filled with good, interesting, worthwhile confident human things.

Only I had that rubbery feeling of nothing at all.

I was so convinced there was a hole in the middle of us that when I saw a transparent plastic model of a human body in a shop window, I just couldn't understand why all the innards filled the entire body. Where was the space in the middle?

Yet for a *nebbish*, I was strangely passionate about life. It was a bit like one of those hope-against-hope love affairs—will the *nebbish* get Life and live happily ever after?

I pictured having a Life a bit like I pictured having brains. Kids used to say to each other: "You got some brains, but they fell out, and you had to go to the back of the line. When you got to the front, there were none left." I thought brains were like straw stuffed into the hole in your head. The more you had, the smarter you were. If you were pathetic enough to end up in back of the line, you sort of deserved not to get any.

In my mind, Life was like that. The more Life you could stuff into that hole in you, the better you were. No matter how frightened I was of something, I would do it if I thought it was an opportunity for more Life. So, though I stammered badly, as this never stopped me from speaking in class. Being frightened and embarrassed wasn't half as bad of being lost and alone, on

285

the side lines of Life, missing out, not where the action is. To me, that was the ultimate shameful failure.

I knew I didn't deserve much, being a *nebbish*. But deserving or not, I was determined to have a lot of Life. I may have had no self-esteem but I was persistent.

Looking back now, I realise I couldn't really have been a *nebbish*. What, then, was that *nebbish* feeling inside, that *nebbish* knowledge, that empty space at the centre of me?

I can feel it now, that be-nothing, know-nothing rubbery feeling inside that I thought was my essence.

I like it.

It's a place in which I can rest, in the crack between all my beliefs about the world. It's the crack from which I stammer, not being sure what I can take for granted. But it is also the crack out of which new things can be born.

I think it is from this place of not knowing that I have learned whatever I do know, and accomplished whatever I have accomplished. Fools and wise people can live in there side by side and no one can tell which is which. My madness emerged from there but so did the miracles.

Without that *nebbish* space inside me, I would never have had the simple foolish courage to undertake my restless never ending painful search for the truth that would set me free, and perhaps set others free too. Nor would I have dared to create projects in the world at a time when I felt so unworthy.

A *nebbish* has nothing to lose—no beliefs, no pride, no sense of what you are and are not, what you do or don't deserve. Like fools and wise people, mad people and miracle makers, you are always at the beginning.

Dear reader, thank you for coming along with me on this journey of *nebbish* wisdom, suffering with me, laughing with me, and hopefully finding a resonance that makes it your story, too. I needed to tell this story for me, but I also needed to tell it to you.

When I was first writing this book, I had an image of being in the afterlife and meeting Jean Paul Sartre. He looked at me challengingly and asked:

What do you have to say for yourself?

For some reason, I didn't feel intimidated. I just said,

I stand by my life.

And I stand with you by your life, too, dear reader.

NOW AND THEN

I'm sitting in my tiny flat by the sea in Hastings where I come to retreat and to write. I am looking back at the younger Dina who started dismantling her life, didn't go far enough, hit burnout, and then dismantled some more.

Her life is not so dramatic anymore, at least on the surface. But of course, the real story of her life—and mine—has always been as much behind the scenes as on the fully lit stage.

There is no doubt that there have always been two forces in me, one that doggedly kept my outer life moving along, and another that equally persistently kept my inner life moving along. Always they fed each other, because every insight had to be taught to others who might benefit, and every external achievement allowed me to feel that maybe, just maybe, I was enough.

And sometimes, every now and then, I have been able to truly rest, and at those moments, neither story is important. At these times, as it says on the calligraphy print by Vietnamese Zen Master Thich Nhat Hanh on the wall of my kitchen:

Present Moment, Wonderful Moment.

So, what has happened in the years since I burnt out?

I found my way through burnout, eventually gaining my health back, and writing a book about the basic lesson of burnout for me.[47] I wrote another book about the steps to new

289

beginnings,[48] an important sequel to the burnout book, because any crisis is a catalyst, and the first step to the new beginning. And now, of course, I am writing this story that you are reading today.

Besides writing, I continue to see clients, run courses, give talks, though not as many or as often or as consistently as I used to. Did I retire? Doesn't sound like it, does it? I would say that I am semi-retired, which means I spend less time working professionally and fulfilling public commitments, and more time choosing freely what I want to engage with.

I have worked my way through more and more of my stuff about men and have managed to create a good and a lasting relationship with a lovely man. I took up the saxophone, put it down, and took it up again. I made new friends and kept the old.

And with the establishment of a committed relationship and a solid sense of self, added to a stable group of family, friends, colleagues, and clients, I have finally stopped feeling lonely.

My son Ari now lives in Switzerland with his wife, Suzy, and three children, Leonardo, Alexander, and Emelie, and my daughter Chloe lives in New York. I wish they lived around the corner, but given what you've read in this book about their parents, maybe it's not so surprising.

We do of course meet and phone and Skype, and, though I am never allowed to give any advice, they sometimes let me do "tune-ins", so I can offer them an intuitive sense of what is under the surface. And Chloe now offers me tune-ins, which she is great at, and I love that.

What is my next project? I'm hoping to live a few months a year in Monopoli, a small town in Puglia, Southern Italy, and to invite family and friends to join me. But also, and this emerged in a visioning I did during one of my groups at the Skyros Centre, I want to start a centre for training professional people-workers in my Imagework approach: The Puglian Centre for Imagework Therapy, Coaching and Consulting.

When my Italian friend, Marina, asked what the actual name would be, the name *Aurora* emerged as if by magic. I discovered it was an Italian word, and it is sometimes rather wonderfully defined as the purple glow between the first light and the sunrise. This is just the kind of liminal space from which imagery emerges.

Side by side with this, I hope to write another book, a handbook of imagery for therapists and counsellors, a kind of textbook to accompany the courses. And of course, I need to learn Italian, which for some reason seems like an enjoyable challenge.

The inner search continues, and the inner struggle, but it is more muted, less desperate, more of a tool for living and understanding than a tool for surviving and overcoming deep suffering. I did have some difficult years in which I had a lot of painful waking-up-in-the-night-making-plans-for-the-past moments, along with the joyful times. But most miraculously, I have now emerged onto a level path, a new experience for me entirely.

Anxious and depressed thoughts and feelings visit but don't take hold. Everyday tasks that I struggled with, from sitting down at my desk to packing for a trip, are almost easy now. I walk regularly, and even have training sessions at the gym. I live much more in the world, whereas before I lived in my mind and my emotions and reached out from there to act in the world. And behind it all, there is a stable sense of myself, that continues to love, observe, smile, trust, and know that this too shall pass.

Some things don't change. I still have breakfast at the café and write little notes to myself whenever I possibly can.

Less focused on my inner life, I am now far more troubled about the state of the world—about who runs it, and for whom, and how much human, animal and planetary suffering is the terrible result. None of what I read in the papers every day is really new, but it seems more extreme and visible, more culturally acceptable, more frightening. Or maybe we just know more. And yet, there are also countervailing forces, movements of people who are listening to the whispering of the world soul, and working towards the good. Indeed, many who used not to be directly involved in the political world, are now feeling that something must be done and they can help do it.

I do what I can, and, not being a natural political activist, I especially like coaching activist friends through bottlenecks in their own lives and work. But it does sometimes feel as if I am fiddling while not only Rome but the whole world is burning.

At least I can now see that the madness is all around me, not inside me.

People often ask me "What worked?" As usual, it depends on your theory. I like the expression, "I did the work." This includes the outer work of making good things happen in the world, the inner work of making good changes in my consciousness, the will to stay open to my own soul and to the souls of those who care about me even if they are saying something difficult to hear, and the persistence to keep on keeping on. Just plain growing older seems to work, too, as all the latest research shows.

Could it all be about work—and getting older? I love the work, that miraculous process of transformation, and I even love growing older. But that must be only half the story. There is also the fact that I've given myself the space to hang out, play, breathe, wonder, watch the sunrise, do nothing, fall in love with life. *Present moment, wonderful moment.*

This is not to say it's all a steady upward climb toward perfect health and happiness. As they say in the spiritual life, "Don't look for results." There are moments when it can feel as if nothing had changed, nor ever will again. In those moments, all you can do is breathe and wait. Then of course, all of a sudden, lo and behold, you come back to yourself. And then there is more work to do once again, but less dramatic work, and more self to do it with.

And there is another, more wonderful, way in which nothing has changed. On some level, I have always been the person I am now, but it took all this time to come to know it and experience the joy of it.

What can I offer younger Dina?

I look at her life, and I say:

"You've stepped off yet another precipice, faced so many of your lurking monsters, and you're beginning to get glimpses of how it might be to overcome loneliness, let go of regrets, be content with your life and yourself. As always, I'm so proud of you."

Then I find myself wanting to tell her a bit about the future, perhaps to warn her:

"Don't expect just to rest on your laurels and sail off happily into the sunset. It will be tough sometimes. Even when it is, don't doubt the path you are choosing. I stand witness to the fact that you can and will get through, and find a new level of inner peace, joy, and security. But I can't promise you plain sailing. Do you remember Hannah Green's novel *I Never Promised You a Rose Garden*?[49] It's like that. Life's good but it isn't a Garden of Eden."

I look at her. She is looking down, upset. I try to reassure her:

"I want you to remember how you always used to say you wanted to live happily ever after, and what had you done wrong that you failed to do so? Then you discovered a poem you wrote as a young teenager which tells a very different story. In this poem, Eve talks of how absolutely determined she is to leave the Garden of Eden.

The poem ends:

> *The leafy sweetness tortured me.*
> *I wanted pain and ecstasy.*
> *I ate from the forbidden tree.*

Maybe "happily ever after" was never what you really wanted. You might have done things a bit differently if it was. Can't you be happy with the fact that all those inner and outer adventures have brought us to a good place, and hopefully there is a lot more to look forward to? Isn't being happy to be yourself whatever happens better than a thousand fairy tale endings?"

I'm talking a lot, probably because I'm getting more and more uncomfortable at her response. Younger Dina seems frightened and a bit angry when she answers:

No. I can't be happy about it. I wanted it to be easy now. I am scared of more pain and struggle. I was hoping for a rose garden. That's the truth. Why not happily ever after? Enough already.

I don't know what to say. Maybe I shouldn't have told her; I've only given her something to worry about. But then she continues:

But what I can do is this: I can pride myself on what I have accomplished so far. I can stand by myself each time I take yet another risk, catapulting myself, or perhaps being catapulted willy-nilly, into a new life. And I can make it easier for myself by remembering that all's well that ends well, and it sounds like you've made a pretty good job of it. That will help when it's the middle of the night and I feel I've painted myself into a corner and there's no hope for the future. To know you're there rooting for me—that's good too. Thank you for coming back from the future to love me.

I have to admit that I'm proud of you, too. You haven't become just like your mother or your father. You're just like you. And just like me but more so. Well done you.

I am touched. Then, as we speak, a beautiful and surprising email arrives from Yannis. He has read this manuscript, which I sent him, and he is worried that all my inner descriptions of pain, self-attack, loneliness, and longing give the wrong impression of me.

He reminds me that I have been included in a book about inspirational women around the world.[50] Why didn't I mention that?

Then he writes, "My own feeling about all this is that viewing your life as you did, you've done yourself a terrible injustice.

You've never been the person you describe. Instead, and since the first day I met you, you've been an interesting, challenging, insightful, and loving person, bright and creative, brave in the face of all difficulties, a gift to the world, and the person I loved and treasured. I was totally behind you in your years of trial, as you were totally behind me, especially during the horrible times I experienced in the seventies. I'm very grateful to you for this. But you know that!"

I am stunned. It is as if we have come full circle, given love its proper place.

When I recover, I tell younger Dina about the email and add, "I could say the same to Yannis. Neither of us were able to acknowledge this to ourselves or to each other all those years ago. Yet, it has always been true. And we did always know it. Can *you* rest in that knowledge?"

She smiles. I smile. We are both okay with all of it.

And I hope you are too, dear reader. Is there something you know but haven't told yourself that would let you come to rest?

Rose garden, shmose garden. How about a nice desert? It's a much more sensible place for a nice Jewish cactus.

REFERENCES

1. Sondheim, S. & Lapine, J. (1987). *Into the Woods* (p. 77). New York: Theatre Communications Group. See also Barton, A (2017). *The Shakespearean Forest*. Cambridge: Cambridge University Press. Anne Barton describes Shakespearean forests as places of transformation where chaos rules and anything can happen.
2. Lessing, D. (1969). *The Four-Gated City*. London: MacGibbon & Kee.
3. Fowles, J. (1965). *The Magus*. Boston: Little, Brown.
4. Dostoevsky, F. (1866). *Crime and Punishment*. Moscow: Russian Messenger.
5. Townsend, S. (2012). *The Woman Who Went to Bed for a Year*. London: Penguin.
6. Cavafy, C. P. (1968). *The Complete Poems of C. P. Cavafy*. London: Chatto and Windus.
7. Cavafy, C. P. (1968). *The Complete Poems of C. P. Cavafy* (p. 27). London: Chatto and Windus.
8. Laing, R. D. & Esterson, A. (1964). *Sanity, Madness and the Family*. London: Penguin Books.
9. Rinehart, L. (1971). *The Dice Man*. New York: William Morrow.
10. Glouberman, D. (2002). *The Joy of Burnout*. London: Hodder and Stoughton.
11. Glouberman, D. (1989). *Life Choices, Life Changes: Develop your Personal Vision with Imagework*. London: Unwin Hyman.

12. Glouberman, D. (2014). *You Are What You Imagine: Three Steps to a New Beginning*. London: Watkins.
13. Glouberman, D. (1977). *A Study of Psychological Differentiation*. Unpublished PhD Thesis. Brunel University.
14. Available online at: https://www.skyros.com/about/press/.
15. Available online at: https://www.skyros.com/about/press/.
16. Andricopoulos, Y. (1974). *1944, Krisimi Chronia*. Athens: Diogenes.
17. Bailey, A. A. (1953). *Esoteric Healing*. New York: Lucis.
18. James, W. (1902). *The Varieties of Religious Experience*. New York: Longmans, Green.
19. Buber, M. & Smith, R. G. (1947). *Between Man and Man*. New York: Macmillan.
20. Buettner, D. (2009). *The Blue Zones: Lessons for Living Longer from the People Who've Lived the Longest*. Washington DC: National Geographic; Dina Glouberman and Josee-Ann Cloutier (2017). "Community as Holistic Healer on Health Holiday Retreats: The Case of Skyros", Chapter 13 in Melanie Kay Smith and Laszlo Puczko (Eds.) *The Routledge Handbook of Health Tourism*. NY: Routledge; *Okinawa Centenary Study: Centenarians* (2007). Available online at: http://www.okicent.org/cent.html
21. Available online at: http://www.dinaglouberman.com/approach/co-listening/.
22. Available online at: https://www.skyros.com/about/press/.
23. Lewis, O. (1961). *The Children of Sanchez*. New York: Random House.
24. Glouberman, D. (1989). *Life Choices, Life Changes: Develop your Personal Vision with Imagework*. London: Unwin Hyman.
25. Glouberman, D. (2002). *The Joy of Burnout*. London: Hodder and Stoughton.
26. Glouberman, D. (2014). *You Are What You Imagine: Three Steps to a New Beginning*. London: Watkins.
27. Plummer, D. (1999). *Using Interactive Imagework with Children: Walking on the Magic Mountain*. London: Jessica Kingsley.

28. Gallwey, W. T. (1974). *The Inner Game of Tennis*. New York: Random House.
29. Available online at: www.theguardian.com/global-development/2017/apr/14/harare-friendship-bench-grand mothers-mental-health-zimbabwe.
30. Thomas, D. M. (1996). *Lady with a Laptop*. New York: Carrol and Graf.
31. Glouberman, D. (1989). *Life Choices, Life Changes: Develop your Personal Vision with Imagework*. London: Unwin Hyman.
32. Salvage, J. (2011). *Skyros: Island of Dreams*. London: Skyros Foundation.
33. Machan, K. H. (2001). *Skyros—little songs*. New York: Foothills Publishing.
34. Alcott, L. M. (1868). *Little Women*. Boston: Roberts Brothers.
35. Glouberman, I. (2015). In: D. Glouberman (Ed.), *A Poem is Anything That Sings* (p. 12). London: Skyros Books.
36. Glouberman, I. (2015). In: D. Glouberman (Ed.), *A Poem is Anything That Sing* (p. 42). London: Skyros Books.
37. Glouberman, I. (2015). In: D. Glouberman (Ed.), *A Poem is Anything That Sings* (p. 41). London: Skyros Books.
38. Glouberman, D. (1989). *Life Choices, Life Changes: Develop your Personal Vision with Imagework*. London: Unwin Hyman.
39. Glouberman, I. (2015). In: D. Glouberman (Ed.), *A Poem is Anything That Sings*. London: Skyros Books.
40. Glouberman, D. (1989). *Life Choices, Life Changes: Develop your Personal Vision with Imagework*. London: Unwin Hyman.
41. Glouberman, D. (1989). *Life Choices, Life Changes: Develop your Personal Vision with Imagework*. London: Unwin Hyman.
42. Glouberman, D. (2002). *The Joy of Burnout*. London: Hodder and Stoughton.
43. Glouberman, D. (1989). *Life Choices, Life Changes: Develop your Personal Vision with Imagework*. London: Unwin Hyman.
44. Glouberman, D. (2002). *The Joy of Burnout*. London: Hodder and Stoughton.
45. Buber, M. (1958). *I and Thou*. New York: Charles Scribner's Sons.

46. Elliot, T. S. (1943). *Four Quartets*. New York: Houghton Mifflin Harcourt.

47. Glouberman, D. (2002). *The Joy of Burnout*. London: Hodder and Stoughton.

48. Glouberman, D. (2014). *You Are What You Imagine: Three Steps to a New Beginning*. London: Watkins.

49. Green, H. (1964). *I Never Promised You a Rose Garden*. New York: Holt, Rinehart and Winston.

50. Gifford, Z. (2007). *Confessions to a Serial Womaniser: Secrets of the World's Inspirational Women*. UK: Blacker.